To Val

Babylorn

Honor Donohoe

Best Wishes

Cathy

Jan 2017

Babylorn
Copyright © Honor Donohoe 2014

Published by Cahar Publications
1st Floor
2 Woodberry Grove
LONDON
L12 0DR

ISBN 978-0-9575203-9-4

For Harry

Preface

The Lorn Trilogy is a fictional portrayal of how the past can influence lives today. The adoption industry in Ireland and abroad became a fertile source of lies, falsified birth certificates, sealed records and lost files throughout the 50's 60's 70's. A language evolved formulated with the intention to mislead. God featured and His will was used as a scapegoat more often, I imagine, than He would sanction.

The legacy of these decades does and will continue affect subsequent generations. The primal wound cannot be dismissed. A deprivation of genetic information is something people raised in 'normal' families cannot fully grasp.

Millions of adoptions world-wide, each a unique story, hold a common denominator, which is they are based in the severance of biological connections.

Pro-adoption language focuses on the gains for the child, while anti-adoption concentrates on the impact of loss on the child/adult.

A salient fact, worth knowing, is that more adopted people undergo counselling in their lifetime than in the general population. The disturbing impact can and does at times derail even the 'happiest' adoptees.

Never did a young pregnant woman give birth to Satan's spawn.
No one should ever have to be a secret.
No mother should fear her secret child will be discovered.
A desire to nurture was never a hideous crime worthy of punishment.

Babylorn

Contents

Chapter 1

Ripples

'Did I hear the phone?' Toby wiped sleep from his eyes as he approached Kirsty who sat at the breakfast bar.

'You did; it was Sam.'

'Who?'

'Sam, my cousin, Matthew's son,' she responded.

'What did he want at such an early hour on a weekend when all sane people are asleep?'

'Aunt Cressida died this morning.'

'Oh,' he replied disinterestedly, helping himself to orange juice from the fridge before asking, 'Was that expected?'

'No.' She placed her empty glass on the worktop, to suggest it could also be refilled. 'She was alright, or so we thought. A heart attack apparently, late last night. According to Maud she'd managed to dial 999 herself and the ambulance took her to hospital in Eastbourne but she died around half five this morning.'

Toby pulled his blue dressing gown over his knees and tugged the cord tighter at his waist. 'I don't suppose anyone knows yet when the funeral might be?'

'Sam will let me know. I imagine the earliest possibility would be the end of this week.'

'Well, I hope it isn't Thursday because I need you to go to a meeting on Wednesday evening. The Buccap crowd in the Eagle Hotel. Just the usual sort of thing – drinks, canapés, networking.'

Kirsty said nothing, her eyebrows knitting into a frown.

'No need to look like that. I can't go; Jo Langford is coming up from London to sign a contract.' He spoke impatiently. 'I need a representative to attend as a PR exercise and all that good stuff. You know the drill,' he said, before adding lavish praise, saying he knew she was greatly respected, and perhaps should consider working for him full-time.

'I'll make you some porridge,' she said moving away from the breakfast bar.

Kirsty stirred the contents of the saucepan absentmindedly as she looked out at the flats opposite. Sometimes shadowy figures moved at the windows so she'd deduced that she might also be observed in her kitchen. She hated not having a sea view from their modern flat in North Berwick. To purchase a property which did encompass waves and boats on the distant horizon cost at least an extra six thousand pounds. Toby refused to pay, not out of any claim to poverty, but he felt there was no point when a five-minute walk could serve the purpose.

*

The previous afternoon Kirsty's car splashed over wet tarmac heading south from Edinburgh on the east coast road. Casually negotiating the final bend of a narrow lane she arrived at the beach, having already anticipated angry brown churning waves crested with cream. To take this detour on her way home and observe the sea in all moods had become a routine, particularly on a Friday.

The broad tyres of her Range Rover crunched over the

gravel car park. Stopping at the end she sighed and silenced the engine before leaning forward to embrace the steering wheel, aware despite such turbulence, the tide was on the ebb. Windscreen wipers flipped intermittently to disperse sea spray and raindrops carried on the wind. Her finger pressed open the window, empowering fierce gusts of salt laden air to dishevel her auburn curls. Sometimes she might walk barefoot, squashing sand between her toes, but not on this day when wind rocked the car and moisture shimmered on black metal. The icy draught caused her to shiver, but was to be endured as an aid to annul the turmoil of a working week and city traffic. She sat, a lone figure contemplating his words, until the greyness of winter twilight grew into to a black starless night. When the churning sea-swell became barely visible, she reluctantly admitted it was time to go home.

The ignition key sparked life into the engine, but before releasing the handbrake she shouted out into a wild January night.

'We are programmed well how to forget.'

To hear Kirsty talk in the school staffroom about her husband Toby, would suggest a degree of pride. He seemed to have flair to invent exactly the right marketing slogan for any product. This, coupled with his artistic ability and ruthless pursuit of success proved a winning formula for growth. He worked independently, running his business from a small office in North Berwick High Street, where this lone venture had rapidly expanded. Toby was slick and efficient, ensuring new work came through recommendation from satisfied customers.

Kirsty enjoyed teaching nine-year-olds at St Mungo's. The age appealed because they were still innocent, but more house trained, as she put it, than her friend Diane's class of five-year-old children. On Friday afternoon they'd enjoyed a visit from a former army officer. It tied in nicely with their current project work on the Second World War, and provided some understanding as to why the army is still needed today. She'd given him the nickname of Mr SAS because something he'd said during their previous telephone conversation led her to think he was not an ordinary officer. He was diplomatic, putting most of his focus on peace and negotiation, deftly avoiding any preference for blood, gore and guns. Carefully chosen words were pitched with candour, appropriate to the age group. He brought pictures of himself in uniform and also a slide show exhibiting a variety of army equipment. While he talked, Kirsty observed his highly polished brown brogues, finding it preferable to study them in detail rather than risk feeling disconcerted by making eye contact. That is, until time ran out for the pupils to ask any more questions. A rehearsed thank you speech was delivered by a girl, which precipitated a spontaneous round of applause. Two of the more responsible children were then delegated to escort Mr SAS to the staffroom.

'I'll join you shortly,' she promised.

Five minutes after the home bell rang, she made her way along the corridor to reconnect with her guest. Mr SAS stood at ease with his hands behind his back by the window observing a tidal wave of children surge across the playground, eager to escape.

'Thank you. I think your talk was a great success,' she said. 'Can I get you a cup of something?'

He nodded, only half turning in her direction, 'Please, tea would be nice.'

Just then Marjorie, who taught Primary 4, rushed in.

'God Almighty, Kirsty, what an afternoon! Please tell me I'm allowed to strangle just one of the little darlings.' She sat down heavily on a chair before noticing an unknown man by the window.

'Oops, only joking,' she laughed nervously.

He remained standing while the ladies sat. Marjorie changed her complaint to how many reports she still needed to write, insisting she'd rather clean the loo than settle to the task. Kirsty half-listened to her colleague, preferring to study the stranger in their midst, wondering what made a man like him want to become a soldier in a crack regiment.

'Well, these reports won't write themselves,' Marjory said eventually. 'I'm going to love you and leave you.'

Mr SAS turned and smiled at Kirsty when her colleague left the room.

'Truly dedicated,' he said, tipping his head to the side, feigning a long suffering facial expression. 'Can't stand people who are half-hearted about their chosen profession. I sense you are not.'

Blushing, she said, 'I know the children will be talking about your visit for days to come.' She tried to fix her face into resembling a smile. It was then she asked the question which had niggled at her throughout the afternoon. 'Have you ever killed another person?'

With no visible reaction revealing any emotion, he responded politely, 'We are programmed how to forget.' Then looking at his watch, he suggested it was time for him to leave, adding how nice it had been to meet her.

*

Kirsty yawned as she scooped porridge from the pan into a bowl. It had been exceptionally early when she'd leapt out of bed to pick up the phone, trying not to disturb Toby's Saturday slumber.

'Aunt Cressida? Dead?' she'd said, surprised by Sam's revelation, and moved quietly to another area of the flat, away from the bedroom where she sat on one of their leather armchairs.

'Yes, totally unexpected, a heart attack,' Sam said. 'She was taken into hospital just after midnight, but died about an hour ago. The precise time according to Maud was 5.40.'

'Oh that's so sad. Poor Cressida.'

'I know. Aunt Maud has asked if I can go to Victoria Terrace immediately to console her. I think Cressida will be sorely missed, she was a great soother.'

'And can you? Go, I mean.' She didn't wait for a reply. 'Yes she was, even if these last few years she preferred her own solitude.'

'Certainly I can go, but I won't get there before lunchtime. I have some days owing and can call the office and arrange to take Monday off.' After a pause he asked, 'How are you?'

'Me? Oh fine. As ever, busy enough, you know the usual round of work, domesticity and all that.'

Sam sighed. 'Who would have thought, Maud would be the last survivor.'

'True, but then nothing with her should ever surprise. We should know that by now.'

Sam laughed.

'Yes indeed. Do you remember when we were children and she made us eat every scrap of food on the plate and you struggled with the kidney in her home-made pie?'

'Oh God, yes I do. The texture made me want to gag, but what was particularly terrifying was imagining being sick all over her pristine lace tablecloth.'

They both laughed. 'Well, at least you managed to avoid such a disaster.'

There followed speculation as to when the funeral might be. Sam promised he would call immediately the arrangements became definite. Also, that he'd be prepared to arrange more days off if needed to stay on longer.

'I shall speak to Aunt Maud later,' she said. 'And remember, if you need any help with anything, I'm here.'

*

There was a time she would have kissed Toby's cheek when presenting a steaming bowl of oatmeal. Any dilemma relieved in finding his focus remained fixed on the juice filled glass.

'It's such a pity it has to be a funeral that brings what's left of the family together,' she said, placing the bowl on the table.

Toby had been her first and only boyfriend. They'd married when she was barely twenty-two with congratulations from those he now ignored. Instead of acknowledging her angst he tried to entertain with tales of sealing a contract with the managing director of Benisom Books. Kirsty followed his lead, understanding the wisdom of taking care to praise her husband's business skills until he glowed.

With every last drop of oatmeal licked from his spoon he sat back saying, 'One thing I can always do is make you laugh. I like to hear you laugh.'

Wiping her mouth on a red paper napkin, she blew a kiss across the table, and carried the dishes to the sink before he moved to sit on the sofa and lifted the remote control to switch on the television. As she tidied, disgruntled sounds suggested that scanning through the channels was failing to find anything which spiked his interest.

'Come and give me a cuddly,' he requested when she'd finished her chores.

'Diane had a funny one,' she started snuggling beside him. 'You know she takes the infant class? Well, she was reading *Cinderella*, with oodles of dramatic effect. When she got to the bit where poor Cinderella was left all alone...'

'Shhh, I want to listen to this,' Toby said, having finally settled on the History Channel. Exerting a gentle squeeze on her shoulder, suggesting she should obey.

'I shall...' she tried to continue.

'Not now, this is interesting,' he insisted, becoming irritated.

Soon her eyes felt heavy, having missed out on extra sleep that morning. 'It's been a big week, think I'll go and lie down for a while, leave you in peace.'

'Okay, on you go. I'll shout when it's lunchtime. This pro- gramme finishes at noon.'

Chapter 2

Eastbourne

'In reality, she was a hideous creature,' Aunt Maud emphasised the word hideous. Intrusive sunlight penetrated frayed window blinds, piercing Sam's eyes as he squinted to focus. He could only suppose his elderly aunt, as usual, assumed she knew best. He would have preferred to feel indifferent, but instead sadness wafted over him because any opportunity to prove her wrong had died that morning with Cressida. It was Sam's stepmother who was being referred to, the one who brought shame on the family by connecting intimately with his father Matthew.

'Be a dear and make me a cup of tea,' requested the old lady as she retrieved a crisp lace handkerchief from her cardigan sleeve, before adding, 'Oh! And a biscuit would be nice, blue tin, left of the kettle.'

The smell of Maud's life was most pungent in the area surrounding three steps leading down into the kitchen. Sam paused for a moment before making his descent. He gazed into a large open cupboard, which resembled a library, crammed full with Mills and Boon romances. Its own distinct musty aroma of damp decaying paper remained exactly the same as remembered from his childhood visits.

Entering the kitchen gave him a brief respite of temporary solitude. Although it was not yet noon it felt like an entire day had elapsed since the early morning summons to Victoria Terrace. The recent death left Maud, the eldest of three sisters and one brother, as the sole survivor. Maud had one daughter, Victoria; Philippa, her younger sister by two years, was Kirsty's mother; Cressida was three years younger than her, had never married, and finally Matthew, the youngest, was Sam's father. Over the years the cousins had little in the way of contact. The sisters formed their own secret society and rarely wavered from weekly phone calls to each other at prescribed times. Thursday at 2pm or Monday at 6pm, always on the chime of the hour and religiously alternated as to who would make the call and who would receive. During his adolescent years Sam had been of little interest to Maud; his father was an outcast and his mother had extracted herself and him from the family fold.

Once Sam matured to adulthood he became useful again, a man in the family. He tried to recollect how this had come about and had to admit it had been his doing more than Maud or Cressida's. There was a rising curiosity in him to know more about his own father and the family whose values he'd apparently condemned in the life choices he pursued. He was a bohemian artist living on pennies with a former actress, a recluse in the mountains of County Kerry.

Sam found himself wishing Kirsty did not live so far away and could be there to dilute Maud's intensity. The reference to his stepmother as being a hideous creature had induced acute discomfort. He calculated there had been fewer than ten meetings with Kirsty over the years, yet it was she who'd registered with him as being in any way normal. Whatever normal might be! he thought, reaching for the biscuit tin which was sitting to the left of the kettle.

Chapter 3

Dream

Modern, efficient central heating ensured the North Berwick bedroom had become stiflingly hot. Kirsty threw open the window before lying spread-eagled on the bed, relishing the touch of cool air stroking her uncovered body. It was a particularly dark, grey day. The breeze caused the curtains to billow, admitting the hint of an orange aura from a street lamp which, for some reason, remained lit. The television had been silenced, which she'd grown to recognise meant Toby was probably on the computer. The interesting programme, not so interesting after all.

Her imagination saw them lying side by side in this king-size bed, between luxurious Egyptian cotton sheets. He held her close and kissed her brow with credible tenderness; it felt so real, as she drifted into sleep. Before long the dream woke her, one which often replayed unaltered, until convinced it was communicating some kind of message for to her to grasp. It was always the same; depicting a slender, handsome woman standing outside a church with a headscarf framing a well-proportioned face. She stood with her back to a chapel door looking down from an elevated position onto a fairground below. Sometimes the image came accompanied by an air of menace which gripped Kirsty, making every fibre of her being tingle with fear.

It was not her first dream she believed to contain a message but the fairground, with its easy charm to mesmerise, had somehow clawed its way inside her mind. She craved to discover the reason why.

Toby dismissed her thoughts when she'd tried to share the experience, saying, 'It's meaningless, no point in fretting over imaginary people. You are so silly sometimes.'

Kirsty hated her inability to understand the dream. She sat on the edge of the bed and shivered, it was cold now. The window should be closed else she could be accused of wasting valuable heat. The bedside clock told her it was nearly noon, so rising to her feet and closing the window before pulling on her jeans and a loose sweater she left the bedroom. Before saying anything she observed her husband as he rummaged in a drawer to find the tin opener. A surge of love for his handsome features, his mop of black hair and the pout of his lips welled up inside her. Watching the perfect physique prompted the unconnected image of Aunt Cressida playing the piano while her mother and Maud looked on in admiration. Sam, the fair haired happy boy who idolised his father, wasn't there. Now it felt that the family as she knew it had dwindled to practically nothing. Toby was her family now and in such moments she accepted no one was perfect. Marriage, she often told herself, was about generosity, tolerance and sharing.

*

As they ate lunch Toby read the newspaper while she tried to convey how sad she felt this favourite aunt, who had always been considered the peacemaker, was gone. Philippa, Kirsty's mother, once said when talking about their brother Matthew, that not even Cressida could make a difference. Aunt Maud referred to her brother, when he was alive, as 'estranged'. She insisted that to say more could heap shame upon the family.

Toby showed little interest, but she continued regardless informing him that according to Aunt Maud, Matthew's unsavoury relationship with some actress type cost him a marriage to a perfectly respectable girl whose father was, after all, a doctor. Then raising her voice slightly in an effort to provoke some meagre response said, 'Cressida was the only one ever to meet her, to actually talk to the woman. Apparently she was quite nice, if a bit different from the norm.'

'The norm!' scoffed Toby from behind his newspaper.

A silence descended between them until he said, 'Right, I'm going for a shower. Just don't ask or expect me to attend any funeral. Far too much going on at work.' Then, over his shoulder as he disappeared out of the room he added, 'And don't forget I need you for that meeting on Wednesday night.'

*

Kirsty fumbled frantically with the front door key, to answer the phone before it rang off. It was Tuesday, which meant a staff meeting kept her later at school. Picking it up and trying not to sound too breathless, she heard Sam's tired voice greeting her from the other end and giving information the funeral was scheduled for Friday.

'It's good to talk,' she said as he unburdened details of the difficulties experienced staying with Aunt Maud since Saturday. She listened sympathetically knowing that it was better he was there because she would not have the same tolerance level for the old lady's irritating behaviour. When his collection of complaints about being treated as a slave ended, she said, 'Thanks for letting me know about the arrangements. See you on Friday.'

'Oh! Wait, nearly forgot. There's a letter for you from Aunt Cressida.'

'A letter?'

'Yes. The lawyer suggested I warn you to look out for it arriving in North Berwick.'

'Oh!'

'Yes, apparently she left a letter to be given to you when she died. I have no idea what it's all about. Anyways, now you know, so watch for it in the post.'

'Does Maud know?'

'Absolutely not, that's why he wanted to post it to you.'

Immediately Kirsty felt a burst of curiosity. Whatever was it about? She tried to imagine what it could possibly be as she prepared supper.

When they had eaten she cleared the dishes before sitting down to mark a pile of school jotters. By the time she'd finished, her head ached. She joined Toby, who sat watching television with both feet on the coffee table and handing him a mug of tea recoiled from the odour of sweaty feet. Accepting the drink, he mentioned a film he wanted to watch, before proceeding to slurp excessively at the hot contents.

'Must you?'

There was no answer.

'Must you do that?' she repeated.

'Yes, I must,' his response was tainted with sarcasm.

Anger welled inside her with a new ferocity which translated to, 'Does it ever occur to you once in a while it would be nice to be asked if there might be something I would like to watch?'

Toby looked surprised. 'Well, is there? Is there something you would like to watch?'

Kirsty struggled to recall what day of the week it was, so had to sink back into defeat. 'I haven't a clue what's on.'

'Well stop being such a sour-faced bitch then.'

She fidgeted in the large leather armchair, creating rasping squeaky sounds. 'Just supposing I was allowed to have the remote control once in a blue moon, then maybe I could look at the programme listings.'

This time she was not giving up, even if her voice started to quiver. Toby's face blackened before he threw the remote control in her direction. His aim was perfect. Smack, it hit her upper arm.

'Oh dear, I'm so sorry, did it hit you?' he smirked.

Tears smarted in her eyes, as she glowered in his direction.

'Oooooo got a little hump on, have we?' he mocked.

From somewhere, Kirsty found the strength to fight back. She had been doing more of that recently and he didn't like it.

'Always Toby, the world has to go the way Toby says, and what Toby wants he must have with never a care or a real thought for anyone. I pity you.' Painfully aware as the word 'pity' fell from her lips it was likely to provoke a severe reaction. Blackness swamped his features. He did not look handsome, or resemble the wonderful Mr Right. He became the man who could only cope when in full control of himself and those around him. A tremor started in her hands and legs, then took root deep inside until she shook uncontrollably. He stood up and stepped towards her but she did not flinch. He wouldn't dare, she told herself; no, he wouldn't dare. Toby towered above her small curled figure. He stood for what felt like an eternity as she waited for the impact of his reaction. All the time she longed to scream at him that she was aware. She knew all about his seedy, tainted, pathetic, degrading, twisted, tragic, insulting, and deeply hurtful other world.

Toby sneered, 'Look at you, if there is pity to be apportioned you have the biggest slice. No, on second thoughts, you have it all.' He paused for a moment, then coldly said, 'Goodnight.' She watched him walk away with his usual swagger. The leather felt cold next to her skin, it rejected her body heat and she shivered violently. Only then did she liberate the tears pressing for release.

Later, when Toby knelt on the floor in front of her, pleading forgiveness with his great big eyes, expressing a desire to kiss and make up, she was receptive to his charm.

'Mmm that was a nice cuddly,' he said, before he rolled away from her and slept soundly. Where had any tenderness gone? She rarely refused him. It was easier not to. Toby had a 'healthy' sexual appetite, sex between them played out three or four times a week, mostly in the dark.

Kirsty accepted the crumbs on offer because among the mire were times they giggled together or cuddled with tenderness. She lived for those moments, because they compensated for the hurtful behaviour, all those derogative comments, which dispensed a vile sensation of anxiety in the pit of her stomach. When he was tender she could forget those bad nights when she felt him thrusting mechanically with increasing rapidity, glad to know that faster meant the sooner it would be over. Toby told her what she wanted. He believed he knew what turned her on, quite convinced he was a sexy man women liked.

Sometimes she consoled herself by retreating in to a fantasy world where a lover, a faceless man, kissed her slowly, smothering her with love. He adored her.

Chapter 4

The Letter

When she arrived back at their flat on Wednesday afternoon she found the letter waiting on the mat, postmarked Eastbourne. It had been a frantic day and remained unfinished, so she slid it into her handbag. Then she started to get ready to attend the 'Buccap' meeting on Toby's behalf, glad the venue was a local hotel.

Only when alone in the bedroom much later that evening did Kirsty retrieve the letter. Inside the type-faced cream coloured envelope she found a smaller pale pink one with italic blue ink depicting her name on the front, instantly recognisable as Cressida's script. She placed it on the bedside table and examined it at a distance for a moment, before snatching it back again to break the seal. It revealed two folded sheets of premium quality writing paper. There was no address or date.

My dear Kirsty,
   Where to begin is the problem, but begin I must.
   For many years I have felt the injustice inflicted on you and feared you may become aware through an outside source. The consequence of which would have been detrimental. This is a

family matter and before I proceed to the crux of my reason to put pen to paper, I want to assure you everything was done with a sincere belief it was correct for all involved at the time.

I am sure you are aware of a rift within the family which occurred many years ago between us sisters and our brother, Matthew. However, it was not always so. There was a time when I, in particular, was close to Matthew and his wife. Yes, the woman whom it chokes Maud to mention. Sam remains within the family circle and a firm favourite of our self-appointed chief. The irony being that his parents were ruthlessly excluded.

Matthew and Marie are both dead and gone, as I shall be if you are reading this letter. It is not possible for anyone now to ask exactly what happened, but I can and will shed a little light. Please appreciate this is so difficult for me to do.

I have restarted this letter several times. You see, something occurred which involves you. Something I firmly believe you should be made aware of and quite possibly will help you to make sense of things which were hard to understand during your formative years.

Marie was Irish, an actress Matthew met somewhere in London, I believe, although I was never sure. She was beautiful, charming and a breath of fresh air to our serious existence. She came from a small village in County Kerry called Balvohan. Regular contact was maintained with her own family, although they rarely visited until the couple selected a cottage high in the Kerry Mountains in which to live. Presumably they had funds from somewhere. Maud believes there was some sort of scandal which precipitated a need for them to leave London, but I do not. Matthew was an artist and Marie, who had grown tired with the glitter of the theatre, longed for a return to her homeland.

At this time, Philippa and your father visited them, three times altogether, and during one of these visits it was all arranged. Philippa was so excited, but first they had to convert to the Catholic faith. As you are aware, your parents were Catholic, and you were raised in the faith, another thorn in Maud's flesh!

This process was fast tracked by a kindly priest located by Marie, a relative of hers, I believe. So Philippa, three or four months later, was pronounced a devout Catholic. Now this is where you come in.

Marie told me your parents visited a Magdalene Laundry where it had been arranged, mostly by her, that they were to collect a baby. That baby was you. Sorry, but there is no gentle way to say this.

You were to become what's known as a de facto adoption. That is where the adoptive parents register the infant as their own, so no one is any the wiser regarding the truth of their origin. Matthew knew and disapproved, Marie urged your parents to think differently, to be more transparent. I know, because she confided in me, hoping I could change their minds on the matter. To my dying shame, I confess to you now, I did not try. I was scared to mention it and pretended to believe what they wanted us to believe, that Philippa produced you herself. This was all perfectly plausible because during those years we saw little of each other. Letter writing and phone calls sufficed to maintain contact.

I did wonder if Matthew or Marie might inform you, but they were, I suppose, preoccupied particularly when Marie became ill. Matthew devotedly nursed her back to health only to then become ill himself. Sam knows nothing of this. Victoria is ignorant of any such facts, and even our self-elected head of family, Maud, remains oblivious. Those who knew are all gone and I escape your wrath being in receipt of such a revelation by communicating from the grave.

Your biological mother was apparently a young Irish girl who came from the same village – Balvohan in County Kerry. She was abandoned at a Magdalene Laundry in Limerick by her own family upon discovery of her pregnancy. In the Magdalene Convent the girl, whom I recollect was named Biddy Duffy, remained long after your birth. What then became of her I have no idea.

I know nothing of your father, only what I relate above. Please, I beg do not be angry with me. Surely this is something you should know even if it arrives as something of a bombshell later in your life.

So here I have given you all the information I can and wish you well.

Have a good life and may you find happiness.

Your loving aunt,
Cressida

Chapter 5

South

The following morning when they met briefly at breakfast, Toby was eager to hear about the Buccap meeting. Kirsty pleased him by delivering a positive report, with assurance she'd managed to speak to everyone he'd previously suggested was of importance.

'Good girl, I am proud of you,' he said, tapping her bottom. 'Oh and I think I have the contract nailed, bar the signature. He's coming to the office later to finalise the details.'

'Good, I am pleased for you. Remember I'm away tonight. All being well, I'll return sometime on Sunday evening, depending on the train.'

'That's okay. I'll keep myself entertained,' said Toby. 'Call me sometime. Let me know how old Maud is these days?'

Having arranged compassionate leave for the Friday, Kirsty made her journey south after school, arriving late on Thursday evening at the pre-booked Eastbourne accommodation. The entire duration of the long train journey was completely preoccupied with thoughts of the disclosure contained in the letter. It was a new sensation to experience the essence of her existence as a falsehood perpetrated by people she'd believed to be trustworthy.

As soon as possible she collapsed into bed, aware the following day could prove to be gruelling. All hope of restful sleep vanished into the quagmire of the revelation. As the night became elongated these thoughts became supplemented with irritation that communication within her marriage was becoming more fatuous and redundant by the day. He should have been there with her now, and at the Buccap meeting the previous evening, but made his excuses with the usual aplomb. Slick and well-practised, like a machine regularly maintained. So often had she gone instead and hated every minute of the fawning, simpering, drooling conversations that festooned such evenings.

Always his life was more important than hers, his needs, whims and fancies. Those who were wiser would have none of it; they would kick, scream and fight every step of the way, or else divorce. She never asked him why. He never offered the answer, not really, just charmed and smarmed his way through life. He was so very sure he had everyone taped, sorted, compartmentalised. Particularly her. She wrapped herself in darkness, the blanket of night. He should be proud of her, an ambassador in his absence. There were those who would say he was hardly missed.

Of course it was simple really, he had to die. Not in the sense his breath might cease, but die in her, cease to exist as any sort of thread which could be tugged. How do you get rid of someone like that? Years etched on a heart, tightly embraced memories of united moments. Some brief, so fleeting the grasp of them might escape until a sweet breeze would rekindle enough to allow the wistful, instantaneous poignancy to fool and tantalise before evaporating again. When she woke in the morning she remembered everything.

*

Showered and dressed, she felt equipped to face the day. Raising the window blind, she saw written in bold letters on the car park wall, a warning to drivers. EXPECT THE UNEXPECTED. With everything she needed in her handbag, she set off to walk to Aunt Maud's house.

Soon her feet started to ache. The shoes she wore were all wrong. A wooden bench begged her to sit a while to contemplate waves rippling over Eastbourne pebbles. It was strange to revisit, the last occasion on the promenade had been with her mother. A child who observed the strange dynamics between three aging women who collectively never spoke kindly about anyone as far as she could recall. Individually, Cressida and her mother were not so vicious so perhaps this made Maud the necessary ingredient for integrity to disintegrate. It provided relief to take the weight off those throbbing feet and raise them in front of her, wiggling her toes inside new red shoes. She loved red shoes, so decadent, but dared not take them off for fear those poor feet refused to be squashed back inside them again.

Philippa, her mother, was in her thoughts too as she recalled how the eldest sister intimidated all her siblings. 'How typical of her to be the last survivor,' she muttered hoping nobody was near enough to hear. She was determined that today Aunt Maud would not be permitted to intimidate. Sun tried to push through a cluster of spit-laden grey clouds. The few pale blue rags, expanded to become more than enough for Our Lady's veil. Visits to Aunt Maud had always been infrequent, even when her mother was alive, but today there was a funeral to attend and no escape. What array of new weapons might have been amassed in the old lady's armoury? She couldn't help but wonder.

Sighing deeply, acknowledging the time on her watch, she knew there was nothing else for it but to continue walking into the wind with bird-like steps to accommodate pinched toes. It was a long way to the end of the promenade and a further five minutes beyond the Grand Hotel to reach Maud's house. Apprehensively she eyed a weighty black cloud drifting rapidly across the sea. It left her with diminishing confidence that she would make it to her destination before rain fell. For some inexplicable reason the stylish umbrella bought to complement her handbag had been left behind in North Berwick.

Crunch; she stepped from the pavement to Aunt Maud's gravel driveway. Having examined her shoes she felt relief in seeing no stones had left any mark on the leather, she tugged the bell cord and waited. Sam opened the door, greeting her with a welcoming hug.

'Aunt Maud awaits,' he said. 'She's in good enough humour under the circumstances, just anxious to get the funeral over with.'

'Have you got some sort of air freshener?' Kirsty asked, stepping into the hallway.

'I have. Lilac. Can you smell it?'

She nodded, but refrained from saying how strange it was not to be met with an odour of mothballs and cooked cabbage.

'Had to do something,' he added.

The elderly lady drummed her fingers on the worn velvet arm of her chair, extending a sarcastic welcome. 'At last! We were beginning to think you might be lost in space.'

'Hello, Aunt Maud,' she responded forcing herself to kiss an aged wrinkled cheek before being pushed back.

'Let me look at you. Goodness, there is nothing of you. Slim as ever, too thin if you ask me.'

Kirsty gritted her teeth smiling benignly, wondering how many other barbed comments she might be subjected to. Sam took over, explaining the arrangements for the day. The funeral was at noon followed by a light lunch in the Grand Hotel. A big turnout was not expected but there would be a buffet to cater for at least twenty people, in case numbers exceeded expectation. The lawyer would meet them all at the house around four, and that was it.

Maud appeared subdued, but it did not prevent her asking about the lovely, handsome Toby. Her niece, who felt determined she should sound upbeat, responded by saying he was as busy and handsome as ever. Then added he sent his condolences and apologies for being unable to attend due to the pressure of work.

'Time off is difficult when you're a one-man band,' she smiled.

A black limousine came to collect the three of them from the house at 11.45. Kirsty had not dared to ask if Victoria was going to attend, but thought it could add clarity to why Maud appeared unusually subdued. Sam solved the mystery as he walked her to the car, whispering that Maud's daughter had arranged to rendezvous with them at the crematorium chapel.

Victoria was instantly conspicuous, wearing red from head to toe. Her outfit paled Kirsty's shoes into insignificance. Cressida loved the colour red, they all knew, but whatever would Maud, in her black funereal outfit, make of her own daughter's added Americanisation, as she would no doubt see it? Cressida had worn a red jacket at Philippa's funeral four years earlier. The rather special hug she gave Kirsty that day took on a new significance in light of the recently received letter. Yes, Aunt Maud would surely blame the New Yorkers for this and all other such changes in her daughter, Kirsty thought as she smiled at Victoria who reciprocated before moving to sit beside her mother. Fifteen people had gathered to say farewell to Cressida, including the minister. He was a short, bald man who mentioned relatives had travelled from as far as Scotland and New York to honour their aunt, as if these places were equidistant. He talked of Cressida's life, as prescribed on the sheet of paper provided by the surviving sister. It was all a bit dry, unsentimental and unexciting. Maud and Victoria dabbed their eyes with dainty lace handkerchiefs. Kirsty was amazed to notice how their mannerisms mirrored each other exactly, rendering any statement made by a red outfit redundant. The sparse congregation learnt where Cressida was born, about her siblings, her school, choice of career, nothing remotely intriguing or even faintly amusing. With a scratchy rendition of 'One More Step Along the World I Go', the coffin glided on a conveyor through parted velvet curtains and disappeared.

On entering the Grand Hotel, what was immediately obvious was just how 'grand' it was. A uniformed porter stood to attention and held the door open, bidding each of them a sombre good afternoon. At the far end of the entrance hall stood an imposing marble fireplace surrounded by oil paintings. Two in particular appealed to Kirsty, one of a lute player, and opposite, on the left, was a flute player. The mourners progressed through a door and along a corridor to be guided into the Norfolk Room set to accommodate the meagre post-funeral gathering.

Lunch consisted of unsubstantial but delicious morsels. She loved the honey-coated sausages and barbecued chicken wings, making several visits to the buffet table rather than heaping her plate in an unladylike way. Maud tutted as she picked at a bite-sized egg sandwich, mumbling something about steak pie being more appropriate. Kirsty chatted to an elderly neighbour who said she hardly saw Cressida and felt sorry for the old lady. The young woman who delivered the meals on wheels said more or less the same. It confirmed her aunt had become reclusive in old age. Two waitresses dressed discreetly in crisp white aprons tied over black uniform dresses ensured the guests were constantly provided with drinks.

Sam was Sam. Tallish, blondish, slimmish, with a charming smile. Kirsty observed him move with ease among the scanty group of ancient guests, noticing it was nothing like the way Toby worked a room. There was something far more genuine in his approach. She wondered why he'd never married. All she knew was he worked as an insurance underwriter and lived in an old woodcutter's cottage on the edge of the New Forest. She felt ashamed not knowing any more details about his life.

At just after two, it was Sam whom Maud beckoned, eager to suggest it was time to return home; asking if he could organise the car to collect them.

Once home, Graeme Carter soon arrived. He struck Kirsty as being long past retirement age. He mumbled and Maud sighed, glowering at him before eventually saying, 'Can you speak up a bit? Some of us are having difficulty hearing you.' The whole process did not take long. Sam, Victoria and Kirsty had each been left the sum of £10,000. Maud inherited all Cressida's jewellery together with the house and a children's charity would receive the residue of the estate, estimated to be around £5,000 once all sundries had been dealt with.

Mr Carter then requested a private audience with Kirsty. He wanted reassurance Cressida's letter had been delivered safely. He explained the aim of posting it was to avert any potentially awkward questions from Aunt Maud. However, when the meeting was over the old lady could not stifle her curiosity, saying, 'Well, what did he want with you?'

'He wondered if I knew his son who works in Edinburgh, that's all.' It was only half a lie, as he had also made such an enquiry.

'I see. You mean there is another one of him out there in the world?' declared Maud with utter disdain.

Chapter 6

Solitary

Kirsty's preference was to spend Saturday alone, having declined Victoria's invitation to lunch, she did however, agree to visit Aunt Maud's house for tea at four o'clock. It would have been rather ignorant not to go. Having eaten virtually nothing for breakfast, following another restless night, she anticipated a walk from Eastbourne to Beachy Head. Then, realising this would be a big task, opted instead to pay £5 for the tour bus. After the bus toiled up a steep hill she got off at the first stop, from where it was easy to walk to the cliff edge. A bright sun shone, enhancing the picturesque scenery. Had it not been for her total preoccupation with Cressida's revelations, it would have been pleasurable. To step from grey concrete onto the grassy South Downs Way brought some relief. Walking further to reach the headland, before stopping to look back at Eastbourne, Kirsty started to enjoy the sea air.

The dramatic disclosure contained in the letter had certainly shaken her, but not in a way which astounded or utterly amazed. While the content had come as a shock, it also served as a confirmation of something she gratefully accepted as having always known. There was comfort in learning why so many previously inexplicable things were becoming clearer. To start with, physically she had never felt remotely like any other member of the family. Sometimes as a young girl she stared at her parents and wondered if a stork really had deposited an infant on their doorstep. Her memories were of course of being with her parents, but now a new curiosity started to grow. She wanted to know more about a girl called Biddy Duffy.

Later, as she arrived back at Maud's house, she wondered about sharing this news with Sam. Yes, it would be good to communicate with someone, and he was the only person who would have any sort of real understanding of the disclosure. Tea was, as expected, rather formal, with Aunt Maud, Victoria, Sam and Kirsty sharing stilted, polite conversation. Victoria enthused about life in New York, Sam was non-committal in his description of work, while Maud remained distant and sad, making reference to how much she missed her sisters. Kirsty observed her 'relations' with awareness of why she saw nothing of herself reflected in any of them. Sam was the only one she felt any tangible affection for. Thinking too of Philippa, and how strange it seemed to put the word 'adoptive' in front of 'mother'. But, on the other hand, it made perfect sense, although she remained her mother in the reality of nurture there now came into being the added dimension of nature. Suddenly a little ditty started going round and round in her mind, *I know something you don't know* repeated in in a sing-song sort of way as she scanned their faces.

'Keep in touch,' said Sam, when Kirsty judged it was the earliest polite moment to depart. Just as she was on the brink of saying something about Aunt Cressida's letter, Victoria thwarted the attempt by appearing in the hallway.

'Before you go let me give you my email address.' Her slight American twang had become increasingly irksome. 'My mother thinks the world of you, both of you.' She looked at Sam who smiled. 'Thank you for being there for her, I sometimes feel guilty being stuck on the other side of the Atlantic.' Then giving Kirsty a farewell hug, she said, 'Come on, Sam, let's get back to Ma before she thinks we've abandoned her.'

With little alternative available, Kirsty left, setting off to walk back along the prom to her hotel.

By the time of her arrival in North Berwick on the Sunday afternoon, more than one destination had been reached. Her aunt's revelation added to the cacophony of thoughts already jousting inside her for supremacy. Encased in a bubble of otherness where reality had become hazy, she managed to retain enough awareness to know there was a need to be extremely careful.

Opening the door to a cold grey flat she found no welcoming convivial warmth from radiators to greet her, only a scribbled note on the kitchen table: Don't wait up, not sure when I'll be back. Meeting Stan Clark.

'My punishment for being away,' she muttered, squashing the paper in her hand before tossing it into the bin.

Poached egg on toast was all she could face before settling to read her letter again. She wanted to commit every word to memory. Then she concealed it carefully in a book which she placed at the back of her wardrobe beneath a pile of jumpers. Utterly exhausted, scared, confused, sad, lonely and desperate for sleep, she lay on their luxurious bed and curled herself into a tight ball, glad to be alone.

Drifting from consciousness into her world of dreams took her to a cottage in the Kerry Mountains. One single ray of sun pierced the window and caught Matthew's heart in a gasp for breath. He longed to paint a portrait with eyes of blue, hair of black, lips ruby red and hues of pink to dab upon burnished cheeks. With deft sable strokes he became committed to revive Marie's spent beauty upon a canvas. He worked all day and barely slept by night. Her body, weary in a fight for life, admired the inner potency of his devotion and through gentle words spoken knew he loved. Each stroke of sable restored until she overflowed with renewed zest to defeat death.

Marie scanned the finished portrait and scowled, finding no greater beauty displayed. He begged she should try to see what he intended. With seductive musings she cajoled, baited and teased until gladness filled his heart and culminated when their youth became rekindled. But then it was he who grew frail, his vigour waned as hers grew stronger. He languished, feeble, drained and vulnerable. She tossed her head, resenting the serenity locked in the portrait he painted.

When he died she lamented, but as winter snow trickled to nothing and green shoots pushed from his grave, a knock came upon her door. The stranger used persuasive words so she bid him enter, rejoicing in laughter until, insidious and consumed, he lay by her side as apple blossoms drifted on the wind. Amid bursting buds she celebrated new liberty and cried to no one there, 'Lucifer be dammed.'

When the stranger viewed her picture she told him lies. He should not know of her disguise. Soft beauty twisted and curled as the mystery unfurled. She watched him stride away, her framed image by his side exchanged for thirty pieces of silver left upon her table. He did not care.

Kirsty stirred restlessly from slumber.

Who has the right to disenchant, to scrape the core of a soul until all traces of its past are erased? No one can, nothing can. She was dark-haired and slim-figured, an outward manifestation of her differences, alien to the heavier-build and blonde-haired family she grew up surrounded by but never questioned. It was there all the time. She had felt it inside so often.

Observation is an old woman's memory. Memory can never die, only be locked behind doors which are not always easy to penetrate, they sometimes shrivel but never die. Perhaps the solution is to throw away the key, she thought. Why does it matter? Really? Let it all sink to the bottom of an ocean deep. An ocean full of good intentions with deepening fathoms to hide dark deeds and suffocate seeds of doubt, should they threaten germination.

Chapter 7

Setback

The following morning Kirsty set in motion the next phase of her life. For the first time the wider world called to her as Mrs Campbell, the headmistress at St Mungo's, reluctantly accepted her resignation. One thing still remained to be done, the most difficult thing she'd ever faced and that was to inform Toby their marriage was over. The number and variety of speeches rehearsed over the last few weeks failed to produce the words she felt expressed her sentiments in a non-threatening, acceptable way. That evening he would be home at six precisely, she knew, because he had to eat before going to a meeting at seven. If nothing else, he was predicable when it came to meticulous timing. Toby was able to boast sobriety for fourteen years, and was justifiably proud of this achievement. He had gained a reputation for being one of the best speakers in the area, which resulted in frequent requests for him to take the chair at AA meetings within their district. Officially, he sponsored one man, but several women talked to him regularly on the phone. 'Save me from alci-women,' he often said when the conversation ended, yet always sounded sincere and compassionate when Kirsty overheard his side of these conversations.

Before now she had never quite managed to break his spell,

always relenting remorsefully to her puppy-eyed husband. She gathered the guilt he dealt for making him wretched. It was because she'd overreacted or it was that time of the month he would eloquently say and like the fool he'd turned her into she believed any disagreement to be her fault. Her moment of epiphany was blurred, a gradual process rather than one event, a culmination of little things led her to acceptance that it was not her to blame when he raged at her or belittled her more often than could be considered acceptable.

'Can you sit for a moment?' she asked. 'You still have at least fifteen minutes before heading out to Aberlady. This won't take long, please listen.'

'Okay. What is it?'

She launched into one of her prepared speeches. 'I have given what I am about to say a lot of thought. In fact, there have been times when I have wanted to say this before but have never managed.'

'Say what? Get on with it,' said Toby.

Taking a deep breath, because there was no gain in dragging it out longer than necessary, she began, 'I want to leave you, leave the marriage, separate or however else it should be put.'

He said nothing but his expression suggested he was expecting more.

'I feel it would be better for both of us. Don't you?'

He cut across her, 'Okay.'

She was astonished not to be met with an insulting verbal onslaught. Instead, he merely shrugged his shoulders. 'Whatever,' his scant response. 'I'll give you peace to pack. I'm going to my meeting now.'

So, no lingering goodbye. No pleading or begging.

Before he returned, her car was loaded with her most important possessions and she was gone, driving straight to Diane's flat where a bowl of piping hot pasta and a bottle of wine awaited.

Kirsty surprised both herself and her dear friend, with how well she appeared to cope during the initial weeks of marital separation. From February until the Easter school break the routine of work, company in the flat and a feeling of relief was all she experienced. Numb was the word she believed best to describe her emotional state. Gradually the bad times with Toby gave way to memories of good times. This subtle change coincided with her obsessing less over Cressida's letter, and she had to admit she missed her husband. A new longing to see him meant she struggled to maintain the outer facade of liberation.

Everything else was going to plan. Mrs Campbell announced just before school finished for Easter that a new teacher had been appointed and would start in May. Kirsty feigned happiness when the date was agreed for her to finish at the end of April. Mrs Kavenagh, the new teacher, visited and proved to be a lovely lady, in her mid-forties, firm but kind; so she knew the children would be well attended.

The exit plan had been nicely taking shape, that is, until one day Kirsty met Toby in North Berwick High Street. Instantly her heart beat faster, she could hardly ignore him, yet did not want to engage in conversation. He flummoxed her completely by looking devastatingly handsome and gushed with charm, expressing softly-spoken sentiments which sent shivers down her spine. He told her he missed her. What a pity their love had to end this way. Did she have any thoughts or even a tiny hope they would or could reconcile their differences? All his good traits, the parts of him she had fallen in love with were on display. Watching his plump lips closely as he spoke she longed to know their touch again.

Finally managing to extract herself, which was not easy, she rushed into a nearby shop. Once inside she found herself trembling uncontrollably, so much so the lady behind the counter fetched a chair, persuading her to sit and take time to recover. That night she booked into a bed and breakfast on the coast using the pretence of more items to be collected from their flat. The cruelty was in her belief, *he still loves me.*

Chapter 8

Turmoil

It was exactly 4.25 a.m. for one second, before two seconds, three seconds ticked by, all gone. In the same way as yesterday, last year and the year before. Kirsty stopped this train of thought, it was becoming too complicated. She sat on the edge of the bed, trying to work out whether she should be rising to face the day or attempt sleep. Her head ached. She slid her hands over the white cotton in an effort to dry beads of sweat from her palms. She turned on the bedside lamp and reached down to the floor to find her faded pink knickers and stepped into them before lifting her bra and cupping her small breasts in lace. Then, with a sudden surge of urgency, she slipped on her skirt and favourite pale blue blouse before snatching a cardigan from the back of a chair. She hesitated briefly to look at the reflection staring back from the full-length mirror fixed to a wardrobe. No more! She of all people should know it was not possible to survive on crumbs of affection. The fool in her had let him seduce her mind again after all the weeks in a position of strength.

April air tinged with the scent of spring wafted temptingly through the open window inviting her to step outside where all was quiet and still. Calm, like the water, when she reached the small harbour. Serenity threatened to dominate another day. Something in this tranquillity disturbed her and she yearned for a brisk, fresh wind to ruffle her curls and spike her eyes with tears. Inside she hurt so much. Toby had pulled her to him and pushed her away too many times. She shivered in the chilled early morning air. It was not yet daylight, but clear enough to follow her route as she continued on to the end of the harbour pier. Dark brown timber appeared worn in places where splinters sheared off into the water which lapped incessantly round wooden stakes. These plunged, into its depths years ago.

Deep enough, she thought, moving to sit with her legs dangling, swinging to and fro in a child-like way over the edge. Sunrise crept slowly across the sky to dispel the residual darkness. Occasionally a car could be heard on the road leading into town. Back and forth she swung her legs, as she glimpsed the outline of a trawler far out across the water.

There was no way of counting how many times he hurt her with sharpened words that seared through her heart. The perverse way he bound her to him, and when she tried to pull away would seductively intensify lavish attention until her servitude was regained. It was then he savoured inflicting pain, as he pushed her away again. Aware of all this, her heart had given in to him again and it caused distress trying to work out why.

The unravelling to expose the extent of his 'other' seedy world had been gradual. At first she believed there had to be some mistake, having stumbled upon some of his computer activity, or at least felt there could be a satisfactory explanation. Probing deeper, she found there could be no plausible excuses manufactured, even by a master of deceit.

How many profiles he had she could not be sure, but did know he weaved his own particular brand of charm anywhere it might have a hope of capture. He did it in the name of seeking a friend, an activity partner, and he even cast his net seeking sexual encounters. It had been hard to comprehend the truth. God knows, thought Kirsty, he had all angles covered with a strange array of names – tabletop, mousetrap, sanyo. The increasing carelessness in covering his tracks led her to believe he knew she knew and in his perverse way taunted her to challenge him. It was a sickness he would of course deny.

She could no longer be sure of who she was. An accumulation of everything was destroying her from the inside out. He would become aggressive and defensive in denial if she dared to question any small thing. Being fearful of her safety made her reluctant to present him with the evidence of his other world.

This man she was joined to in matrimony, was no more than a creature in search of self-gratification, an abuser devoid of normal feelings. Where other people had a soul this space was occupied by a black chasm, an empty vacuum.

The water gently whispered its offer of freedom. An escape, a final exodus from the mental torture of hating him but longing to be near him, hold, kiss, love him. Vindictiveness did not come naturally to her, even now she bore him no malice for his merciless spiteful acts. Kindness was alien to him, a pretence to gain control. Love was not a sickness, there never had been any love. What was this thing people called love? She didn't know.

Tilting forward, she closed her eyes and imagined how cold it would be engulfing her, filling her lungs, as oystercatchers circled overhead.

The road had become host to more vehicles. A tractor with a round bale of hay carried on large spikes clattered and jangled, while others still lay in bed delaying the arrival of Monday morning. Today the pavement would not feel the patter of young feet or hear the squeak of leather shoes as mother and child engaged in idle chatter carrying school bags. Easter brought respite from the world of classroom and teacher.

With the tractor's interruption she turned to find a lapwing staring, curious and inquisitive, trying to figure out why a shape with which it was not acquainted sat at the end of the jetty. The bird did not flinch, it did not fly. Water lapped in corrugated ripples composing a melodic tune and she wanted to feel its chill, but suddenly the bird flapped its wings and was gone.

Kirsty rose to her feet as if to follow the bird; with a new certainty her life would not become his prize.

Chapter 9

Distraction

Aunt Maud communicated with Kirsty having decided Cressida's house should be sold. Before it could be put on the market it first needed to be cleared and cleaned. The elderly lady felt unable to sanction thoughts of a stranger 'poking about' among her sister's possessions, so approached her niece and nephew with a request that they complete the task. It was the legacy left by Aunt Cressida which had given her the impetus needed to start making changes, therefore she felt it would be dishonourable to refuse. Several phone calls later and after lengthy discussions with Sam, Easter bank holiday weekend became mutually agreed as the optimum choice to unite and face the task. It would provide a welcome opportunity to escape from Scotland for a few days.

Diane had been concerned since her friend's admission following the encounter with Toby. The emotional content on display made it patently obvious he still held a perverse sort of power to derail Kirsty's plans for escape. With unwavering persistence, she tried to persuade her dear friend to change her mobile number. Or at least to block him. 'Damage limitation,' she said. Enforcing total non-contact with someone like Toby, in her opinion, was the only way to progress. 'It's like taking the sticking plaster off a wound, seeing him again, particularly in the way you did. He's not finished manipulating you yet. Be warned.'

'I'll change it soon, when I find a moment,' promised Kirsty.

This time she'd opted to drive to Eastbourne with a vacuum cleaner, mop, bucket and assortment of cleaning fluids. It took nine hours but nevertheless she stuck to the original plan of detouring by Cressida's house to drop off the cleaning items. It also provided an opportunity to inspect the magnitude of the task they faced. Aunt Maud had insisted on offering accommodation with her, but they would have to fend for themselves as she did not cook much these days.

Adopting the aura of an intruder, Kirsty opened the front door of Cressida's home using the key Maud posted to Edinburgh the previous week. A faint musty, un-lived-in smell followed her from the narrow hallway into the sitting room, where straight ahead stood the marble fireplace with distinctive pink and blue Victorian tiles. The hearth looked dowdy, dejected and cracked beneath an abandoned solitary brass poker. Dust formed a grey shadow over all former glory. The upright piano remained, its lid raised to expose several keys stripped of their white ivory. Peeping from the space between piano and wall, several framed pictures protested their careless abandonment. The three-piece suite which had caused boundless excitement on its arrival with vivid pink hues, was tired, threadbare and sad. Kirsty pressed three piano keys to form a musical chord, wincing at the clunky sound from the 'special' piano which in a past life produced melodic tones of Beethoven, Bach or Cole Porter. Matthew played by ear, Philippa told her when as a child she'd wondered why he had no need for books of music. Apparently he listened to tunes, learned them and then could play them beautifully without having to read a note.

Until this moment Kirsty's memory of Matthew was vague, but now she could see him sitting at the piano. Blonde, perfect white teeth, shirt sleeves rolled up to his elbows exposing strong tanned arms. The gold chain of a fob watch dangled from his waistcoat pocket and a pint glass half-full of burnished liquid sat upon the piano above his head. A small blonde boy beside him rested a hand on his father's leg. It had been Cressida, she recalled, who played Beethoven sublimely, while Maud stood at her shoulder flicking page after page of music. When did such family gatherings disintegrate? The bigger question had to be why. Was it because of Matthew and his Irish adventure?

No more grandiose reds, blues and cream could be appreciated on the Indian rug, which lay tattered and threadbare. The gold carriage clock presented to Cressida on retirement from the council offices managed to maintain something of its former glory, but had stopped ticking one distant day at twenty minutes past one. Kirsty remembered, her deceased aunt delighted in turning a key the back of the clock exactly nine times, sufficient to mark the passage of time for another seven days. The adult world of this, the original family house, was never that simple.

Stairs creaked as, one by one, as Kirsty ascended. Each of the four bedrooms appeared to be in a desperate state. She quickly resolved that no serious attack could be accomplished without wearing dust masks. All the rooms within this tired Victorian house appeared so much smaller than she remembered.

The remainder of her journey to reach Aunt Maud's was made on foot, carrying a small suitcase. The old lady greeted her niece warmly, being disarmingly charming and effusive.

Kirsty told her she had detoured by the house to leave cleaning items and the car where parking restrictions did not apply.

'Oh you are marvellous. Well done you, driving all the way from Scotland with a Dyson. Sam will be here, all being well, early morning, and is eager to get his sleeves rolled up.'

Kirsty smiled with amused embarrassment, wishing her

cousin was there already. However, it was easy to retreat and remain respectful, saying with truth that she needed an early night after such a long drive.

Sam arrived at Cressida's house just before ten the following morning and did indeed get his sleeves rolled up, quickly bagging a heap of rubbish and making a first journey to the tip.

'We make a good team,' he said, smiling. 'That's me ready to get rid of a second load,' his strong arms making light work of the piled-high black bags. Kirsty worked hard gathering the detritus of an unknown life. Sam presented her with 'rewards', such as bottles of Lucozade and bars of chocolate, purchased at the garage shop on his journeys to and from the tip.

'You're my kind of friend,' she joked, gratefully accepting the supply of indulgent calories.

'Can't have Aunt Maud complaining you're too thin,' he said.

'Look at this,' Kirsty exclaimed and lifted a very large beige corset from the wardrobe. 'You want me to end up having to wear one of these?'

Sam laughed. 'It's a bit personal, poor deceased Aunt Cressida. We shouldn't be mocking.'

They worked methodically through each drawer and cupboard and soon between them gathered an increasingly large number of what they classified as 'sentimental items'. Neither had any idea what they should do with it all, but some things, mainly trinkets, ornaments and pictures, held significant memories and could not be just be dumped into a black bin liner destined for the tip. There was one particular teapot Kirsty knew she wanted to keep for herself, as a memento of her childhood visits. Sam crinkled his nose. 'Yes, I remember it too. You're most welcome.'

'Thank you, kind sir. One day, if you ever come to my house wherever that may be, I shall brew you a cuppa in this very teapot.'

'And then we can raise our cups in a toast to our dear old aunt.'

His blonde hair fell over his brow with a boyish haphazard attractiveness. She noticed how neat his ears were, his clear fresh skin and lovely blue eyes mischievous but there was something much more conveyed in the sincerity they held.

The dust masks Kirsty had purchased that morning, it was agreed, had proved to be an absolute necessity. Frequently throughout the day mild hysteria manifested in them collapsing into convulsive giggles when finding items like a mummified mouse or an eight-year-old tin of Spam. Sam described the need for such hilarity as a 'stress buster'. Eventually, feeling grubby and extremely tired, they returned to Aunt Maud's.

'Whatever am I supposed to do with that lot,' she complained, seeing three large cardboard boxes deposited in her hallway.

'Sentimental items,' said Kirsty, feeling the words thank you would have sounded better and not such an obvious lack of appreciation. She found herself doubting if Maud had ever in her entire life worked so hard in one day.

'Go through them at your leisure and decide what you want to keep or give to a charity or bin,' Sam said.

The old lady sighed and tutted, prompting her niece to excuse herself to take a shower before saying something she might regret later.

'You're looking well.' Sam kissed Kirsty formally on the cheek when she came back downstairs. He looked thinner, she thought, casually dressed in jeans and a loose navy wool jacket. He smelt nice as he stooped to rest his lips briefly on her cheek.

'We won't be late, Aunt Maud. Please don't wait up. We can see you in the morning.'

'Enjoy,' said the old lady with beguiling sincerity.

They sat amid a melee of fellow diners surrounded by plastic grape vines intricately woven between low wooden beams.

An assortment of copper kettles, ladles and strips of Italian bunting dangled above their heads positioned with an air of studied carelessness. They shared good wine and food, while conversation continued to flow easily. For the first time in months Kirsty felt totally relaxed with a male companion. On several occasions she nearly told Sam about her recently discovered status within the family, but it seemed wrong to spoil the shared humour and warmth. Similarly, she related only a briefest outline of the situation regarding her marriage breakdown. To labour on these serious issues was not compatible with the ambience of their evening together.

'Thanks for being good company,' he said, turning the key in the lock to let them back into Maud's house.

'I enjoyed it too, thank you.'

'You know, I'm thinking of heading for Ireland to have a change of scenery,' Kirsty revealed.

Chapter 10

Departure

Kirsty casually observed a man seated on his own, he looked familiar but she could not think why. The waitress handed her the menu before asking if she would like something to drink. 'Fresh orange juice with no ice, please.' It was the highly polished brown brogues which gave him away, suddenly it came to her. Of course she knew exactly who he was. As if sensing her gaze, he briefly raised his head, peering across the restaurant to where she sat, before returning to the magazine which lay open on the table. *Oh God, now he thinks some random woman is making eyes at him.* Her mobile phone bleeped discreetly. It was a text message from Diane: Sorry. Running a bit late, on way now, should be with you in 5.

Mr SAS beckoned to the waitress, requesting his bill. A brown leather wallet materialized from his inside jacket pocket. She watched his long fingers extract a crisp twenty pound note and place it on the circular silver dish. Standing up he repositioned the chair with military precision. Tall and straight backed, the cut of his jacket flattered a fine figure. It took some effort not to appear alarmed when he made a deliberate detour via her table on route to the exit stopping beside her to say, 'Forgive me, but I feel I know you from somewhere?'

Kirsty blushed. 'I'm a teacher. You visited my class and talked to the children last term.'

'Ah yes, that's it! I do remember now, but I meet so many people and when someone is out of context, it's not always possible to make an immediate connection.'

'Absolutely,' she nodded in agreement.

'Are you waiting for someone?'

'Yes, my girlfriend should be here shortly.'

He gestured to the vacant seat. 'May I keep you company until her arrival?'

'Please do.'

His sharp, angular features seemed more pronounced than remembered.

'So where is it you live?'

'Home is where the heart is,' she responded and tried not to sound irritated by his intrusion.

'So they say.' He sat back in the chair, staring straight at her. 'Are you married?'

She scrutinized his neatly pressed blue shirt and tie, with some sort of regimental motif, then noticed the immaculate gold cufflinks peeping from the sleeves of a cream linen jacket.

'You don't need to answer that,' he said.

'Yes, I am married.' She was aware she'd paused longer than necessary, quickly adding in a rehearsed way. 'My husband is in advertising. He works freelance from a base in North Berwick. A very successful business and highly sought after.'

'I see. I wondered about you after my visit to St Mungo's.'

Kirsty knitted her brows and tilted her head, to question why.

'Because you asked had I ever killed anyone. No one has asked me that before. Maybe people just assume,' he shrugged.

'I liked your answer,' she admitted.

'You did? Well we are programmed to forget and return to civilian life with no memories of any atrocities or war zones, all of it erased! That's if you wish to believe all they want you to believe.'

'You sound a tad cynical,' she spoke to the table because his steely grey-eyed stare was becoming unnerving and made the gold cufflinks all the more fascinating.

'When we are sent for therapy, a form of rehab I suppose, they tell us when an unpleasant thought intrudes, or we have a flashback to some hideous moment, we are to replace it immediately with something pleasant. Sounds a bit trite, but believe it or not, given practise, it does work. A technique often used to treat post-traumatic stress disorder, I believe.'

She raised her eyes and felt she'd misjudged him. His voice was quiet, his demeanour self-assured, but his eyes, she hated, they epitomised steely determination with something of a psychopathic quality.

'Did you have counselling?'

'I did.'

'Hi, sorry I'm late.' Diane stood beside them slightly red faced and breathless.

Kirsty, who only knew her companion as Mr SAS, floundered briefly, but her friend helped by extending a hand and saying, 'Hello, I am Diane.'

Mr SAS stood and shook hands. 'Hello, and I'm John Headley. Very pleased to meet you.'

Then lifting *The Economist* from the table, he said, 'I shall leave you in peace.' He appeared to bow from the waist and almost clicked his heels before turning to Kirsty. 'It's been lovely to meet you again.'

When he had safely left, Diane smiled at her friend. 'Well? A fine figure of a man, as my mother would say.'

'Not as far as I'm concerned,' responded her friend. 'There's something about him I find unnerving. Anyway, we're not here to discuss him.'

'OK, subject closed. Let's have a look at the menu.'

They dined extravagantly with only sparkling water to fill their glasses raised in a toast to new beginnings. Kirsty ordered a particularly good bottle of rosé wine, requesting it remain corked and presented it to Diane to enjoy at home to mark the eve of her departure to new shores. With determination she stated Ireland had always been on her list of places to visit, rejecting any concerns voiced by her best friend. Kirsty insisted it would take her away from any danger involving Toby. Diane had to agree and offered reassurance that her spare room would remain available as a base to be used any time.

'Have you remembered to pack everything you need?' she asked.

'I hope so,' responded Kirsty. 'There is little room in the car for anything else.'

Two hours later they hugged and parted company having exchanged mutual promises to keep in regular contact.

As the month of May dawned, Kirsty joined the early morning queue of cars waiting to board the ferry sailing from Cairnryan to Larne. The previous night had been comfortably spent in a small hotel in Portpatrick. On this, her first ever visit to Ireland, she anticipated meandering down the country, stopping when or where the notion struck before eventually arriving in Kerry. Beyond that, her plans remained a blank. The combination of Aunt Cressida's money and the Range Rover, to which Toby had made no claim, gave her scope to wander for a while. Time was her friend, without pressure to be anywhere or to do anything in particular gave her a sense of release from the confines of life in Edinburgh.

County Wicklow hosted her first night on Irish soil where she found suitable bed and breakfast accommodation near a place named Avoca. She had not eaten properly throughout the day so by ten in the evening she felt peckish. Having searched her handbag for chocolate, she remembered it was in the glove compartment of the car. Although it was cold she ventured outside with no coat. Flicking her thumb on the key ring the car lights flashed exposing a man who was walking into the driveway. Beside him a spaniel pulled hard on its leash, their breath visible as small clouds of silver vapour.

'Brrr,' he said, 'it's a cold one alright. Not seasonal, but then it would not be the first time a frost has caught us this late in the year.'

'It is,' she shivered, regretting not wearing a jacket.

'I'm Mr Feeney,' he held his hand outstretched as the dog gave a faint whine in protest at being held on a shortened leash.

'How do you do,' she shook the gloved hand, trying to avoid total exposure beneath a beam of light radiating from above the front door.

'You're staying the night with us I believe, are you out for a smoke?' he asked.

'No,' then she mumbled an explanation about a chocolate bar in the car.

'Ah ha,' he laughed, 'you know what they say, a moment on the lips and a lifetime on the hips.'

She smiled.

'Still, I'm no man to talk,' he said, patting his rotund waistline.

Kirsty bent down to stroke the dog. 'At least you have this one to keep you active,' she smiled.

'I do. Well, I'll leave you to enjoy the chocolate. Anything else you need just ask, always happy to oblige.'

'Thank you.'

The dog pulled him away, clearly eager to be indoors.

In spite of the chill factor she lingered outside and sat on a bench, holding the bar of chocolate in her hand. Stars above competed for space as she thought of the one who gave her breath of life begrudgingly, an unwelcome child she did not seek. Kirsty became 'given'. Such expectations, hopes, and manipulations ensued in the name of love. Her first tears came large and wet, followed by a salty cascade that brought no relief. Her shoulders felt heavy as realisations spilt in a desperate search for resolution *into this world we arrive alone, and depart alone.* Beneath these stars each person searches with restless turpitude for the 'thing'. That elusive 'thing' which hides itself but can solve, heal, absolve, cosset, and covet what we long to have and hold. Huh, she thought, 'they' espouse so many words of wisdom, but does anyone ever listen? They say it's quality not quantity that counts, less becomes more. All of it wrapped up in a facade of contentment and gratitude for money, health and family, but what about the journey? When we are old and frail and before the end who can say 'yes I did it well', or were the choices made and their consequences something we had to live with?

All this carried with us under a thin veil which rarely becomes transparent for fear of what others might say. No one knows, no one can, but no one really cares, for life weaves its own tenuous path and we become gripped by an inner fear the veil might fall. They say this and they say that, all is vacuous, second-hand, unproven dubious wisdom. When lost, who will find? Who will seek? No one will, for there are just too many components in each mind to hold another near.

Frost-covered mountains rose to meet clear starlit skies as icy air penetrated her bones below a universe full of lonely stars which 'they' say are angels poised to protect. 'They' do damage, pontificating such things, she shivered and returned to the warmth of her small bedroom and lay on the bed with her thoughts: when I walk jauntily down the street to be greeted with 'how are you?' no one wants to hear, no one wants to know, so 'grand' or 'fine' will serve to hold the thin veil over my eyes. Three legs on the stool. Take each leg one by one and the stool is gone. Soon forgotten in the myriad of fleeting moments it takes to live one life.

Eventually, flicking through the television channels to find RTE1, Kirsty watched the end of *The Late, Late Show*. A young girl was being interviewed about her recent time in Iraq as an aid worker. The magnitude of the situation and her graphic descriptions of the plight faced by so many innocents served only to reinforce the fragility of humanity.

The following afternoon Kirsty arrived in Limerick with a

plan to locate Clare Street. She stopped and asked a man for help. He knew exactly where it was, directing her with ease. She parked the car near a large sign for St Joseph's Convent and walked the length of its outer stone wall, stopping several times to lay her flat palm onto the bricks. By doing this she believed some sort of osmosis could enable access to dark secrets, tales of girls who came here disgraced, some to die in childbirth and all the poor babies who never made any sort of journey beyond these walls. Largely forgotten but their restless spirits might be held in the fabric of the bricks. Too many unmarried pregnant girls hidden away from the world with no option but to trust the care of religious orders. These mothers wept and their children cried. Their mother knew why she wept but her child did not. A mother given her baby to hold wept all the more as the infant suckled eagerly on her breast. They wept because one day the nun would come and take the child from the mother's arms and give it to a new mammy and daddy who they claimed would provide a good life. The mother had to believe the nun; it was time to leave it all to history. A profound sadness tugged at her heart. Such a waste, these poor girls condemned by those who claimed God's love as their own. The brides of Christ motivated by who knows what because she was very sure it was not the God she knew.

Chapter 11

Kerry

That night she stayed in a pleasant bed and breakfast on the edge of Lough Derg in a town called Killaloe. The room had a balcony overlooking the beautiful lough, and for the first time in months she slept soundly.

The following morning after managing to eat a hearty Irish breakfast, she continued weaving a route along Irish country roads through County Clare. Arriving at the Kilmur ferry she crossed the Shannon to enter County Kerry. Balvohan beckoned. A sense of urgency dissipated those original thoughts of meandering along a slow route, she was anxious to be there. To walk the streets where Biddy grew up could become a form of connection with her roots.

Just after three in the afternoon she reached the edge of the village. From here new, modern looking houses lined her route on either side until she reached a church. Opposite it, she noticed a hotel and having managed to secure a room for that night, returned outside to wander around in the village.

Outside the post office, which she noticed doubled as a shop, she paused to read the contents of a glass-framed cabinet fixed to the wall. Inside it displayed a chaotic array of post cards and pieces of notepaper advertising items for sale, coffee mornings, carpet cleaning services, puppies free to a good home and a fete in Killarney. In the section labelled job vacancies there was only three post cards. One was looking for a chef in Killarney, another for a waitress in the Turrets Hotel, which was momentarily considered as a possibility. The third, however, was more interesting, looking for a temporary housekeeper for an elderly lady in the village who had recently undergone a hip replacement operation ending with 'apply within'.

With little hesitation Kirsty entered the shop to find an elderly woman sitting behind the counter knitting. 'Well, what can I get you?' she asked, barely looking up.

'I'm interested in the job you have advertised outside for a housekeeper. The lady who had a hip replacement.'

'I see. And who would you be exactly? Not from these parts judging by the accent?' The woman spoke gruffly, and was now viewing this interloper with suspicion.

'My name is Kirsty McHardie. I'm from Scotland and would like to apply for the post.'

'I gathered that,' came the terse response.

Knowing that this less than charming lady could be of assistance Kirsty had no choice but to remain polite.

'And what would be your job in the past?' asked the woman.

'I'm a teacher, but having a sabbatical in order to travel.'

'I see. So you're not a nurse?'

'No, but the advert says housekeeper and I can cook, clean and am totally trustworthy. I can provide good references.'

'I see.' The woman appeared to be softening slightly. 'I'm Mrs Morriarty. The lady who needs cared for is Mrs Devlin. It would be her son who placed the advert because he has business in Dublin most of the time. He takes good care of his mother; she wants for nothing.'

'I see,' said Kirsty mimicking the woman to quell her rising irritation. 'Would it be possible to give me a contact number, or any idea how I might apply for the job?'

'Well, I could give her a ring for you now and see what she says. What's your name again?'

'Kirsty McHardie.'

The woman laid down her knitting and limped to the phone, clearly audible as she explained there was a girl in the shop, about thirty she thought, then asked, 'How old are you?'

'Thirty-three.'

'Yes, alright I will. Perhaps, but you'd be the best judge. Yes I will, straight away.'

She replaced the receiver. 'You've to go to the cottage, she's expecting you.'

'Now?'

'Turn right out of the door, and do another right at the corner and hers is the fourth cottage on the right. Last one before the path to the strand, you can't miss it. The garden is beautiful and tidy.'

Thanking the woman and leaving the shop, she wondered if she was presentable enough wearing jeans, a blouse and cardigan. Stopping at the corner and rummaging in her handbag to find a hairbrush, she hoped sleeker hair would make her look a bit better. The cottage was lovely, as described, pink blossoms bedecked two cherry trees and the hedgerow was full of green buds fit to burst. Taking a deep breath, she rang the bell and stepped back waiting for an answer.

'Come on in,' said a voice. 'Come right in.' She opened the door and entered the house. 'In to the left. Good girl. There now, let me have a look at you.'

Kirsty need not have worried. The elderly lady was gracious and immediately likable. Mrs Devlin chatted and asked her to make a cup of tea, and then after half an hour said, 'Yes, I think you will do nicely. Why not just cancel your stay at the hotel and move in immediately? The room is ready. I believe you and I shall share a good relationship.'

Kirsty recognised in this lady wisdom borne out of experience, expressed in Mrs Devlin's large brown eyes, knowing when not to probe too deeply.

Yes, here I shall be alright and all things shall become well.

The house was neatly tucked behind Balvohan's main street in a cul-de-sac. From here a footpath continued for a short distance before arriving at the strand and the Atlantic Ocean. A climbing rose weaved and twisted to reach Kirsty's bedroom window and as the cycle of summer progressed, scent from pink petals drifted into her bedroom, lingering throughout each day and night.

She was accustomed to the sound of gulls crying at dawn in North Berwick, and the distant sound of rolling waves which lulled her to sleep at night. Mrs Devlin, she decided early in the proceedings, was a gem of a lady. Gentle in manner with a sharp humour, attractive with the appearance of someone younger than her years reflected in beautiful translucent skin. She used only a faint touch of pink rouge to accentuate her high cheekbones, with no heavy mascara or face powder; she captivated the essence of dignity.

It was easy for Kirsty to be efficient and professional when following the job specifications. The two women shared a lively sense of humour, chatting and giggling over silly absurdities or tales told of past characters long gone from the village. At other times a companionable silence sufficed. The expected duties consisted of general housekeeping and assisting her charge in the shower who, once seated, washed herself but needed help to dry and dress. A printed sheet of paper detailed a physiotherapy programme, which was adhered to rigorously.

Mrs Devlin liked to rest for at least an hour each day after lunch, which quickly became established as Kirsty's time to walk and explore her new surroundings. The charming, well-maintained house contained every conceivable labour-saving device, which meant her remit was more that of being a companion than a housekeeper or carer. The cottage was also hoovered and dusted twice a week with all bedding changed every Friday by Mrs Clancy. This lady lived in the village and had been attending to these chores for the last five years, and would probably continue long after Kirsty's job ceased. A tiny dynamo of a woman who talked mostly to herself, she whizzed around leaving a trail of highly polished furniture and spotless floors. Friday was also the day a generous salary was paid by Mattie Devlin from a Bank of Ireland account in Dublin into an account in the local post office set up for the purpose.

Supper was easy, usually something simple like a boiled egg or sandwiches. Initially, numerous eggs lay rejected in the bottom of the pedal bin, but within the first week she had it timed perfectly to Mrs Devlin's satisfaction. The ancient radio still worked perfectly and each evening after supper was tuned to the six o'clock news preceded by the Angelus Bells. The radio was the one thing Mrs Devlin refused to have ousted by a modern replacement. Neither of them worried too much if they missed the chimes and neither recited the prayer.

Gradually the two women got to know each other better and for different reasons relished their relaxed companionship. Most days a visitor dropped by to provide an update on village gossip. Kirsty knew if the elderly lady wore her turquoise blue jumper adorned with a red necklace there was the expectation of, at the very least, a scone or assorted biscuits. A powder-blue blouse and a neat pearl necklace were reserved for those considered to be more important. They required sandwiches, cake and tea. Kirsty was primed to obediently interrupt after an hour to announce Mrs Devlin needed to take her medication. It worked every time and the guests took their leave.

All her promises made to Diane and Sam to keep in touch had not been forgotten.

Kirsty - GOT MYSELF A JOB IN KERRY

Sam - THAT'S A SURPRISE SO U STAYING IN IRE THEN?

Kirsty - YES FOR NOW

Sam - YOU HAVE ME WANTING TO VISIT

Kirsty - FEEL FREE TO COME ON OVER

Sam - WHAT PART OF KERRY U IN

Kirsty - BALVOHAN IT'S LOVELY

Sam - NEAR KILLARNEY HEARD MY DAD MENTION IT NEVER BEEN THO

Kirsty - LOOKING AFTER A LADY AFTER AN OP ON HIP

Sam - SO NEED TO CALL YOU FLORRY THEN

Kirsty - ???

Sam - FLORENCE NIGHTINGALE DOZEY!

Kirsty - LOL

Sam - TAKE CARE AND KP IN TOUCH

Kirsty - WILL DO NIGHT NIGHT

She then sent more or less the same text to Diane who responded enthusiastically saying how delighted she was to hear things were going well.

QUITE AN ADVENTURE LOL WOULD LOVE TO TALK

Kirsty replied to her friend promising a phone call soon.

Chapter 12

Balvohan

The routine and slow pace of life served to soothe Kirsty's troubled mind. Her daily walk usually took her along the strand, where she often removed her shoes and socks, and enjoyed the melodic sounds of Atlantic surf in her ears. Bathing was restricted to the far end of the beach, between red flags, patrolled by a lifeguard who sat high on an observation chair. 'Strong undercurrents,' said Mrs Devlin, 'need stringent safety measures.'

Sometimes Kirsty opted instead to walk through the village or head uphill towards the mountain top. Many times she was tempted to try and find some information about Biddy. She imagined there could still be people living in Balvohan who might remember the Duffy family. The parish register or the priest might be a help, or Mrs Morriarty or even Mrs Devlin. Kirsty had not mentioned her ancestry to anyone and to cross the bridge from locked secrets to disclosure proved hard; although she did not fully understand why it should present her with difficulty. It was a continual regret that she did not share the discovery with Sam, the only person she knew who had a tangible connection to her truth.

She had been trying to use the technique described by John

Headley to help her forget. It was not proving easy to banish intrusive thoughts of her husband. His recent silence was becoming spooky, because this was not true to his character. It also saddened her and she found herself wondering what kept him occupied. At times, conflict raged beneath a calm exterior. She had suggested no contact, but it felt like he was punishing her by sticking to the request.

She and Diane chatted on the phone at least twice a week. Her good friend continued to maintain it was not healthy to dwell on Toby whenever his name was mentioned, particularly if the question involved whether or not there was any other woman in his life.

One day Kirsty entered the village shop to see three ladies huddled at the counter talking to Mrs Morriarty. 'I feel an Irish girl would have served the purpose just as well if not better. Our own should be employed before interlopers.'

'Shhhhhhhhhhh,' Mrs Morriarty hissed at the bird-like woman, who had wisps of grey hair failing to cover her flaky scalp. Flecks of dry skin sat like snow on the collar of her navy-blue blouse.

'They do say Dan Boyle has plans for a third pump,' chirped the other customer, clutching a tatty nylon bag devoid of contents to her pink-bloused chest.

'Is that so? I did hear nothing of that,' said the bird-like woman suitably distracted.

Mrs Morriarty directed her gaze at the newcomer. 'Can I help you? We could talk all day and I know you're probably in a hurry to get back to Mrs Devlin.'

'Could I have packet of digestives and four small bananas, please?'

'You will have settled in fine, I have no doubt.' The biscuits were virtually thrown onto the counter. 'Help yourself to the fruit, there might just be four left in the box at the door. That will be three euros and seventy-nine cents altogether, if you have the right change it would be appreciated.'

Kirsty paid and smiled congenially at the ensemble. She'd become quite decided never to ask any questions about Biddy in the post office. She walked on up the road until she reached the 'Welcome to Balvohan' sign, where one road led to Killarney and the other named by the tourist board as the coastal trail. From here she turned and walked back, stopping at the church, debating whether or not to go in and light a candle.

The hotel sat in a triangle between shop and church, to the left a narrow road climbed steeply up one of the Kerry mountains. The pasture consisted of mottled coarse grass, dotted with sheep and grey boulders. Sometimes from a distance it was difficult to differentiate between the two. The candle idea was rejected in favour of a coffee sitting outside the hotel and watching the world go by. The Turrets could boast clientele from elite sources, the rich and famous from across the globe enjoyed food served in its five-star restaurant. Photographs were proudly displayed in the bar including the entire cast who starred in David Lean's *Ryan's Daughter* filmed in the area.

In her line of vision was a yellow cottage with dark-blue woodwork, numerous window boxes and hanging baskets, each brimming with colourful flowers. Two elderly men leant on the gate, deep in conversation. 'Grand day. How are you?' said the tall one when she passed a short time later. She paused briefly beside the parochial house, Father Carlin, the parish priest was a 'good man' according to Mrs Devlin. Kirsty wondered about him as a possible confidant as she ambled back to the house, which was starting to feel like home.

What had become a daily ritualistic walk after lunch she viewed as valuable thinking time. Initially, she reminded herself of the unpleasant events experienced with Toby, but gradually the old pattern emerged where these images converted to the happy moments they shared. It was this subtle change which found her longing to see or at least speak to the man she'd married. Feelings of agitation reactivated a desperate need to hear his voice. It had become challenging to maintain resistance to the strong grip of temptation to dial his number.

Mrs Devlin unwittingly came to the rescue with a request for Kirsty to collect a pair of made to measure curtains from a shop in Killarney. The tourist season was not yet in full swing so the town was quiet. On her way back to the car and carrying two heavy bags she noticed 'G. Maloney, Psychotherapist' etched on a brass plaque outside a townhouse. She walked on and put the curtains on the passenger seat of her car, before returning to the house. I would be anonymous here alright, she thought, and rang the bell. A first appointment with Mr Maloney was booked for the following Monday at three. Mrs Devlin need not know, as this could be claimed as her half-day off, which until now had never been taken.

*

Kirsty arrived fifteen minutes before her allotted time and was escorted by the receptionist into a book lined room. 'Mr Maloney will be with you shortly.' Several paintings adorned one free wall, each depicting stormy seas or tranquil flower gardens. Soft chairs draped in loose covers of cream, with muted green scatter cushions were placed either side of a low beech wood table and a yellow rag rug complemented the bare floorboards. A large bay window lined with cream curtains all combined to create a serene environment. Mr Maloney entered quietly with soft soled shoes and introduced himself before sitting opposite. He was in his mid-fifties, with a grey beard and unruly thick coarse hair and wore steel rimmed spectacles. He was casually dressed in a blue denim shirt, cream trousers and sandals which combined into a warm, crumpled appearance.

Their session lasted approximately an hour. His relaxing manner made Kirsty feel at ease to discuss almost everything which troubled her mind. The psychotherapist made suggestions which reinforced John Headley's words, providing further techniques which she could use as an aid to banish Toby from her thoughts. 'To kill him off bit by bit in her memory,' he said. It was important to revisit her memories of the bad times as a reminder of all the emotional reasons she originally had for wanting to be free of him and leave the marriage. 'Good times were an illusion and pleasurable associations were no more than a cruel trick, a distorted truth. Kirsty talked a lot and Mr Maloney listened, so what took place was essentially between her inner and outer self. These meetings immediately became established as a routine occurrence scheduled for each Monday afternoon.

Late in their third session Mr Maloney said he believed Toby exhibited traits of a pathological personality. He went on to explain these were complex characters with sociopathic, narcissistic and psychopathic tendencies. The boundaries were blurred and often they embraced combined traits. He was of the opinion that when dealing with such personality types the only way forward was to make a complete break. To have no interactions, negative or positive, as it was not possible to reason with them in any rational way. Their existence was based in manipulative tactics to meet personal needs and no one else mattered. The cruel truth was they mimicked real emotion but were not capable of experiencing love or honesty as most other people did.

Diane agreed wholeheartedly, expressing how delighted she was that someone else, a professional, was endorsing what she'd always felt about her friend's 'former' husband. She laid a particular stress on the word former, hoping the implication would not be missed. She also expressed her relief that Kirsty was finally receiving professional guidance, begging her to promise when, because she believed he would, Toby tried to call or text she would not, under any circumstances, respond.

*

One afternoon as Kirsty sat to enjoy the sun beside the water pump outside the chapel she observed a nun pass by. An empty brown hessian bag flopped back and forth rhythmically accompanying her business-like walk. Ten minutes later the nun re-emerged from the chapel and crossed the road to Mrs Morriarty's shop, this time bidding Kirsty a good afternoon in passing.

Mrs Devlin told her the nun was Sister Mary Cecelia, who was at home having been released from her convent in Dublin to take care of her terminally ill brother Callum. Their family home was the little white cottage on the hill overlooking the strand. The elderly eyes moistened as she added, 'So terribly sad. My Mattie would be a good friend of Callum's.'

'My Mattie' was often mentioned, but the absence of family photographs struck Kirsty as peculiar. Only one black and white picture rested on the mantelpiece, depicting a solemn young man with black curls. 'Yes, that would be his father alright, my husband,' said Mrs Devlin. 'I don't see my two boys as being particularly like their father, although they would have his hair, I'd say.'

One afternoon, having spent time studying headstones in the cemetery but finding no mention of anyone called Biddy or Duffy, Kirsty retreated to the chapel where she pressed a fifty cent coin into a metal box before lighting two candles at Our Lady's altar. She then sat on a chapel pew to observe the blue core of the flickering flames. Hail Marys and the Momorare discarded; she became lost in her own thoughts.

'Hello. Kirsty isn't it?' A rotund middle-aged woman startled her. 'I'm Siobhan. I help Father organise the church cleaning rota and such. My turn this week.' She talked amazingly quickly. 'It does come around again soon enough. I don't suppose I could interest you? No, no of course not, you would be fully committed already. Silly question. How do you like Balvohan?'

'I'm enjoying it a lot,' she answered, immediately warming to the lady.

'Good, glad to hear it. I'm just after leaving himself watching sport on television. It's all he does – watch sport, any kind of sport – all day every day.'

Kirsty wondered if Siobhan could answer a question for her, although it was not the one she asked. 'What time are confessions in Killarney?'

'Killarney?' Siobhan sounded surprised. 'Before ten o'clock Mass on a Sunday. And 6 to 7 p.m. on a Saturday.' She carried on talking of her husband. 'Well, I like to paint, not pictures, to decorate. I got paint the other week in Killarney. Folks come from far and wide to buy paint and wallpaper at Rafferty's interior design shop. The one on the corner with a blue door. I bought gold wallpaper but didn't use it in the end. I'll have to take it back sometime, should get a refund, or at the very least a credit note. They'd be decent enough that way.'

Kirsty hoped she was not about to suggest being a travelling companion to town.

'Father Carlin does confessions here. Absolution is absolution, I don't think it would be any better in Killarney.' The woman smiled. 'Anyway, I painted the sitting room last weekend and himself came in saying that's a grand job of the hall you've made.' She raised her eyes skyward. 'So I says to him, open yer eyes ye idiot, it's the sitting room I'm after doing. Now I might just have slipped another word in front of idiot but couldn't be repeating it in the Lord's house.'

Kirsty laughed. 'I'm sorry but I'd better be off now. Mrs Devlin will be thinking I'm lost.'

'Well, nice to meet you.' The woman shook her hand and returned to cleaning, still talking about wallpaper and paint without a care there would be nobody to listen any more.

On her walk back to the cottage a thought occurred that perhaps the best plan would be to write a letter to the priest. Fountain pen, so much nicer, he would respect a letter handwritten in ink. The strengthening breeze ruffled her hair and made her eyes water. Real ink flows from the heart like blood spilled from a corner of the soul.

She did not know the status quo was about to change.

Chapter 13

Mattie

'Have you opened the window in Mattie's room to allow a bit of air through?'

Kirsty gave reassurance all was ready, repeating for the third time the window was wide open and plenty of fresh air was circulating.

'Good, that will please my Mattie. I always say he must have been born in a field.' Mrs Devlin's face creased around deep-set brown eyes at her own joke. Glancing at the gold carriage clock on the mantelpiece she said, 'I imagine he will arrive soon. He called before noon to say he was nearly half way.'

Mattie, who inspired awe in all who spoke of him, was to finally return home. Kirsty excused herself and went upstairs to freshen up. Twenty minutes later from her window she noticed a red Jaguar turn into the driveway. A man clambered out.

Was this the wonderful Mattie? He was overweight, not tall and not handsome. His shirt buttons strained over a very large belly. He did have hair though, copious amounts of it for a man his age, a mop of dark grey curls.

Slipping her partially composed letter inside a book, she returned downstairs, hoping to prove worthy of the fine salary her employer paid. A luxurious tan leather suitcase lay in the hall and she could hear Mrs Devlin laughing and cooing with delight. Retreating to the kitchen she filled the kettle with water, setting it to boil.

'Kirsty? Kirsty? Come, a gentleman wishes to meet you.'

Wiping her hands on the kitchen towel she obeyed.

'Ahhh, welcome, my dear,' said Mattie, approaching with an outstretched hand. He squeezed her hand firmly and looked directly at her with deep-blue eyes. 'Mammy has been telling me on the phone how well you're looking after her, I'm grateful. She can be the very divil.' He winked.

Kirsty smiled, uncertain of any other appropriate response.

'An old lady has earned the right to be a divil,' responded Mrs Devlin, loving every moment as she looked adoringly at her son.

'So tell me, how do you like our Emerald Isle?' He gestured, inviting her to sit on the floral sofa beside him.

'I love it, and have to say your mother is a model patient. I have yet to meet the devil.'

'Good, glad to hear. You must be bringing out the best in her,' Mattie winked at his mother.

'Can I get you a cup of tea or coffee?' Kirsty asked.

'I would hate to put you to such trouble,' he said before adding with a mischievous grin, 'so half a cup would do.'

Mrs Devlin laughed. 'I'll have tea, thank you, and we may partake, all three of us together. I hope you will join us.'

She looked questioningly at Kirsty who nodded.

Mattie talked a lot. Mrs Devlin laughed indulgently as Kirsty observed the stocky figure with rather nice blue eyes and had to admit there was something disarming about his smile. He was clearly a man with well-practised awareness of his assets. The greatest of which could only be described as an unquantifiable charisma.

A short time later he stated he was not hungry and would like go to and visit Callum. The ladies were left alone as he headed to the Flannigan cottage with a bottle of Irish whiskey in his hand. Mrs Devlin was in great humour, delighted to have her son home, saying his visits were going to become more frequent because he wanted to spend time with Callum, adding how sad it was an ill wind brought what she most wanted.

'Did I tell you he's a great singer?'

'No. I would love to hear him sing sometime.'

'He needs little persuasion. Remind me and I'll ask him.'

Once supper was finished they settled to idle compatible chatter. Then Mrs Devlin clicked through the TV channels and declared it a disgrace that with so many to choose from she could find nothing to capture her interest. 'Could I trouble you to put the rug over my legs? It gets cool around this time.'

Kirsty tucked a soft rug carefully over Mrs Devlin's lap asking, 'How did Mattie become involved in the motor trade?'

'I'm proud of my boy, but it's a long story,' she replied wistfully.

'I'm sitting comfortably so you can begin,' Kirsty grinned.

The old lady required no further encouragement to divulge the pride she had for her son. 'Mattie was such a good-looking young man. Raven black hair and those beautiful blue eyes. He arrived in Dublin with nothing, we were not at all wealthy, in fact quite poor, he thought it the most exciting place on God's earth. He desperately needed to find work.'

Kirsty shifted forward in her seat, to assure her companion she had a captive audience.

'Then in time he ended up married to a woman called Veronica who always had great ideas about what she should wear, where they should live and where the children should be educated.' Her voice and face revealed distaste. 'When Mattie first met Veronica he came home, with a great big smile, saying he'd spent an evening in the company of the most beautiful woman he'd ever seen.' Patting the plaid rug on her knees, her face contorted slightly. 'From our first meeting I could not take to her. My Mattie worked long and hard to provide all the material things she craved. She never asked or cared where the money for her next extravagance came from just so long as the never ending wish list was indulged.'

'So does he live in a big house?'

Mrs Devlin nodded. 'From the start I could see it was lust and not love. But the young think they know better. Four months later Veronica announced she was pregnant and my Mattie, being an honourable man, did the right thing and fixed a date to marry. All done and dusted before any hint of a pregnancy became obvious.' She stared wistfully into the empty fire grate.

Then forcing herself back to the present moment continued, 'The bride had her white wedding and I have to admit was stunningly beautiful. With her long auburn hair, high cheekbones and immaculate pearl-white teeth she'd bagged one of the best men a girl could ever find. I wept, for all the wrong reasons, seeing them hand in hand at the altar and a priest pronounced them man and wife.'

There must be photographs somewhere of the wedding, and the grandchildren, Kirsty thought. If they were hidden, was there a reason? Curiosity grew as to why no family photographs were on display. Mrs Devlin continued and Kirsty listened closely for any hints 'Their first son, Declan, was born six months after the wedding. He's twenty-four now. Susan was born two years later, and is even more beautiful than her mother. She'll be twenty-two, and Francis is the baby. He's a clever boy studying to be a doctor. Veronica is apparently in the throes of planning a big party for his twenty-first.'

Then she seemed to drift into a place of her own, talking to no one in particular just giving voice to thoughts. 'Veronica was never faithful to Mattie, a string of men all younger than her. But they never lasted. They all tired of her demanding personality until this one. A Spaniard.'

She sighed deeply. 'Veronica somehow managed to manipulate an annulment so she could have a second white wedding.'

Kirsty could never quite grasp the concept of annulments, particularly when there were children involved. It all seemed such hypocrisy to her, and shared this belief with Mrs Devlin. The ladies agreed, but who were they to question judgments from Rome?

'My dear, let's have a glass of wine. Or better still, port. Yes, a small glass of port would be lovely. The ruby red stuff in the squat decanter nearest the window.' Mrs Devlin waved her hand in the air as Kirsty moved towards the table in the corner. Several decanters sat in a row, all of which held some coloured liquid. Having settled her companion with a glass of port, opting not to take a drink herself, Kirsty suggested the old lady continue her story.

'There were lots of applicants for that job, you know the one at the garage you asked about earlier. Mr Rafferty saw qualities in my Mattie straight away and he became like the son he never had.' Taking sip of port, she smiled. 'Goodness, you will have me singing with such a large measure. Oh I do love having him at home so much.' She yawned, before emptying her glass and declaring it was probably time for her to retire.

Later that evening Kirsty sat curled on the sofa wrapped in the plaid rug. She was lost in memories of her own wedding day when she heard the back door open and shut. Mattie walked straight into the sitting room. It was obvious from the rush of whiskey fumes a large quantity of alcohol had been consumed.

'Hello, my dear. Is Mammy gone to her bed?' he slurred and swayed towards the drinks table to decant a large tumbler of straw-coloured liquid. 'Oops.' He knocked into the table, causing the collection of crystal to tinkle musically.

'She is, and sound asleep. She persuaded me to give her a drop of port.'

He sat down heavily in an armchair. 'There we are. Oh, blast. Be a honey, put some music on will you? *Blue Moon*, Ella Fitzgerald would do.'

He watched Kirsty scan the shelf. 'Top left,' he said impatiently. Having located it and pressing the play button, she sat gathering the rug over her again enjoying its soft texture.

'The doc says Callum should be getting out and about so yours truly and his trusty Jaguar are required. Tomorrow I have promised to take all for a drive round the Ring.' He waved the hand holding the tumbler in the air in front of him and belched.

'Oops, slipped out, beg your pardon. Mammy must come too. She would enjoy that. Be nice that, yes nice. Will you come?' He didn't give time to hear Kirsty's response. 'That poor bastard, excuse the language, is dying, you know, and there is sweet FA any of us can do about it.' He stood up and moved towards the drinks tray again, stopping for a moment, to lean against the door, making an effort to look casual and sober.

'Come,' he said. 'I'd like it, dear lady, if you would join me with a night cap.' He drained his glass, and managed to stifle a further belch.

'I'm not much of a drinker, but perhaps a small something,' Kirsty responded reluctantly.

'A drop of Irish?'

'No, no thank you, a sherry would be nice. Just enough to wet the glass.' She might as well have talked to the birds in the trees as she watched him filling a wine glass to the top with sherry, and then pour a large measure of Irish whiskey into his own tumbler, with a tiny squirt of soda water.

Handing Kirsty her drink and holding the crystal tumbler tenuously in front of him, he said, 'Mostly water! Cheers! Who or what shall we toast? We have to have a toast!'

'To your mother's speedy recovery?'

'Yes indeed, but as soon as she recovers you will leave us.' He pulled a pretend sad face. 'To Mammy.' He gulped a large mouthful before thumping heavily back into an armchair.

'To Mrs Devlin,' she echoed quietly and sipped the sherry, which caused a shiver to run over her spine.

Mattie swilled the contents of his glass gently round and round. 'So are you coming with us then?'

She declined politely, explaining there was an important letter she needed to write. Then she stood up, holding the sherry glass, with a plan to dispose of the remaining contents upstairs, adding, 'I feel very tired; will you please excuse me.'

'I see. Nice that, writing letters, I like to get letters. Will you write me a letter one day? Yes, you do what you have to do.'

Standing up he swayed a bit, belched again, saying, 'Excuse me,' as if it helped. 'Night, night. Lovely to meet you.' He lifted her hand to his lips, kissed it. 'I enjoyed our little chat.'

*

When Sunday morning dawned Kirsty was there as always to help prepare for the day. Mrs Devlin wore her beautiful blue dress, enhanced with a string of pearls complemented with matching earrings, her grey hair swept into a neat bun at the back of her head. Keen to prove to Mattie she was well worth the salary he paid she served scrambled egg on toast for breakfast, astonished when he insisted on a large portion with no hint of feeling the slightest bit queasy. She heard him telling his mother he'd booked lunch for four in a restaurant called The Duck. 'They do a great Sunday roast with all the trimmings and afterwards we can have a leisurely drive round the Ring.'

'Sounds just lovely,' cooed Mrs Devlin happily. 'I plan to enjoy every minute. I believe Callum will really appreciate a run out in the car.'

A short time later Kirsty escorted Mrs Devlin to the front seat of the Jaguar and then waved until the car disappeared out of sight before returning to her room. It felt good having the house to herself for a while and she lay on the bed falling asleep briefly but was soon disturbed by the familiar dream of the woman with her back to a church on a hill overlooking a fairground. It was disconcerting and it had been a few weeks since the last visitation. The frustration of not being unable to work out who this woman was returned to her. She longed to know why there a need for this image to persistently revisit her subconscious.

Getting up from the bed and lifting her jacket, she left the house and walked to the strand. In a trance-like state she watched the tide inch its way over golden grains until ripples kissed the rock on which she was sitting skirted with slimy, shiny seaweed and clusters of mussels and limpets. Gently the water lapped and gradually rose higher as she enjoyed the chill water washing over her toes. When it reached a level above her ankles, she moved and started walking back to the cottage. It had finally happened; she deleted a text from Toby without reading it. It had arrived before breakfast that morning. Mr Maloney and Diane predicted it was only a matter of time. The prolonged silence following their damaging encounter in North Berwick High Street had been broken.

Small, busy birds darted back and forth across her path. Such a heavy heart failed to rejoice at the sight of a bright coloured butterfly basking in late afternoon sun. Arriving at the house she lay on a sun lounger on the patio in the rear garden, flicking blindly through a magazine. Only when she heard car doors banging and voices did she delete Toby's second message, unread, aware there should never have been any hesitation.

'What a wonderful day. It's such a pity you didn't join us,' said Mrs Devlin, smiling.

'And I'm starving,' said Mattie. 'It's been a long time since lunch.'

'My goodness, you and that appetite. You know, he was born hungrier than any other baby I ever knew.'

'Kirsty, we missed you.' Mattie winked and brushed her arm as he passed her in the hallway. She did not flinch, turning to Mrs Devlin saying, 'Come on, let's get settled. I want to hear all about your day. I have prepared a salad, it's in the fridge so ready whenever you want it.'

There followed excited talk of dolphins spotted off the coast and tourists who talked too loudly in a chapel and a wonderful roast beef lunch. 'Oh yes, I also have some good news. Sister Mary Cecelia is coming to visit tomorrow afternoon, and is keen to meet you properly,' said the elderly lady with a smile.

After they'd finished supper Mattie jumped to his feet and started gathering up plates and cutlery, following Kirsty into the kitchen. She felt her cheeks burn, hoping no one else noticed. 'Must say you look very pretty with pink cheeks,' he commented.

'It's been muggy here all day. I feel warm. Did you have a thunder storm this afternoon?' she stuttered.

He shook his head saying playfully. 'Nope, no thunder where we were. Nothing pleases me more than loading the dishwasher,' he said whilst tossing a tea towel in her direction and flicking grains of sugar from the work top impishly in her direction. He flirted shamelessly, but was entertaining and she could not help but giggle encouragement as he fired one corny joke after another.

'Did you hear about the man who went to the dentist and said I think I'm a moth?'

Seeing her reaction was a smile, he carried on, 'Sir, I am a dentist and fail to know why you come to see me.'

Then gleefully, he delivered the punchline. 'Your light was on.'

Abruptly he ceased all this frivolity, saying he had to go out for a while, that his mother was tired and could she be sure to get her to bed early. Such a sudden change found her wonder if anything she'd said or done had caused offence.

Once the elderly lady was settled in bed, Kirsty read aloud another chapter of *Pride and Prejudice*. Mrs Devlin was not unfamiliar with Jane Austen, having seen both *Pride and Prejudice* and *Emma* as films, but had never read the books.

She loved this innovation, having someone read to her in instalments, relishing this time spent in the company of the Bennet family. A fanciful notion evolved that Mrs Bennet would have liked to introduce her Mattie to one of those fine daughters. After barely ten minutes, the excitement of the day caught up and she was snoring softly.

Kirsty tiptoed outside and sent a text to Sam.

Kirsty – ANY NEWS. HOW ARE YOU?

Sam - ALL GOOD HERE NO BIG NEWS JUST THE SAME OLD. HOW R U?

Kirsty - GREAT B GOOD TO CHAT

Sam - AGREE WILL CALL SOON. WANT TO HEAR ALL.

She had a hope he would call immediately but did not feel bold enough to make the suggestion.

Chapter 14

Visitor

Before Sister Mary Cecelia's visit Mrs Devlin insisted fresh cut flowers from the garden be placed in a vase on the hall table and the furniture polished until it gleamed even more than usual. In the midst of it all, Kirsty, who was tired of hearing how Sister Mary Cecelia was a wonderful baker, meticulously followed a recipe for a lemon drizzle sponge.

Prompt at three a loud rat-tat-tat from the brass door knocker reverberated in every corner of the house.

'Come on in,' shouted Mrs Devlin.

Before Kirsty reached the door she heard it opening and a woman's voice say, 'Hello, hello, Mrs Devlin. It's only me, Sister Mary Cecelia.'

'Come away through, Sister. I'm in the sitting room.'

The elderly lady sat in her favourite pink floral armchair which sank into the luxurious golden carpet. Her dress of lilac, embroidered with tiny white flowers, was complemented by the special pearl necklace reserved for important guests.

'Come, my dear, how lovely to see you again. Please do have a seat.'

Mrs Devlin asked about Callum and how Sister Mary Cecelia must stay and talk to her as, 'Kirsty has everything under control in the kitchen. Go through and say hello, give her your cake then hurry back.'

'How do you do?' said Kirsty to the nun who appeared in the doorway holding a brick-shaped object wrapped in silver foil that shined brightly against the muddy brown drabness of the religious habit.

'How do you do? Nice to meet you.'

She accepted the foil brick graciously and then the ladies shook hands.

The nuns in her past life at school wore black, with white spongy wimples. Not that black was a cheerful colour, but it somehow looked better than the brown she now observed.

Sister Mary Cecelia had good skin, although Kirsty noticed it was a bit red and shiny over her nose in comparison to the paler cheeks. Her hair was harshly drawn up and tucked beneath a dowdy wimple of brown cloth. An effort had been made to soften this effect by delicately exposing a curled tendril on the right-hand side.

'It's a lemon drizzle sponge,' said the nun enthusiastically.

'Gosh. We must be telepathic, I baked today,' said Kirsty as if it was a regular occurrence, 'and of all things, would you believe it, a lemon sponge. No worries, it'll be great to have two. One can easily be saved for later; there's always a stream of visitors and need for cake.'

There was no reaction reflected in the nun's brown eyes. She must be boiled in that lot, thought Kirsty dropping her gaze and observing thick nylon stockings crinkled at the ankles below the calf-length habit. The nun excused herself saying it would be good to have a longer chat sometime.

Placing her own cake on a plate with three slices cut in readiness, quite determined her first ever attempt at baking would be appreciated, Kirsty felt everything was ready.

A short time later Kirsty entered the sitting room carrying the tea tray.

'Who's going to be Mammy then?' said Mrs Devlin, rubbing

her hands together, looking at Sister Mary Cecelia.

'Perhaps Kirsty should pour as she made the tea. I remember you and Mammy used to say it brings bad luck if the person who made it doesn't pour.'

A full cup was handed to each lady, and a plate and a napkin before offering a slice of cake. As she left the room, Kirsty overheard mention of the younger son.

'Sister, you will never guess. Mattie has arranged for Peter to come and stay next weekend. It's all sorted. The three of us can have a lovely reunion. I'm so excited.'

No comment on the sponge yet, thought Kirsty, stepping outside the back door to cool down. Then she heard, 'I must say this is a beautiful cake, Sister Mary Cecelia.'

No response from the nun.

Kirsty smiled.

'I am so lucky to have found such a lovely girl to help me recover from the op. She's good at her job, we chat about all sorts of things. It's great having company and a bit of young life about the place too.'

Kirsty smiled even more.

There was no need to watch the clock and make an entrance after an hour because forty minutes later, Sister Mary Cecelia announced it was time she got back to her brother. She overheard promises to call again soon or perhaps Mrs Devlin could come to the Flannigan cottage one afternoon to see Callum.

Later that evening, just before starting the next chapter of *Pride and Prejudice*, Kirsty said hesitantly, 'Mrs Devlin?'

'Yes, my dear.'

'Do you or did you ever know anyone called Biddy Duffy in Balvohan?'

'Biddy? Let me think. No, although Duffy rings a bell somewhere in my fog. The only Biddy I can think of is Biddy Early who lived in Clare who reputedly cured illness with her special potions. No, sorry can't help.' She paused in concentration then added, 'There would be a Brigit lives in Lavender Cottage at the foot of the village.'

'Oh! How old would she be?'

'Goodness. I have no idea. Not young but not that old either. Actually, I feel very tired tonight. Could we leave the book until tomorrow?'

'Of course.' A bookmark was slipped between the pages and it was placed back on the bedside table.

Mrs Devlin yawned a 'Night, night,' and snuggled between clean pink sheets.

Around ten o'clock a text arrived on Kirsty's mobile. She let out a sigh of relief seeing it was from Sam.

WHERE R U? CAN U CALL?

Without hesitation she pressed Sam's contact number and he picked up immediately saying, 'Hello, Kirsty, are you alright?'

'Yes, OK, thanks. Why do you ask?'

'Been wondering about you; bit worried. Leaving a big relationship, one as big as a marriage, is never easy, even when you want to.'

'True. Never thought I'd be forced into such a decision. All for the best though'

'So tell me, are you really OK?'

'Well, sort of. It is good here, quiet, no pressure. Suits me for the moment anyway.'

'Good, glad to hear.'

'How are you?' she asked.

Sam chatted on about how he was coping and work was just about tolerable, although he would really like a change. He increasingly felt like a 'square peg in a round hole'.

After about ten minutes he ended the call saying, 'Don't feel you are on your own, phone anytime.'

'Thanks, that's appreciated. I do still speak to Diane regularly.'

'That's good. I do mean it, call me anytime.'

'Thanks again. Talk soon, bye.'

'Bye.'

Another night passed without finishing her letter to Father Carlin.

Chapter 15

Brothers

Mattie had arranged Mrs Devlin's stay overnight with a friend in the village in order to permit the brothers some time alone together. She was happy to oblige, recognising that her elder son was the peacemaker and better placed to restore harmony between the three of them. The promise of all day Saturday and part of Sunday devoted to the enjoyment of having both sons at home filled her with joy.

'Jeez, you're some cook, Mattie boy,' he talked to himself, sprinkling contents from a green and white cylinder marked 'mixed herbs' into a steaming casserole. Stirring methodically before raising the wooden spoon to his mouth, he flattered himself, 'Mmmmmm, perfect.' He then returned the dish to the oven. With arms flailing and short rapid steps he moved to the sitting room, parting the curtains to peer into a starless foggy night.

'Come on. Hurry up, Petsey,' he said, letting go of the curtain and scuttling back to the kitchen, stabbing a knife into the contents of one of the two saucepans bubbling on the hob.

'Good, good, at last,' he said hearing a car stop outside. The tea towel which balanced precariously on his shoulder was tossed carelessly onto the green marble work surface before rushing to the front door to greet his guest.

'Come on in, quick as you can, let's try and keep the heat indoors,' he said as the warm air gathered in the hallway escaped and mingled with haar-laden darkness.

'Hi, big bro.' Peter self-consciously slapped Mattie on the back as he shook his hand. The canvas bag he carried dropped onto the floor beside the coat stand with a dull thud. 'By God, it is a cold one, and it's supposed to be summer.' Then moving from the hallway to the sitting room he expressed his delight. 'Jeez, isn't it grand to see a real fire?' Rubbing the palms of his hands together over the heat he said, 'I thought I was never going to get here. Horrible thick fog all the way down country.'

'Welcome.' Mattie repeated the word three more times in a preoccupied way, 'Welcome, you are most welcome.'

'Will you look at that turf glow, just what the doctor ordered.' Peter sat himself in the armchair closest to the hearth. 'Now a glass of something would go down a treat,' he said smiling.

'Wine or beer?'

'Oh, let's have a beer to start with, good man.'

Mattie scuttled off to the fridge, pleased everything seemed to be going well.

'Now that's getting better. I can feel me toes start to tingle,' said Peter, before taking a swig of beer from his glass.

Both brothers were blessed with a head of curls most men their age would envy. Mattie perched himself on the edge of a chair and barely sipped any of his beer, and after a few moments jumped up again, saying, 'Let me dish up my little culinary delight! It's all ready and waiting. Come, follow me.'

Peter sat at the table with his back to the door, something Mattie found hard to do, he felt a need to always face the door. As the meal progressed his guest was regularly plied with refills of wine. Their conversation ranged across work, the government, people they both used to know and where and what mutual friends were doing now. Lilting Irish brogue wafted through the house as the brothers became increasingly relaxed in each other's company.

Replete, they returned to the fire, which immediately generated a soporific effect. Peter yawned. 'Sorry, the working week and the journey's catching up with me.'

'How's the family? You know you are a lucky man,' Mattie said feeling that this topic could now be safely broached and lead into a discussion aimed to heal the rift between Mrs Devlin and her younger son.

'I am, I am indeed,' he paused, 'and be sure I do appreciate my luck.'

Mattie sighed. 'I really don't give a damn these days about my marriage or lack of it. Come on, can I tempt you to have a drop of Paddy's?'

There was little persuasion needed and after Peter gulped a mouthful of spirit from the glass he asked, 'Now then, what's this really about? I cannot recall ever having had a summons before for the two of us to meet alone like this.'

Mattie leant forward. 'I have…' he started slowly, staring directly at his brother, '…concerns.'

'Concerns about what?' Peter's voice starting to develop an alcohol induced slur.

'Be patient, let me continue, all will become apparent. More whiskey?' Peter drained his glass and held it out for a refill.

'It's Mammy I have concerns over.' He shifted from leaning against the arm of the chair to sit opposite his brother. 'I would like to know that if anything should happen to me you will be there for her.' He paused. 'I need to know you're willing to mend the rift.'

Peter was only half listening, busy loosening his tie and releasing several buttons on his shirt. 'Jeez, it's warm, the old turf gives out a fierce heat.'

'Will I open a window to let air circulate for a bit?' Mattie moved steadily with no hint of intoxication.

'Better?'

'Will be in a moment, thanks.'

He sat down again. 'I do wish you would visit her more often, let her get to know the children. Not just rely on your occasional letters and phone calls.'

'Are you going somewhere that would mean Mammy's golden boy might not be there regular as clockwork, available to tend to her every need?'

'I'm not planning on going anywhere,' said Mattie impatiently. 'But we're none of us are getting younger and things happen.'

'Have you a health issue; is that what you are leading up to?'

'Not exactly, but I have been giving thought to a lot of things recently. Maybe turning fifty has something to do with it, I don't know. Anyway, please hear me out.'

Mattie cleared his throat to deliver his rehearsed speech, 'Mammy loved you every bit as much as she loved me. The difference, if there has to be one, is that when Da died she leant on me because I was the older boy. I had to grow up quickly while you still had your childhood.'

Peter stared thoughtfully into his whiskey tumbler. Mattie accommodated the silence until his brother spoke. 'I'd say it's all possible. Let me sleep on it.'

'If your wife wants to stay away that's alright, I know she's at the root of this estrangement – although I never understood why dear old Mammy upset her. You and the children could visit. Or just you on your own.'

'I hear what you're saying.'

'Mammy does not deserve to be deserted in her dotage by her younger son or his family.'

'I said I hear what you are saying, now can we leave it, I'm tired and need to sleep.'

*

The next morning the brothers burst into the kitchen return-ing from an early walk, both apparently wide awake and fresh faced. Kirsty was introduced to Peter who declared he'd forgot-ten how a blast of sea air was the best cure for a hangover.

'Is Mammy back safe and had her lunch?' Mattie asked, turning on the cold tap, letting it run to chill then filled a glass which he handed to his brother before repeating the process for himself.

'We should all do that every day,' said Peter. 'Empty our lungs of all the stale air and refill with good clean air.'

'Yes, your mother is home, lunched and now resting.' And she also replied to Peter, 'I've heard something of the sort regarding our need to inhale deeply.' The brothers were physically similar although Peter was slimmer and fitter in appearance.

'Which fork did you take at the top of the hill?' she enquired.

'Hey Mattie, herself wants to know did we fork off?'

Mattie smiled maintaining eye contact with his employee for a few seconds longer than was necessary. He was to be dis-appointed when she begged to be excused, saying there were chores to attend to.

The brothers continued to talk of their school days con-gratulating themselves on doing well in life from a humble beginning. Not everyone in the village had gone on to great things. Their voices became quieter and more concentrated. It was all becoming intriguing. 'After all, blood is thicker than water,' she heard Mattie say as she climbed the stairs.

'Rafferty is elderly but mentally sharp. My boy Declan is in the business, my daughter Susan would like to be and Frances never will be. I may have a need to go abroad for a while. I want to know you will be here for Mammy.'

'Mattie leaving Ireland, unbelievable,' said Peter. 'You on the run?' To which she heard no answer. Then Peter spoke again, 'Yes alright then. of course I promise to be there for Mammy.'

'I thought we could take Mammy for a run in the car to

Dingle this afternoon. Over Connor Pass,' said Mattie.
   'Sure, she'd like that, I'm up for it.'

Chapter 16

Disconcerted

On Sunday evening, as far as Kirsty could see, the three Devlins were very close and the weekend had been a great success. Peter gave his mammy a hug, vowing to return with the children on a visit very soon. For her too, personally, it had also proved a good weekend. Aside from the additional catering arrangements she had time alone in the house in a way unknown since her arrival. Added to this she'd found strength to delete texts from Toby and as a result felt buoyed up and positive about her future. She decided she would try and phone Sam later; sometimes it did feel a bit lonely for her in these new surroundings.

It came as an added bonus when Mrs Devlin was ready to retire early after the excitement of her weekend. Kirsty left the house and walked to the village pump where she sat on the bench and tried to call Sam. No answer, so she left a voicemail saying she would try again later. Diane was up to speed with everything that had been going on, although not the latest development about the texts from Toby. She called Diane but again no one picked up so once more she left a voicemail and made her way back to the Devlin's.

'Please sit with me. You don't have to make conversation. Read if you like.'

Mattie's portly figure sat by the window in the sitting room. Kirsty obeyed his request, the house seemed so much quieter that evening as the sun set on the horizon.

She pretended to read but instead watched a far distant ship silhouetted against the red sky. The spell interrupted only by sips from the whiskey tumbler lifted periodically from the table. Loud snoring came from Mrs Devlin's room, as if trying to shake the whole fabric of the house. Kirsty thought that Mrs Devlin was a good woman, one of the best. The elderly lady had shown nothing but kindness and empathy since Kirsty's arrival. There had been no prying only genuine interest in anything Kirsty opted to share.

'I like you,' said Mattie, leaning back and closing his eyes. When she heard his breathing change to snoring softly, she tiptoed to the door.

'Don't go, my dear. Sit with me, please.'

She did.

They sat.

In silence.

Until he moved deftly to kneel by her chair.

'I want to kiss you,' he said.

She let him.

It was soft and practised. Then snapping her mind back to reality, she pulled away.

'What's the matter?' he whispered. 'It's alright, I promise.'

She could smell the whiskey on his breath. Sensuously and tenderly he stroked one side of her face with his finger.

'*Ta tu go h alainn?*'

His low resonating tone spoke to her in Irish and sent a shiver through her body.

'*A chuisle mo chroi.*'

Then her loneliness slipped a hand round the back of his neck, pulling him closer.

'That's more like it,' he whispered.

He stroked her hair, uttering intimate words using the language of his homeland, taking her briefly to a place of imagined love. In this moment he validated her as a woman. She became hypnotized into a fantasy of belief that he understood her pain.

But suddenly it all felt wrong. 'Mattie, I am sorry, I can't do this.'

'Do what?'

'This. Please don't try to seduce me any more.'

She felt tension rise in his relaxed body, but he said nothing. She trembled with a horrible sense of déjà vu, uncertain what might happen next. Many moments experienced with Toby flashed before her.

'Please don't think badly of me.'

'Why are you shaking?'

'I'm not,' she snapped defensively.

His arm tightened for a moment before relaxing again. This small gesture gave her courage.

'I hope you'll agree it is for the best. I think I just had a bit of a blip,' she pleaded.

'Fair enough.'

'We can be friends. I would like to think we could be friends,' she desperately appealed.

'Surely. You can be friends with anyone if you set your mind to it.'

'I would like to go and sleep now. Alone.' She stood up.

He kissed her brow tenderly. 'Good night, friend.' Holding her wrist for a second and knowing her to be familiar with one of Ireland's greatest poets, he said, 'I trust you, because I believe you understand W.B. Yeats *world more full of secrets than we can understand.*' Then released his hand.

As she left the room she was aware of his silent tears.

Chapter 17

Discovery

Mrs Devlin smiled for the entire week following Peter's visit, repeating over and over that he was a good boy too, and wasn't Mattie great building bridges to restore the family. The morning in the immediate aftermath of the kiss, Mattie apparently left early due to an unexpected summons to a business meeting in Dublin. 'Oh, and before I forget, he asked me to give you this,' the old lady had said, handing her a sealed envelope.

'Thank you. Excuse me a moment. I need to unload the washing machine.' Kirsty retreated to the kitchen and immediately opened the letter.

Dear Kirsty,

I want you to pay attention to the ramblings of a drunken man. I'm making a big effort here to make sure my writing is legible. Have been thinking about what you said. You know, the friends thing, and want to apologise for being offhand. You hurt my pride. I am not made of stone, you know.

I do want your friendship. Yes, in fact, need your friendship, but most of all I trust you.

Maybe we can still help each other.

Chat soon.

Your friend!

Mattie the Blip.

Although unsure what to make of the content it pleased her he had communicated. Any awkwardness between them would not help with their shared priority which was caring for his mother. She liked her job and was certain she was not yet ready to move on.

*

Kirsty obeyed Mr Maloney's suggestion to walk briskly for at least half an hour daily. To work up a sweat was the key. Because, he explained, an increased level of effort would pump more oxygen to her brain and release endorphins. The theory was to evoke a feel-good factor, lift her spirits and therefore be able to cope with any intrusion from Toby either real or in her thoughts. She devised walks of different lengths - thirty minutes, forty minutes and an hour - and soon appreciated starting to feel fitter physically. An added bonus was for increasing periods of time she managed to exclude her husband from her mind.

Sometimes she saw a man sitting on a bench beside the ice cream kiosk which nestled at the foot of the cliffs. Most times he had a plaid rug over his legs and a cushion behind his back. They always exchanged a general greeting when she passed. If the weather was cool or dull he was not there and she found she missed him and felt concerned, hoping nothing was amiss.

*

'What happened between you and your husband?' asked Mrs Devlin one day.

Feeling slightly unsettled but not sure why, Kirsty told her a simplified version.

'The closeness we shared when first married had gone.' To

verbalise even this attempt to deliver a brief account of the pain made her feel sick.

The old lady looked sad. 'I'm sorry, remember bridges can be mended and all the other clichés are true, you know. It does not need to be permanent. It happens in a lot of marriages, and can be overcome but you both need to want to make it work.' She spoke in a way only wise old ladies can.

Kirsty quickly and successfully diverted the conversation by sharing her plan to drive over the mountain pass to Killarney on her next half day. It was too complicated to try and explain that bridge-building did not, simply could not, apply when dealing with a personality such as Toby. Lately she had become increasingly grateful their union never created a child.

Mrs Devlin immediately became enthusiastic at the mention of the Kerry Mountains, adding that Mondays were a wonderful choice for a half-day because there was always a good film on in the afternoon.

'*Gone with the Wind* is on tomorrow. I love nothing better than a good weepie.'

The tourist route to Killarney led along a winding road which climbed higher and higher into the mountains. It became tortuous in places, but the water-filled corries and lakes bathed in sunlight were an extraordinary vibrant shade of blue. She found herself stopping regularly to take photographs. Sometimes landing beside a coach tour she mingled amid tourists of all nationalities, united in awe and all clasping and clicking cameras. It had to be a special kind of driver, she thought, to venture over these mountains in something as large as a coach.

Eventually arriving in Killarney, she saw the familiar jaunting carts waiting near the cathedral entrance. It was depressing to observe these horses relegated to a life clip-clopping through the streets, obedient to their master's bidding. A few were fortunate enough to have a nose bag containing a tasty morsel to munch before the next flick of the whip came to set the wheels in motion.

Finding she was early for her appointment with Mr Maloney, Kirsty decided to drive to the town boundary where she stopped beside a picnic area. Getting out of the car she followed a sign pointing to a public footpath. She felt particularly pensive and alone because she was not making as much progress in eliminating Toby as she wanted to. She weaved a route between lofty gnarled oaks standing proud and noble, holding onto their stories from countless seasons. Wearing only sandals, the soft mud felt cold squelching between her bare toes. The remains of shrivelled primroses lined the route, their time to be vibrant ended. Pungent damp smells clawed in her nostrils, as twigs broke with a dull and barely audible sound beneath her feet.

The walk proved frustratingly incomplete, for no matter how deep she penetrated the woods, car engines and voices remained audible from the nearby town. She needed to think, she wanted silence. Deeper into the wood, on and on until the path finally became an impassable quagmire, forcing her to turn and squelch back to car.

It was then she read it. All resolve to delete texts from Toby finally failed. This one had arrived sometime during the night. There had been none during the interim period since her inner strength succeeded in deleting two.

I MISS YOU

Then almost as if he knew he'd gained her attention, a second arrived, and she read it too.

I STILL LOVE YOU

Her stomach somersaulted, breathing became rapid and shallow as sweat trickled from her brow.

Her finger hovered over the phone, knowing that to reply would invite him to call.

Within seconds she could be listening to his voice. A part of her, a part she was rapidly losing control of wanted this. Logic stepped into her mind and shouted, stop! Don't do it, think of the consequences. It would be a disastrous scenario. His smooth, seductive rhetoric would continue until he was satisfied he had her hooked again. Damp sweaty finger marks were visible on the plastic casing of her phone as she switched it off and zipped it inside a compartment of her bag, narrowly avoiding any sort of response to him. Feeling quite shaky when she got back to the car, she delayed for a few minutes before heading into Killarney for her appointment with Mr Maloney. After several minutes and a few deep sighs, she ignited the engine and returned to the car park beside the cathedral. 'Oh, Toby,' she said wistfully before getting out of the car. The church brought to mind her enquiry about confession times but she remained disconnected having difficulty recollecting why she'd felt the need to seek absolution.

Mr Maloney did not hold back his disappointment when she confessed her recent weakness, even assuring him the other texts had been deleted unread. 'This is predicable behaviour. Toby understands you well. He knows how vulnerable you are right now.'

Kirsty left the consulting room an hour later. Full of re-morse and promises given to delete any further messages, she also had vowed not to answer a call, under any circumstances. Fine-spoken sentiments, all uttered with the best of intention but failed to dilute the inner yearning to hear Toby's voice. It was easy to grasp the concept that a clean break from her husband's type of personality was the only way; she knew that she had to persevere and would eventually make Toby's power a redundant force. Such choices were ultimately in her hands.

Kirsty was in no hurry to return to Balvohan and retraced her journey over the mountain. Stopping half way at a gift shop, she browsed among the locally produced crafts finding a beautiful jug, glazed with an unusual blend of red, blue and yellow. Having purchased it as a gift for Mrs Devlin, she ordered a coffee, deciding to sit outside and enjoy the view. She wished she could blame all her turmoil on the frustratingly full waste bin in her room. The letter to Father Carlin remained incomplete. Each repeated attempt found her increasingly aware of the potential for such a communication to be inadvertently left where a housekeeper or visitor might catch sight of its contents.

Every time she thought she might tell Mr Maloney about Biddy the words stuck in her throat. So far, not one living person shared her secret. Sam knew nothing, but of all people he should be told. After all, it had been his father who helped her parents gain a child. Maybe he did know something but was afraid to say. It was with regret she remembered the missed opportunity to share when in Eastbourne. *It was so typical of Victoria to butt in on the potential for a private moment alone with Sam.*

*

Upon her return to Balvohan, her needs became the centre of a spontaneous event. With no pre-meditation she stood on the doorstep of the parochial house and pressed the doorbell. There was no immediate response and she was about to walk away when a kind-faced, grey-haired man opened the door. To her amazement he knew immediately who she was. It appeared everyone in the village thought they knew who she was, but how could they when she did not know her true self? The priest invited her to enter, anxious to know if all was well with Mrs Devlin. Once reassured that was not the reason for her visit, he asked how he could be helpful.

Father Carlin had to decipher the jumble of words which tumbled out of his visitor - Biddy Duffy, Kerry cottages, adoption, letters, uncles and actresses. Gently, he suggested she slow down and start again at the beginning.

'You'll treat what I say with the sanctity of the confessional?' she pleaded.

'Of course I shall if that's what you wish.'

She managed to repeat the information rearranged into chronological sequence. This opening of the floodgates brought a huge sense of relief which detracted from the intensity of Toby's intrusion. Father Carlin barely flinched at these revelations, quietly suggesting they should check the registers of baptisms, first communions, marriages and deaths. 'If there is anything to know it will be recorded in one of those.'

Flicking through the pages of a large book containing birth entries he talked as he looked. 'I've only been in the village this last ten years. Father McInally would have been the man to help, he would surely have known the family, but sadly he's deceased.'

The baptismal records revealed seven possible entries for the name Duffy, two boys and five girls. But none of them was named Biddy. Methodically, he continued lifting more registers from the shelf and just as he was beginning to say it was doubtful another would be found, he enthused having come across an entry for a baby girl named Bridget (Biddy) born a full eight years after the last of her siblings. 'There we have it,' he said with delight. 'Let me write this down for you.'

Eight children, she had seven aunts and uncles.

'Where ever are they all now?' she asked.

'I cannot say. The only thing we can be sure of is none of them live in this village. I wonder would it be worth asking Mrs Devlin? She is a good sort, you know, and would not go talking to anyone if you asked her not to.'

This idea did not sit easily with Kirsty. She did not want to bring the relationship with her employer to such a personal level. Not yet anyway.

'I understand,' said Father Carlin handing her a piece of paper with all the Duffy names written in order of age.

'Is there an address?'

'Bramble Cottage, Balvohan is all it says here, and in truth I have no knowledge of a Bramble Cottage. It's possible it has become derelict over the years. There are two crumbling ruins up the hill here behind the church.'

Motivated by his findings, the priest replaced the baptism registry and lifted down a second set of books to check first communions. These suggested all the children still lived in the parish at this stage. However, when he checked further volumes for marriages or deaths, nothing more was found.

'No deaths and no marriages tells me they were not permanent or long established residents in this village. It suggests they probably moved to another town, county or even country.' He smiled compassionately.

It was difficult to accurately select an age for Father Carlin, anywhere between fifty-five and seventy, but Kirsty liked this kind man with his thinning grey hair, thick-rimmed glasses and soft voice. Having thanked him very much for his trouble she left, heading straight to the strand for some sea air.

Later in the evening, Mrs Devlin commented her carer seemed particularly quiet, asking if everything was alright. An urge to ask about Bramble Cottage welled up in Kirsty but her response was only, 'It's nothing an early night will not put right.'

Later she received a message from Sam.

Sam - WELL HOWS U?

Kirsty - TICKETY BOO

Sam - CALL TO GIVE ME UPDATE SOMETIME PLEASE

Kirsty - WILL DO

Chapter 18

Callum

The figure who often sat beside the ice cream kiosk at the end of the strand was Callum. Kirsty had playfully named him the 'rug man' due to the plaid rug always wrapped over his legs. One afternoon a conversation developed between them beyond a polite hello or comments about weather.

As he knew, it seemed, exactly who she was, and she by now suspected who he might be, there was hardly need for a formal introduction. He invited her to sit, saying, 'It would be great to have a bit of company.'

She sat on the bench, worried about the possibility of being sweaty after vigorously striding out along the beach. He told her how he loved to watch children play because it reminded him of when he was a lad. 'Mattie and I used to run races on this very strand.'

He asked if she had visited Kenmare yet, if not, it merited being added to her list of things to do while in Kerry. No direct reference was made to his illness, only a mention of how he would love to be able to step out along the strand but his tired legs were not up to it any more.

Kirsty was startled when the question fell out of her and lay in front of him, full of expectation.

'Did you ever know someone called Biddy Duffy?'

'I did surely.'

'You did?'

'Why do you ask?'

'Just wondered,' she stumbled over what else to say without telling a lie.

'She was the year or maybe it was two years below me at school. I had a bit of a crush for a while.' Callum smiled.

'Oh,' she said, trying not to sound like a strangled chicken.

'Yes, I did. She was lovely. Went away somewhere, I seem to remember, quite suddenly and then the whole family moved from the village not long after. Well, I say whole family, but the older ones were already up and gone. Biddy was a bit of an afterthought, a late baby Mammy called her, but her parents doted like she was an only one. I do remember Mrs Duffy was never done telling everyone how clever her daughter was and all the teachers said she would be going to university. Why do you want to know?'

Kirsty panicked, wishing it had not been mentioned to someone she'd met only five minutes earlier. Suddenly it seemed foolhardy in the extreme. She didn't know what to say. 'I–' she started and stopped. 'I just won–' she stopped again. Then had no choice but to either tell the truth or lie.

Callum was looking at her in a strange way. 'What age are you, Kirsty?' he asked.

'Thirty-three.'

There was a long pause as he continued to study her face. It felt uncomfortable so she mumbled it was probably time to return to Mrs Devlin.

'Are you the reason Biddy left the village and had none of the going to university her mammy predicted? There were rumours at the time.'

'Me?'

'I do know something of what went on for some unfortunate girls in this country of ours,' he said.

She could either run away or finish what she'd started, but could he be trusted?

'Please, I beg don't mention anything of this conversation to anyone. And I really must return to Mrs Devlin now.'

'Don't worry. I'll say nothing. Nice to meet you, perhaps we can chat again sometime. Please give my best to Mrs D.'

She walked away quickly, anxious to put distance between them, wondering what possessed her to have exposed her most private secret to a random Irishman sitting on a bench in Kerry. *Please, please don't let him say anything to anyone.* Biddy had suddenly become a real person, someone remembered. Kirsty had aunts and uncles she did not know and probably never would.

Then she wondered why this should matter. They would not be aware of her, and it was a new thing for her to be aware of their existence. She imagined they probably still lived in Ireland. Although another thought was prompted, it was always a possibility they'd moved to America or Canada which would make it harder to find them. Anyway, even if she did, what then? They may have no notion to know her or could even be hostile towards her. They were not a priority, and could be relegated to a corner of her mind.

*

The following day the strand was avoided completely and replaced by a walk up the hill behind the church. Climbing steeply she could see no evidence of any derelict cottages, but on the descent she noticed something behind a group of mature trees and straggly bushes. Leaving the road to battle through overgrown ferns and barbed wilderness, she reached the remains of a house.

How seven or eight children and two adults lived in something so small was unimaginable when gazing at the dimensions of the perimeter wall. Through a gap in the foliage the Atlantic was clearly visible. Kirsty placed the flat of her palm upon the ancient moss-covered, crumbling chimney breast, which stood higher amid the other relics of stone. She imagined children skipping up or downhill, arriving home to be welcomed with a pot of soup simmering on the hob and glowing turf in the grate.

Then battling back through the jungle of briars she continued her descent. A short distance downhill stood a modern pristine white bungalow where a man worked in a neatly tended garden.

'It's been empty for years,' he said as she passed. 'I dare say that planning permission might be made easier by the fact there is a building of sorts in situ.'

'Oh,' she said.

'I saw you having a bit of a look. They all went from there before my time. Been abandoned this last thirty years or more. Duffy they were called. He was an engine driver.'

'He drove trains?' asked Kirsty.

'No, that was the title of someone who worked the farm machinery. Sort of general farm work for a contractor and such like.'

'Who owns it now?'

'Belongs to Paddy Sullivan. He bought the few acres and cottage. In fact, here he comes now.'

An ancient red tractor clattered downhill towards them. It stopped outside the white bungalow.

'Sean, good man, I'm reminded to say you were missed at last week's quiz night in the Turrets,' the driver shouted from his seat. 'I hope you'll manage this Thursday, we need you.'

'I will surely, we had the grandchildren staying last week and the wife was not keen I go off gallivanting.'

'Fair enough,' laughed Paddy.

'I was just telling the young lady here you own the Duffy cottage.'

'I do. So?'

'I was telling her because she asked,' he shouted above the din of the tractor engine.

'Why would that be?' said Paddy, looking at Kirsty.

'Just happened to see it there among the trees.'

'So you don't want to buy it?'

'No, thank you. I don't want to buy it; please excuse me, but I have to go now.' She left the men to chat, hoping they were not discussing her.

Reaching the bench beside the old water pump she sat down. Everything felt surreal. Somewhere in this village, or at least near it, was where she'd been conceived. With very little knowledge about Biddy, but a lot more than she had two days ago, she thought about the girl and pitied her plight. There existed an army of blood relatives who knew nothing of her. Biddy's parents, her own biological grandparents, knew and of course her mother, but what of her natural father, whoever he might be? Questions and more questions. What now?

'Good afternoon, Kirsty.' Sister Mary Cecelia passed, appearing to be in a great hurry.

'Good afternoon, Sister.' She observed the nun enter the shop before dragging her feet into action and heading back to Mrs Devlin.

Late evening when all was quiet, Kirsty went outside and sat in the garden among the night-scented flowers. An owl hooted in the distance. Moths fluttered nearby, attracted to the light from the kitchen window.

'Hello, Sam.'

'Kirsty, how nice. I've been hoping you would call.'

'Did try before, left a voicemail. You can always call me.'

'Not sure about your work schedule and all that. Wouldn't be normal hours, I expect.'

'Well don't be afraid to try. I can always call you back.'

'OK. Any news?'

She tried to talk normally about her daily routine, taking care not to mention the Devlin brothers in case she was overheard.

'And?'

'And what?'

'Well I can't help feeling you didn't call to tell me what a nice hoover and washing machine Mrs Devlin has, and how all mod cons are a blessing.'

Kirsty hesitated and was on the brink of saying more, but her stomach knotted and she just couldn't get to the point of her call. 'Sorry. Is it all a bit boring?'

'No, no, not at all,' Sam was quick to say. 'I like to hear about things in Kerry. Non-domestic things,' he laughed.

He then went on to repeat how disillusioned he felt with his job and how he had started to seriously look for something else.

Chapter 19

Toby

Mattie returned from Dublin and was soon fussing and fiddling to get his new purchase of a computer set up and operational. Mrs Devlin complained it resembled an alien watching her from the corner, like an intruder. Her son laughed saying everyone had a computer these days and it was time his mammy was up to speed with the modern world. It would be useful for him to do work if he was going to be spending more time at home. Once she got the hang of it she would wonder how ever she managed without one.

'Remember television?' he said in a way which suggested his mother had rebelled against it too. 'Plus, when Peter and the children visit and we have our Kerry rain you will have the very thing to keep them entertained.' He explained several other uses for the computer, including being able to talk to her grandchildren while being able to see them on the screen at the same time.

'Now that I don't believe,' protested his mother.

Kirsty quickly commandeered the computer early each morning for her own use before the daily routine began. She found a plethora of websites on the topic of adoption. While browsing she kept a note of any which could be relevant, saving the links in a folder stored in her private email account. Perusing these adoption websites provided a distraction from something which had now become a daily occurrence, a text from Toby, which had all been confidently deleted. That's what she told Mr Maloney, omitting to mention a few moments of hesitation. Communication with her solicitor in Scotland, Joanne McDonald, confirmed her fear that the divorce proceedings were still painfully slow. The reason for this was Toby's delay in responding to any written communications.

The promises made to Mr Maloney of not reacting to any attempt at interaction from her husband thus far had been diligently adhered to. On the subsequent Monday afternoon visit he congratulated her but reiterated how much easier it would be to change the phone, rather than test her psychological strength every day. He presented her with his own mobile number to call should she feel tempted, or did in fact succumb. 'Speak to me any time day or night.'

Kirsty wondered at a later date if this generous gesture acted as a subliminal suggestion, because that evening she lost resolve and read a text from Toby.

FOR THE HUNDRETH TIME CAN WE TALK PLEASE

Immediately she called Diane and confessed her lapse, feeling too ashamed to speak to Mr Maloney.

'What in God's name did you do that for?' her friend shouted. 'That has to be detrimental. Why? Please tell me why?'

Diane was angrier than Kirsty had ever known, giving oodles of reasons she should change her phone. In her frustration Diane let it slip that Toby had been seen out and about in the company of several different women.

This information should not have surprised Kirsty, but nevertheless it seared through her with agonising intensity. She trembled, sweated, felt nauseated while her friend said that it really was time to get rid of him once and for all. 'Remember all the bad times, the horrible, vile things he said to you, the abuse, the way he used you like a doormat. You can't possibly yearn for any of that back in your life?'

But Kirsty hardly heard.

Of course she understood her best friend's wisdom, but this new pain became excruciating. Images of Toby caressing and charming other women was more than she could endure.

Even Mattie, who clattered around in his own world of endless things to do noticed something was wrong, asking if she was alright. When Mrs Devlin enquired too, she made a huge effort to sound upbeat, proposing they could start reading *Emma* suggesting it was every bit as good as *Pride and Prejudice*.

Then a text arrived:

I MISS YOU I LOVE YOU WE HAD GOOD TIMES, DIDN'T WE?

She typed: IT'S OVER. LEAVE ME ALONE and pressed send.

This time she had to call Mr Maloney. 'You should not have interacted at all. Why will you not be rid of that phone?' he said raising his voice. At his insistence a meeting was arranged for the following day.

During her visit to the psychotherapist Toby had called. When she realised he'd left a voicemail she became frightened by the power her emotions. She felt swamped by this vulnerability which found her listening to the voicemail when she got back to the car. Toby's words were loaded with venom. She was, according to him, 'A sick, sad, lonely cow.'

It was late evening when with no hope of sleep she resorted to the computer. She wanted to cry but no tears would come. There was need for distraction, anything to avert the danger of responding to the poisoned voice message. While it would possibly help to talk to someone, she could not bring herself to call Diane, Mr Maloney or even Sam. Particularly the latter because it mattered to her that he should not view her as some sort of emotional cripple. Her world had become a place of complete chaos, and she despaired at her own inadequacy. To uphold her carefree facade was rapidly becoming an impossibility. She typed Magdalene Laundries into the search engine. A plethora of information appeared on the screen. The content in each of the links proved profound and compelling.

She learned that more than 43,500 domestic adoption orders had been made in Ireland since the introduction the Adoption Act of 1952. At least 100,000 children had been separated from their birth parents through adoption and fostering since the foundation of the Irish State. A considerable number were illegally registered as if they had been born to their adoptive parents, in a practice known as de facto adoption. Historically, the Catholic Church had been highly influential, running numerous institutions. It was all too commonplace for pressure to be exerted on pregnant girls by parents, priests, nuns, social workers and doctors to ensure any child born out of wedlock was adopted. It was seen as a solution to a problem for both the infertile couples and the unmarried mother.

She stopped reading and slumped in the chair, muttering, 'One of them was me,' before continuing.

In 1974 Paddy Cooney, Minister for Justice, proclaimed: 'I think we are all agreed that the consensus opinion in our society is to the effect that adoption is the better option for the illegitimate child than being cared for by its mother'.

It was obvious to her that Mr Cooney had not been adopted.

The facts as she understood them were that Ireland maintained closed adoption records, a legacy from the 1952 adoption legislation. Records at this time were routinely shrouded in secrecy and still remained locked in a restricted system. Archaic arguments from politicians upheld these outdated laws. A right to privacy law to restrict access through a belief it has to remain as laid down in the constitution. Other arguments said: 'Ireland is a small country and therefore the mothers and their families need protection'. The USA and Canada and Australia also endorsed laws to restrict information.

Kirsty discovered the history of Magdalene Asylums goes as far back as the Middle Ages and they were named after Mary Magdalene. They were originally created for repentant street girls and prostitutes to be rehabilitated. The Magdalene movement was readily accepted by the Catholic Church in Ireland and several laundries quickly became established. What was meant to be a short-term refuge became long-term institutionalisation for a large number of the 'penitents', who to all intents and purposes became slaves in the laundries in return for their keep. For some it was to become a lifelong 'penance', while for others their days came to a premature end and were interred within the convent grounds in unmarked graves.

The Magdalene Laundries network operated independently in Ireland from the 1920s to the mid-1990s. The whole truth about the cruelty within this Irish 'child penitentiary' system is still unfolding. Irish girls would be abandoned at the Magdalene Laundries by their own families, particularly if they were pregnant and unmarried. This was true even though for many of the girls the pregnancy was a result of incest or rape – in some cases by a member of the clergy. The view expressed was that the girls had inflicted unbearable shame on their family, which could never be exposed. For others it was considered necessary to hide them from the world because they were considered to be too pretty and could become a temptation to men, or those who were wilful and strong minded individuals who refused to conform. The handicapped were also hidden from the world for fear exposing the family's genetic pool as suspect and would spoil the chances of other children finding a spouse. Authorities would be known to send young girls with 'attitude problems' into the Magdalene Laundries and a nightmare beyond their wildest comprehension. There was some crossover between government run industrial schools and Magdalene Laundries. Although some politicians still try to maintain the governments were not involved with the Magdalene's.

The Church, it seemed to Kirsty, ruled the state, its power knew no constraints.

There were no limitations on the list of reasons a girl could be sent to a Magdalene Laundry. Most were from 'devout' Catholic families that did not question Church rulings. Physical, sexual and emotional abuse became rampant within these institutions. A survivor recounts that one day after school, she was sexually assaulted. Her mother called the police to report the rape and was stunned when the police came and arrested the girl. A judge deemed the attack her fault and sentenced her to life in a Magdalene Laundry. For the most part these institutions were unregulated and not subject to any educational requirements and were exempt from labour laws and safety standards.

The nuns stripped these girls of their given name assigning a new one which they selected. Some became known by a number allocated to replace their given name. The girls were forced to work long hours and endure strict silence with only a meagre nutritional nourishment to sustain them. Punishments could include severe beatings or being locked in a cell for days. The content of words spoken by former inmates, she found extremely emotive.

Babies born out of wedlock were most often taken without consent from their mother in order to be adopted by infertile couples. The mothers had no say in what became of their child and pleas for mercy were ignored as the infant was wrenched from their arms. It is estimated more than 30,000 women passed through the doors of these institutions in Ireland alone and for some it was to be a journey from which they would never return. In the region of 4,500 infants are believed to have gone to American families, often illegally with falsified (de facto) birth certificates in exchange for generous financial donations to the religious order.

The tears which had been locked behind Kirsty's eyes flowed. This parallel existence from which she had come and the scars it left could not be measured in any rational way against what these women endured. What was best? Who has the conceited dogma to dictate these things? Why were they blindly obeyed?

It was so difficult to comprehend. The enormity of the crime against humanity and the trail of suffering left in its wake. Had she and Biddy remained together as mother and daughter, what would her world hold now? Love? Perhaps financial hardship? She would never know. What would Biddy's world have held for her, without the pregnancy, without the Magdalene Laundry? Her life would undoubtedly have been better. Some cruelties were incomprehensible. What could words do? Only fail to dilute the profound impact on so many.

Her world was OK with her parents, Aunt Maud, Cressida, Matthew, Victoria and Sam. They were the only family she ever knew. But she also knew she was not them, they were not her. All different. It cannot be considered wrong to wonder where she came from, she decided. There is a need to know more.

Kirsty wiped away her tears and blew into her handkerchief, then forced herself to continue reading:

In August 1993 workers in North Dublin, Ireland discovered the bodies of 155 young women in a mass grave. The grave was on property once owned by the Catholic Church and the Sisters of Charity. Records of the deaths cannot be found and only seventy-five of the women could be identified. Finding the grave, forced open a 150-year-old secret – the anonymous internment of women who had been residents of a Magdalene Laundry run by the nuns of Our Lady of Charity.

These same nuns doggedly denied any abuse and protested that 27,000 missing documents relating to girls in their care were destroyed in 'accidental fires'. So, for too many Irish born and subsequently adopted children there is little hope of finding their truth.

Kirsty could not help feeling all of this was merely the tip of a large iceberg.

Aware that to sleep would be impossible; it was far too late to phone Diane. Kirsty typed 'narcissistic personalities' into the search engine. Instinctively she knew to become more informed, or learn about others like her and how they dealt with it would be a step nearer to understanding. Identification could be a good place for healing to begin. Prior to meeting Mr Maloney she'd been unaware any such definition existed, the concept these personality types being officially recognised had become intriguing.

Of particular interest was a questionnaire she found designed to act as diagnostic criteria for narcissistic personality disorder. Methodically and with total honesty she ticked the boxes applicable to her husband.

Scoring: five or more true answers may qualify the person as having narcissistic personality disorder. If the person scores higher than ten, be careful.

A pervasive pattern of grandiosity, need for admiration, lack of empathy, a grandiose sense of self-importance. *True.*

Is preoccupied with fantasies of unlimited success, power, brilliance, beauty, or ideal love. *True.*

This person loves competition but is a poor loser. *True.*

This person has achieved more than most people his or her age. *True.*

Holds a belief that he or she is 'special' and can only be understood by, or should associate with, other special or high-status people (or institutions). Requires excessive admiration. *True.*

Has a sense of entitlement, i.e. unreasonable expectations of especially favourable treatment or automatic compliance with his or her expectations. *True.*

Is interpersonally exploitative, i.e. takes advantage of others to achieve his or her own ends. *True.*

Can turn on the charm offensive when he/she wants something from someone else. *True.*

Lacks empathy and is unwilling to recognise or identify with the feelings and needs of others. *True.*

This person thinks that most criticisms of him/her are motivated by jealousy. *True.*

This person regularly disregards rules or expects them to be changed because they are special. *True.*

This person becomes irritated when other people don't automatically do what he/she wants them to do, even when they have a good reason for not complying. *True.*

Uses sex as a means of control. *True.*

Sexual seduction and unfaithfulness within a supposedly committed relationship is all about seeking adulation from and control over others. Repeated adulterer. *Probably.*

Views anything less than adulation as rejection. *True.*

Has arrogant, haughty behaviours or attitudes. *True.*

Gradually she grew in awareness of how absolutely correct Mr Maloney was in his deductions regarding Toby.

There was also an article on co-dependency and another on forgetting the past. She read them all, together with the comments and responses from people, ordinary people, like her sucked into the world of a narcissistic personality.

She discovered how the narcissist likes their victim to believe everything is their own fault. They are masters at turning any argument around so the accuser ends up believing they are to blame.

She reread one article – 'We Must Remember' – several times. John Headley, Diane, and even Mr Maloney did not have it quite right, she imagined. Kirsty now believed that to forget completely was an impossible task, also to remember meant being able to recall the horrific details from her marriage to Toby. To evoke such images could prevent her slipping back into fool's paradise. One writer claimed her brain had been 'fried to a crisp' by the malignant narcissist in their life, and they felt to take responsibility lost all meaning when applied to their situation. The first mantra she should accept was 'it's not my fault'. 'None of it happened because of what I did or said; it would have anyway as long as I was prepared to stay in the toxic relationship'.

'Not my fault,' Kirsty repeated quietly. All those times she accepted the blame for precipitating 'a rage' were about Toby not her.

She read on:

Narcissists often target those who are gifted or talented in some way, as they like to be reflected in the glory. It is not the weak co-dependent personality we are all led to believe they target, but anyone who is of use to them who can be sucked into their strange and fantastic world. One which is not in the mindset or ethical code of the majority of people.

Another woman said: I looked evil in the eye, to know it and see it is to understand. Only then it can be turned away. Once I had educated myself, suddenly it became a no brainer. Yes, we loved them, but they are incapable of love, we were never loved by them, we were used.

Some men also commented on being the victim of a female narcissistic person, but it was the words from this woman she welcomed more than all the rest:

The 'no contact' rule can only work when a person is ready. If it is forced upon someone then it will probably fail because the prey has not yet become informed enough to see clearly all the nuances of the narcissist's behaviour for themselves. Only when they can stand back and predict the pattern of behaviour and remember the previous mental cruelties can they break the ties to this evil in their life.

Many posted about their *pathological* in a way Kirsty found strange. It was as if the real name of the person had been substituted with the word *pathological* as if it *was* their name. 'My pathological this' or 'my pathological that'. Nameless, faceless individuals who inflicted hideous cruelties.

Her head ached when she went outside to get some fresh air after midnight. She walked to the strand, and when the distance from the house was sufficient to ensure complete privacy, she phoned Mr Maloney.

'This was what Toby wanted, to have you in turmoil,' he said without hesitation and in a calm voice.

Kirsty became distressed, it was spooky how Toby seemed to know, texts beeping their arrival on her phone in quick succession. It was uncanny, his need to regain her attention. He even tried to call again.

'It's eerie, like he knows I'm talking to you,' she said.

'In his own perverse sort of way he probably does.' Coolly Mr Maloney challenged her to finally admit the time had come to get rid of her phone. He advocated she walk to the sea and be prepared to lob her phone into the water.

It was a beautiful balmy night, no anger in the soft creeping waves which greeted her. As she stood at the water's edge he said, 'Don't hang up. I want to hear the phone drop into water. You must cut this man out of your life once and for all. That's what you're paying a solicitor to handle, settle all negotiation required on your behalf.'

Several times in quick succession she repeated, 'It has to be now. Toby wants interaction, negative or positive. What Toby wants he won't get from me.'

Her heart thumped, her hand trembled and her mouth felt dry.

'I'm ready, let's do this. After three… one, two, three.'

She drew back her arm.

'I am doing this for me. This is my "now" and NOW feels right.'

Gathering as much strength as she could find in her arm she hurled any connection to her husband into the mouth of an incoming wave. The phone flew through the air landing with a satisfying plop, sinking into the ocean.

Immediately she spun round and ran beneath a moonlit sky across the sand back towards Mrs Devlin's cottage. She hurriedly shut the door and leant against it for a moment; sweat trickled from her brow into her eyes. On tiptoe she went to pick up the house phone, hoping no one would hear her speak to Mr Maloney.

'Well done. Congratulations. Come and see me tomorrow

afternoon as planned. I have an old mobile you're welcome to use until you get a new number sorted.'

*

'You look awful,' Mattie said the following morning.

'I think I am fighting a virus. Not feeling the best.'

'Right then, I say you need a day in bed. There is nothing I can't do around the house.'

Thanking him for his concern, she made no protest in acceptance of this suggestion. She devoted the morning to trying to rest in her room before the visit to Killarney in the afternoon. Having feigned a doctor's appointment to Mrs Devlin she made her way to see Mr Maloney. Kirsty hadn't planned to share her secret but this day was to become the one she told her story of having been adopted. He listened intently, unable to hide his concern. To finally talk about it with him stirred difficult emotions particularly when he cautioned that to find her biological mother would not necessarily provide a cure for anything that was wrong in her life. In his experience an approach of this nature should be made from a strong emotional platform.

Late evening, when all was quiet in the house, she revisited the computer to read more articles on the complexities of narcissistic personalities. It served well in the struggle to fortify her life without Toby. No more fretting or endeavours to fathom why he did this or that, such thoughts had power to derail her again. Moreover, the twisted, evil mind processes he employed were not something any sane person could identify with. Kirsty felt relief she never shared any of the information contained in Aunt Cressida's letter with him, he would only have converted it into another weapon to inflict angst.

The lady from her dream world who stood outside the church viewing the fairground visited again in the eventual fitful sleep she lapsed into. This time the menace in her dream was replaced by the lady appearing content, smiling. Her lips moved but did not translate to any sort of words Kirsty could understand. Then Toby stood by the woman's side, not at all handsome, his face twisted and contorted, spitting poison in globules of saliva sprayed from his mouth as he shouted abusive comments about his wife.

Chapter 20

Possibilities

'You look better today. See, Mattie boy is good for something after all, is he not? A day off was all you needed. I'm not a just a blip after all.' He laughed.

Kirsty wished it was that simple but smiled into his deep blue eyes, saying, 'Yes, thank you. It seems to have done the trick.'

'Well, I'm delighted because there is a favour I need to ask.'

She wondered what he was about to say.

'Sister Mary Cecelia wants to go back to the convent for a couple of days in a week or so. The Cardinal is visiting and she'd like to be there for the big occasion. I suggested perhaps you could sleep at the cottage and care for Callum, making sure he is fed and has his medication etc. I have spoken to Mammy about it and she insists she will easily cope in your absence.'

Kirsty observed Mattie as he spoke and decided she did like him, and his good qualities should be appreciated. Certainly he had strange foibles and his flirtatious manner could be irritating. But, at the same time, he provided a refreshing interval between all her heavy thoughts about Toby and Biddy. She did not feel in any way tempted to share these things with him but instead tried to annul their impact by entering into exchanges of light-hearted banter.

'Mammy says she's almost back to independence, but I was not to tell you because she enjoys your companionship. I won't argue with that.' He winked. 'I like having you around too.' This was the first time there had been any hint of flirting since the evening of the kiss and her dismissal.

Kirsty laughed. 'And I enjoy your mother's company too.'

'And also find her son endearing, I hope.'

'Yes alright, you too,' she conceded smiling.

'The plan is I drive Sister Mary Cecelia to Dublin, attend to some business matters and then bring her back to Balvohan.'

'When exactly does all this happen?'

'Not until a week on Friday. Sister Mary Cecelia suggested you come across one afternoon or evening to meet and get to know Callum beforehand.'

She agreed without mentioning having already chatted to Callum.

'Had a wobble, but back on track,' was all Kirsty divulged to Diane when they spoke again. Sam also called saying he definitely wanted to revisit Ireland and could he accept her invitation. She did not recollect having issued one but tried to sound enthusiastic. Although she enjoyed Sam's company the idea of him coming to Kerry seemed strange. Balvohan had become her sanctuary where no one really 'knew' her even if they thought they did; he belonged to another world. Their conversation closed with him saying he'd be in touch to firm up on dates available to take leave from work.

'Okay then I can book you into the Turrets,' she offered.

'Great. Talk soon.'

Upon waking each morning, the first thing Kirsty did was to reinforce the benefits of not having Toby cluttering her life. It had been almost six weeks since she'd arrived in Balvohan and the thought of having to leave with no further information about Biddy or her roots filled her with dismay. Tenacity took hold, to raise her domestic diligence even higher and become an indispensable employee. She made a conscious effort in her friendship with Mattie. It worked well, apart from his delight in making her laugh at his corny jokes, they also started to talk about all sorts of things. This relationship worked well and acted as a distraction.

Mattie visited Callum every day when he was a home. Then came the evening he invited her to accompany him and they arrived at the little white cottage on the hill together. Sister Mary Cecelia welcomed them effusively, being exceptionally hospitable. Kirsty felt perhaps she had unjustly bracketed her with some of the nuns remembered from schooldays.

Stepping inside the little cottage brought an unexpected wave of Biddy. Was it the old blackened grate, the scrubbed wooden table, or the smallness of it, every inch used wisely? A dresser with plates and trinkets stood slanted on an uneven stone floor, the halved door with its top part pinned back to let sea air mingle with onion stew. All of it brimming with the exclusivity of charm, held by a home serving generations and their stories.

Callum appeared frailer than when they'd chatted by the strand. Sister Mary Cecelia fussed around them taking care she stressed her gratitude several times to Kirsty adding how she looked forward enormously to the Cardinal's visit. With a mischievous twinkle in her eye she said her brother was 'not a lot of trouble and quite well behaved, considering he's a man'.

Mattie scoffed and pretended to sulk at any suggestion men ever conducted themselves badly. Soon they all laughed and conversation flowed until Mattie gave a conspicuous nod to Sister Mary Cecelia who readily picked up on his cue proposing it would be a good idea to let Kirsty and Callum talk while they went for an evening stroll.

Left alone together, initially the conversation was mundane until Callum, compassionate but direct, resurrected the topic of Biddy Duffy.

'When you asked me about Biddy was it because you're connected in some way?'

It felt natural to trust Callum, so she confided the contents of the letter from Aunt Cressida, aware he could be a source of help.

'I suspected something of the sort. You actually look similar, you know. She would have a job to deny you.'

Apparently he'd been giving thought to the situation since their earlier discussion. He had taken the liberty of mentioning Biddy, but not any connection to Kirsty, to a couple of the older characters who visited him who might remember. If they asked why, he told them it was the ramblings of a sick man who once had a crush on the girl. One of the people he asked remembered and apparently knew the whole story.

'Biddy was pregnant. A shame on her family, and her such a nice girl, they all thought.'

He told Kirsty that Biddy was taken by her mother, as requested by her father, to one of the Magdalene Laundries and abandoned 'to rot with the devil'. Callum stressed these were not his words. As far the village inhabitants were concerned, she had supposedly gone to Dublin to work. The pretence, which some recognised as such, was accepted for the sake of poor Mrs Duffy.

'Would that tie in with what you already know?'

All she could say was, 'Yes.'

'The next thing I want to discuss may not please you, but listen and don't just dismiss the suggestion out of hand. It could be an enormous step forward to finding out more.'

Kirsty became intrigued rather than worried.

'I have a friend who moved to London. He was adopted and searched for his roots. The recommendation made to him at the time was to use the adoption agency social worker as an intermediary to make an initial approach.'

Before she could chip in that her adoption had not been through an agency, Callum pre-empted her. 'My sister is a nun, you may or may not have noticed.' He smiled, encouraging her to relax. 'The fact that she is a nun means she is a good person, although when I think about it, why should that follow, who knows? Anyway, trust me, I know her better than anyone else and she's a good person. One of the best. But my belief is because she is a nun she may be able to access information more easily, things which might be unavailable to you. Are you with me so far?'

She nodded, but felt unsure where this was leading.

'Of course, I have not mentioned anything to her yet. Nor will I without your permission. Actually, it would be better if you could speak with her yourself.'

'I couldn't,' her response was definite. 'I don't really know your sister at all.'

'Okay. I understand. Well, how about if the three of us sat down together and you can explain any of your concerns and see what she says.'

Kirsty hesitated. Callum had such a supportive way of offering reassurance she intuitively felt safe in consenting to his judgement. She saw a good man, who was genuine and completely understood the necessity for discretion.

'Honestly, I promise anything you shared with my sister would be like the confessional,' he said, as if reading her thoughts.

'Oh, alright. Go on. Why not, I would dearly love to find out more.'

He looked pensive and after a long pause said, 'It's probably also worth telling you of the difficulties so many Irish adopted people face when searching for their heritage. You may be more fortunate in that your aunt has at least given you a name to go on. In this country secrecy and sealed records still prevail. It's to do with the privacy law and government ministers feel the need to honour this or some such thing.'

She already knew that but let him continue. 'Whatever, the reason, this deprivation of information means angst and

frustration for numerous hundreds of people who had severance of biological connection forced upon them by the church
and state.'

Kirsty was surprised by how much he knew on the subject.

'I know of one lady who had gone through the correct
channels but the agency took an eternity to process each stage
and very sadly her mother had died only three weeks before
finally tracing her.'

'Is it really so common in Ireland? You seem to have come
across a few people in similar situations.'

Callum sighed. 'Yes.' Then he sighed again. 'Sadly it's more
commonplace than most folks either know or want to believe.
The secrecy thing helps to ensure the illusion of adoption
being relatively infrequent.'

Now he appeared to be having difficulty saying more,
Kirsty remained quiet to enable him to formulate whatever it
was he wanted to add.

'For a substantial number,' he stopped. 'Yes, for too large a
number the information, should they manage to find it, can be
distressing.'

'Oh!'

'Yes, some horrible things went on. Need I say more?'

'Oh,' she said again as angst knotted in her stomach. She
had not given thought to the potential for ghastly scenarios.

Then they heard the others returning so he quickly suggested she think it through and if she still wanted to speak to
his sister before the Dublin visit, she was to return alone on
Thursday evening. The three of them could talk privately then.

Chapter 21

Secrets

Mattie did not ask any questions when Kirsty left the cottage on Thursday evening. She was aware of his figure by the window watching her as he decanted a whiskey and presumably imagined she was going for a walk.

'Oh dearie me,' responded Sister Mary Cecelia as she listened to the unfolding story. 'Let me see, what could we do? Oh dearie me.'

Kirsty found this irritating; she wanted to shake her to come up with something constructive, her variations of oh dearie me did not hit the spot.

'Now then, let me consider this carefully.'

'Come on, sis, you of all people can surely think of something. Who do you know that could be a source of more information? All these nuns you live with, do any of them have a connection to a Magdalene Laundry somewhere in their history? What about the elderly ones?'

The nun touched her face and tucked a stray wisp of hair to the left. 'Oh dearie me, I wonder, yes, Sister Consumpta might. Let me think. Yes, I believe she would know where the records, if they still exist, can be located.'

A brief silence followed. It was broken by Callum saying,

'Well then, why not talk with her? In confidence, of course.'

'Oh, dearie me, I do know that it's said some of the laundry nuns were very naughty. They claim thousands of records were burnt in accidental fires.' Her expression became pained as she shook her head. 'It makes me sad they brought shame on the Church we love.'

Kirsty didn't elucidate why she found it difficult to share the sentiment, of loving the institution of the Church. She had developed a genuine affection for Sister Mary Cecelia and had no wish to offend her sensitivity.

'Will you leave it with me please? I'll see what I can do.' She smiled reassuringly at Kirsty, adding, 'With the utmost discretion, of course.'

'Thank you. I'd welcome your help,' Kirsty looked at Callum, who smiled and nodded.

That night she imagined one bright star weave a path across the Milky Way, filling her with optimism as it came to rest on her pillow.

*

Two days later Mattie burst into the house having returned from Dublin a day ahead of schedule. 'Kirsty, Kirsty, come on. We've shopping to do,' he shouted.

Quickly peering in the mirror and pulling a brush through her hair, she replied, 'Be with you in a mo!' before searching the wardrobe to find a clean blouse.

'Is that alright with you, Mammy?' she heard him say. 'I can chat properly later and tell you all about Dublin. Promise.'

'Sure, you go on ahead,' said Mrs Devlin from her room. 'I'm grand here, enjoying a siesta!'

Kirsty arrived in the kitchen, noticing his portly figure darting about was deceptively slim from behind. 'Your backside is very neat,' she said impishly.

Turning and smiling broadly he said, 'Come here you.' He walked over and started unbuttoning her blouse.

'Excuse me!'

'You're odd,' he said looking at her.

'Odd?'

'Yes, the buttons, I'm only trying to be helpful.'

Giggling they left the house making their way to the car where Mattie held the passenger door open for her.

'But you're looking well today, my dear,' he said with a broad cheeky grin.

'Where are we going?' she asked before clicking the seat belt it into place.

'Cash and carry in Killarney. We lads are having a bit of a do for Callum.'

As they started on their journey he then informed her that Sister Mary Cecelia was staying an extra day in Dublin. 'Someone to see or something to do, so I left her to it. One of us has to meet her at Killarney station tomorrow afternoon at three.'

'I'll go,' she volunteered casually.

'Perfect,' he said turning the volume of music louder as the Jaguar sped along winding country roads. It would take a braver person to tell him to slow down as she gripped the seat with white knuckles. It was out of character for him, as previously whenever in his car she found him to be a good steady driver. Faster they went and the music seemed to grow louder until, spotting a Garda car at Killarney's town boundary, Mattie slammed his foot on the brake until they were hardly moving at all. Kirsty relaxed her grip and without asking turned the radio volume down. Able to converse again she said, 'I think it's a lovely idea to have a gathering for Callum. Can I be barmaid?'

'Of course, my dear, but please understand it has to be large measures all round.' He winked at her and she smiled.

Parking the car with carelessness in the cash and carry car park Mattie sped off to fetch a trolley. His stocky legs scuttled up and down the aisles of the superstore and in no time it was filled with bottles of beer, Irish whiskey, sherry, vodka and Guinness. Kirsty meanwhile went on a food foray with a second trolley. Items which could be stored for the meantime in the freezer were collected in quantity. The lad on the checkout joked, saying he wanted to come to the party, and his tipple would be a large rum and Coke. All of this was paid for with a flourish of euros peeled from a large wad pulled out from Mattie's trouser pocket. 'Take it for your trouble,' he said, handing his companion fifty euros. She hesitated. 'Call it a bonus or whatever you like, it's yours.'

'Thank you, much appreciated,' she said slipping it into her handbag.

With supplies loaded, Mattie drove at a leisurely pace on their return journey with no music blaring. Instead he chatted on about the special evening for Callum and how he wanted to make sure it was a great success, to prove in some way how much his friendship over the years was appreciated.

'Father Carlin is the brains behind it. Called me last night. Of course, I agreed straight away and secretly wish it had been the idea of yours truly and not a daft old priest.'

*

Promptly at three, the following afternoon, Kirsty stood checking the arrivals board at the station which confirmed Sister Mary Cecelia's train was on time. She suspected from the fact there had been no interim contact it probably meant attempts to locate someone named Brigit Duffy had proved futile.

It was not difficult to see the nun as she stepped from the train onto the platform pausing to exchange pleasantries with the ticket inspector, before Kirsty stepped forward. As they walked to the car they talked casually about the trip to Dublin and the Cardinal's visit. The nun enthused, how the celebratory Mass had been packed, with some people having to stand outside and hear it relayed through loud speakers. Their journey back to Balvohan became frustrating, peppered with dialogue covering everything but not the burning issue.

Sister Mary Cecelia insisted the car be halted at the foot of the hill and she would walk from there. Only then was Biddy mentioned.

'I know you're probably desperate to know if I had any luck finding information about your mother.'

Kirsty could not disguise the restless anticipation in her body language or the angst in her eyes, with an expectation her need for good news was about to be thwarted.

The nun reached out to touch Kirsty's hand. 'I have to tell you I do have a result but it may not be the one you were hoping for.'

'Continue, please.'

'Well, I was right. Sister Consumpta was able to help, and to cut a long story short Biddy has been located living in County Louth not far from Dublin.'

'Really!' Kirsty almost shouted. 'And…?'

'Well, she is quite frail apparently, both mentally and physically. She resides in a sheltered housing unit where a warden is on hand to keep an eye on the residents.'

There followed a long pause. The nun slipped her hand into the frayed tapestry shoulder bag which lay on her lap. 'I'll get straight to the point. It ended up that I took the liberty of going to see her yesterday and she, Biddy, gave me this.' The nun withdrew a large bulky brown envelope from the bag. 'She wants you to have it.' Holding the envelope outstretched, for Kirsty to accept.

'What was she like?'

'Very sweet. Just a nice little woman who appeared a bit lost, but content in her way. I was told by Sister Consumpta that the Good Shepherd nun mentioned Biddy has had mental health issues in the past. Depression and anxiety, I believe.

She's much better now and able to enjoy life with her friends. I also spoke with the rather nice warden, who clarified she still sees a psychologist regularly and takes medication, but mostly appears a happy soul.'

Sister Mary Cecelia appeared to become uneasy.

'Oh dearie me, this is difficult to tell you.'

'What is?' Kirsty's mind was spinning as she tried to compile the new information into a format that made sense. Her hand was placed protectively on the large brown envelope cushioned on her lap. 'Just tell me, please.'

'Oh dearie me, I'm so sorry but Brigit was a bit shocked, well more traumatized in fact, to hear you were looking for her.'

The nun paused and squeezed Kirsty's hand.

'I'm afraid she was adamant there could be no reunion. She begged me to persuade you to understand and has no desire to cause you pain, but feels unable to open "old wounds". She did ask for your contact details, to know where to find you should she ever change her mind. I could only give her my own but intend to make sure a correct address and phone number is forwarded, if you would like me to.'

It had become stiflingly hot in the car.

'The words Biddy used were "I'm not able for it. Please respect my wish".'

Kirsty looked down at the envelope. 'What's inside?'

'A diary or journal of some kind. She said you would find her reasons for refusing contact in it. I know nothing more of the content. My visit was not long, as it was obviously distressing for her.'

For a number of minutes the two ladies sat in silence. All perception of time became lost.

Poor Biddy, was all Kirsty could think, poor woman, yes it would be excruciatingly difficult for her. She gently stroked the envelope and wondered at the content and why her biological mother should choose to present it to her daughter.

'Are you alright, if I go now?' Sister Mary Cecelia asked.

Kirsty nodded.

This imperfect interaction combined sorrow with an optimism that when the preliminary shock wore off Biddy would want to meet her adult daughter. The primal bond they shared could never be erased.

'How much do you wish me to tell Callum? He's sure to ask.'

'All of it if you wish,' she responded without hesitation. 'He's a good man, I trust him implicitly,' then looking at Sister Mary Cecelia she added, 'and I trust you too.'

The nun smiled. 'I wish there was more I could do. Are you sure you're alright if I leave you now?'

'Absolutely. Thank you for this.' Kirsty patted the envelope.

'Has my dear brother behaved?' she spoke in a tone suggesting an effort to lighten the conversation.

'Yep, impeccably.'

Chapter 22

Journal

Later that night it took all her courage to break the seal of the envelope. It scared her to imagine what it could contain. Inside she found an A5 notebook with a frayed blue cover. First flicking through the pages without reading she found each filled with a steady and slightly old-fashioned script, disciplined in formation. 'Well, I certainly did not inherit the handwriting gene,' she muttered, aware her own could be a bit shambolic.

On the inside cover, written in bold lettering which had been gone over many times, making it heavily black, were the words Biddy's Book. Thereafter the entries were not dated, only showing a day of the week. There was no way of knowing the time scale from start to finish. Propping a comfortable pillow beneath her head Kirsty lay on the bed and started to read. It became compelling, only pausing when a handkerchief was required to dab away tears blurring her vision.

Biddy's Book

Monday

This is all to do with getting me settled to life outside the convent walls. That's what he said anyway. Apparently it will be good for me, to write my thoughts in a journal, things I remember.

When they gave me freedom from the laundry the real world felt like a stranger. I knew nothing else but sheets, steam and nuns for so long.

I says nothing to the therapist man. It's him who says to me it would be good to write things down and keep it for my eyes only or burn it. Never did say anything to anyone before because no one would have listened. There was there, and before there was before, my past, it's all supposed to be forgotten. Most times I don't want to think about my life in there any more. I am here now, and here is better, but I am not full of hope like before it all happened.

There, that horrible steaming sweat shop, a God-forsaken hole of a place where the nuns wanted us to believe everything we did was done in God's name. The nuns had us wash the sheets for God. Does God need clean sheets, or any for that matter? I think not.

In there you would be able to find the odd nun who was of a mind to be kind to me and the other girls. Not many, most just wanted to control us and see nothing or know nothing of the people we really were meant to be. God never intended for us to work in a sweaty, horrible laundry. A prod in our ribs with a wooden crucifix stuck on the end of their rosary beads was our reward for working too slow.

But one thing about there was that I always knew what to expect.

Tuesday

Before I went there I was normal.

Here the folks are kind. It is a good enough place to live and I get to the shops and out for tea, bingo or the cinema odd times. We went to see a film last night. We, that's Martha and me. She lives in the same sheltered housing block and is a good friend. She was never there but the poor lamb is a martyr to arthritis, so needs to live here with a warden on site for she fears having a fall. I have never mentioned there to her. I am not sure she'd believe me if I did, anyway it is easier not to.

We all have nice apartments here. Independent yet plenty of company and a warden to make sure we're not dead. We can buzz the buzzer we wear on a cord round our necks anytime and someone will come to help. They call the buzzers 'a spider' for some reason which escapes me.

When I was at school all those years ago my teacher said I was clever. She said I should go to Dublin and study at college or university. I longed to go, but I ended up leaving school without any of the qualifications needed. Everything in my life went wrong just after my sixteenth birthday.

Such memories.

There was a party to celebrate my sixteenth, a great party it was too. I can see it all as clear as yesterday.

Father McInally stood outside the church hall as a Kerry mist came rolling across the mountains. 'You would tink they were announcing the coming of Christ,' he says.

'You would, Father,' says I.

He was a kind man. 'Well Biddy, here you are now, take the key to the hall so you and your mammy can come and go as you please. I hope parish business spares me the time to join everyone to wish a beautiful young lady well on her sixteenth birthday.' He was a plump man with big rosy cheeks on him. I suppose he'll be gone to meet with his maker long since.

'Now Biddy,' he says, 'look at you, on the brink of adulthood *and a grand future ahead of you. Just don't forget your roots in this little Kerry village when you hit the big city lights. You go to university like your teachers tell you and study well, for knowledge is a God given and wonderful thing. The world will welcome you.'*

I walked the mile home and the mist made me shiver. Signs of spring were all about, crocus shoots, snowdrops and aconites. Mammy was busy in the kitchen and I rejoiced in the glow of a turf fire in the grate.

'Grand timing,' she said.

I took off my coat and hung it on the hook. 'The sea's calm today, Mammy,' says I to her. It was a favourite pastime of mine to watch waves come up the strand and fingers of foam nudge between the rocks.

'Shepherd's pie for my birthday girl, your favourite.' She smiled.

I can smell the meat, gravy, potatoes and carrot, right this moment. My mammy made the most delicious shepherd's pie I ever tasted.

Funny thing she said that day to me was 'a woman never forgets her labour and the moment of giving birth. And you, my sweet Biddy, were a beautiful baby, sure are you not still lovely.'

'Hardly a baby now, Ma,' I protested.

'Ye are to me. I'd be so proud, so proud if a daughter of mine went to study in Cork or Dublin. Yer Da would never be done telling them all down at the pub.'

Wednesday

Carla came to the house before my party. We spent an age getting ready with all our chattering and giggling. We washed our hair and even got to borrow a bit of Mammy's lipstick. My dress was new, bought for the occasion, and a lovely shade of pale green. Mammy said it suited my dark hair and turquoise eyes.

'You're not coming like that I hope?' I said to my daddy who

came in and sat at the table in his tatty working trousers, his shirt with a rip to the sleeve.

'Are you ashamed of your father?' he said with a glint in his eyes. 'Some of us had to fix the hencoop. Mrs Folen lost hers last week to a fox. I'll not be taking chances. Your mammy relies on the money she gets selling the eggs to buy the likes of you fancy dresses.'

'Now, now, children,' said Mammy, 'no squabbles.'

She looked so proud, when we were finally ready and came downstairs, seeing me in my new dress.

'Will you just look at my girl, beautiful.' Then she said a bit bitchy like to Carla, 'What a lovely shade of pink, did yer mammy make it for you?'

'She did, Mrs Duffy.'

"Well don't you have a clever mammy? Come on, Da, time you be ready.'

The church hall was decorated with streamers, balloons and pictures of the best bands in Ireland. The table was piled high with sandwiches and a great big chocolate cake with sixteen candles on top. The girls from school fussed and gave me presents. Simple things like a handmade tea cosy, a length of ribbon, a sewing wallet with needle and thread for emergency mending at university. That's what Carla said handing me a neat parcel with a blue ribbon wrapped round. I also got a manicure set, some nylon stockings. I loved them all.

The boys stood sort of embarrassed peering at us from the far end of the hall. The adults sat and watched and drank tea. Connor's band played then some of the boys got brave enough to dance and if a girl had no boy she just danced with another girl. It was great. When the band took a break, we ate. The boys piled sandwiches on their plates while we wanted to look dainty and be ladylike so only took two at a time.

Father McInally, as always, was true to his word and arrived in time to lead the toast.

'We are gathered here...' he says and we all hushed up. He

was a man who commanded respect. '...to celebrate the sixteenth birthday of a special young lady.' That was me, the special lady, he didn't use the word girl.

'Sixteen is a watershed on our journey through life. Some of you might find this hard to believe, I can remember being nine years old and not wanting to go into double figures. I can be guilty of not wanting birthdays even now. But, really what I want say to you all, the increasing wisdom each birthday brings to us should be welcomed.

'We celebrate Biddy at sixteen years old, the world is her oyster. Her experience of life so far is limited, but the same as for all of you gathered here today, it is based in a solid foundation knowing the love of God's family through your own families. 'Tis this foundation which will help you through life, so never undervalue it, treasure it and use it as your platform to explore the world.'

He spoke well and had me wanting to cry. I could see Mammy with a tear in her eye too. It was different from his usual sermons in church on a Sunday.

'In life, God will continually present you with choices; He has probably done so already. With these choices we have to use our God given free will to decide which path to take. There is something good for each one of you in the world. So consider well and make wise choices, do not lose sight of the solid foundations. Some like Biddy will go to university in a city. There the temptations may be greater but those of you who stay must also deliberate wisely.

'Now let us pray together for God's strength to help us on the next stage of our journey through life.'

All heads bowed.

'Heavenly Father, we ask you to bless Biddy on her birthday and all of us here, help us to make our choices in a manner fitting to being a member of your family. Amen.'

'Amen,' we all said.

Remembering these good things makes me feel so sad.

Thursday

All this has me in a spin. I tossed and turned last night plagued with images of me at a dance. I used to pray, before I was there in that horrible laundry where we were forced to give thanks for our lot. That would make you laugh if you didn't cry first, I don't bother with prayers any more.

It was the night of the dance with Joseph Meechan I pictured. There we are, finally the courage to write down that name which can't be spoken. I hate the way he creeps into my head and scares me till I can't even scream. The dankness of there, that place Mammy and Daddy sent me to with grey walls, grey floors, everything was grey. A roster was made for the whole week. You might have to wash floors, or the stairs, clean out bedrooms, hoover. This was apart from working in the laundry. All of us had our hair cut the same, shaped like a pudding bowl.

Sometimes one of the girls would have a visitor. It was always a prearranged appointment requested by letter and had to be between the hours of three and five on a Sunday afternoon. The nuns made other unmarried mothers, who still had their babies, stand out on the balcony and hold up the infant to show their shame and the physical evidence of their sin to those from the outside world.

When the nuns had the priest calling they looked on it as an honour, he was seen as some sort of superior being. They were in awe of him so if he did anything untoward, like touching up one of the girls no one noticed. We all had to curtsey to a nun or a priest. Some of those babies in that place were spawned from clerical loins. Were they the devil's spawn in the eyes of the church? I used to wonder about that, or were these babies considered different, better than the rest or was it the victim of these assaults was just called a liar?

The laundry was a sweat shop which laundered sheets and shirts for the local people. The washing had to be sorted through and some of it was not very clean. It could be horribly dirty and we were not allowed to wash our hands. The sheets were better; I didn't mind them so much. There was also a lace room, I used to go there odd times and have a peep at the sewing machines. Limerick lace would have been well enough known across the length and breadth of Ireland.

One poor soul who was profoundly deaf and dumb was dumped in there at sixteen years of age because her parents didn't know what else to do with her. And it was there she remained until the day she died at a young age a few years later.

There was another who'd had a son; when he grew old enough to wonder, he asked a lot of questions about his mother. Eventually he found out she was still in the Limerick laundry. From that day he worked all hours scrimping and saving till he had enough money to buy his mother's freedom. I used to see her sometimes after we were all away from there, she apparently told her son to take his children to see what the place was like because what we lived through should never be allowed to happen again.

A lot of the babies went to Americans who came with a ball of money able to offer handsome donations in exchange for a healthy child. What happened to them? Those babies, would they ever know the truth of where they started life and who gave them breath?

One angry nun used the strap a lot. Sister Martina, one of the kinder ones, would try and stop her hitting us girls. Then there were the hell holes as we called them. Cells to be locked in as a punishment. Tiny and square with a pull down bed chained to the wall. The toilet was a bucket in the corner and slopping out was horrible. Once a friend of mine was told off for being slow on the compressor and the nun brought it down on her hand.

Of course they deny such things happening. Believe me they did happen and girls died and babies too. No one seemed to care much what fate did to those of us who lived behind the high walls. The dregs of society.

Sister Martina's parting words to any girl lucky enough to leave were always the same, 'Don't let any man touch you.'

Saturday

Four nights in a row. Why I ask does he have to haunt me now?
He's not a welcome guest. I am awake but it is dark outside and if
my pen moves across the page turning thoughts to written words
it might get rid of him. An owl can be heard in the distance. I
can hear waves lapping but am not near the sea. The moon is
big, round and bright. But I cannot cry the tears I crave to bring
relief.

   I liked him once. Really, it's true, I liked Joseph Meechan.
All the girls thought he was good looking. All the girls wanted
to go out with him. He didn't appear brash and bold like some
of the other boys. His father had just started work as gillie at
Caragh. Sometimes I would see him walking home from school.
One Wednesday it occurred to me I'd never heard his voice. He
chatted alright with the other boys but never within my hearing.

   That's why on the Thursday, the very next day, when some-
one said 'hello' from behind me I didn't know who it was until
turning round to see it was HIM. My dark-haired blue-eyed boy.

   'Hello,' says I all coy.

   He smiled at me hesitantly and said, 'My name is Joseph.'

   'I know and I'm Biddy.'

   'I know,' he said.

   My joy was complete to think he'd been interested enough to
find out my name.

   Joseph fell into step beside me with a smile. But really he
looked as nervous as I felt.

   'We walk the same route home every day,' says he. 'I thought
we might talk together and you would let me protect you from
all things bad.'

   I giggled, then we both relaxed a bit.

   'Would you be thinking about going to the dance in the vil-
lage hall on Saturday night?' he asked.

   'No,' says I.

   'Well I was wondering if you might like to think of it? To go,
with me?'

The Good Lord knows how my cheeks burned hot and my chest felt tight. What would I say? Yes or no?

Then he said, 'Of course if you'd rather not, doesn't matter, doesn't matter at all, sure it doesn't.'

In that instant my mind was made up.

'Thank you, I'd like that, I'll go to the dance with you.'

Joseph smiled, such a beautiful smile.

Then he says, 'You know I've been wanting to speak to you for a while but wasn't sure if you'd be keen to speak to me. I'm shy really,' he pretended to look bashful. I couldn't help but giggle at his antics.

'Well will you look at these two lovebirds,' Angela Murphy's voice cut into our blossoming conversation. Angela accompanied by that horrible boy called Aiden, a rangy lad, the undertaker's apprentice.

'Well,' she said making the wellllllllllllll last forever and giving Aiden a look. 'Should I tell her what I know or leave them at it?'

'The way I see it, you just have to tell. You've got me curious now,' Aiden grinned showing horrible yellow teeth.

Joseph was staring at her with a black 'don't you dare' expression.

'Remember, Joseph, I know you well, how many times have I been in your house?' She was enjoying this teasing and taunting.

'It would be a few,' hissed Joseph.

'W-e-llll,' she dragged out the word again even slower, 'Biddy, let me tell you he keeps all manner of pictures under his bed, not cars or planes and certainly not of the Virgin Mary.'

Smiling broadly, she spat her poison.

'Ah shut up will you,' Joseph's blue eyes flashed with anger.

'Come on, Biddy, we don't need to listen to this.'

We walked on along the road leaving Angela and Aiden to laugh.

I remember feeling uncomfortable, I'd never liked that Angela Murphy. A troublemaker I used to believe, always bitching at or about someone or something.

'How is it she's been to your house?' I heard myself ask him. Like it should be my business at all. But he didn't get cross with me.

'She was pally with my sister Julie.'

'And not any more?'

'No; she's just an old tart, don't go listening to her.'

'Were you friendly with her too?'

'I wouldn't say friendly, but let's just say she has a way with her, but I soon learnt it's best to keep her at a distance.'

We walked on with me questioning how much I really did like him. Then we got chatting again, he made me laugh and he was so handsome so I forgot all about Angela Murphy with her goings on.

Monday

I like to read magazines and stories about how people live in Ireland these days. He, the counsellor, said to me it's alright not to pray, when I told him I don't want to and he doesn't mind. Isn't it great to find someone who doesn't worry if you don't have a notion to pray? You see when I did, and begged the Lord to help me, nothing happened. So my idea is that things happen or don't whether you pray or not.

Thursday

I remember the day I told Mammy. That moment changed my whole life.

Da took the belt from his trousers but Mammy screamed NO. They both decided the solution was to send me to the nuns until it was all over, that's what they told me. The folks in the village would be told I'd left school to take up the offer of wonderful lucrative employment with some cousin called Orla who was supposed to live in a grand house in Dublin. I never met any cousin called Orla.

Mammy said to me when we were on the train, 'Now you write to us at home telling all about Orla. She's a good woman in her fifties who lives in Ballsbridge, the best part of the city, in a grand sort of house. She has silver cutlery and silk dresses, do you hear?'

That had me feeling confused but I nodded anyway.

'It wouldn't do for anyone to know any different. I can show your letter to Mrs Morriarty and then the whole village will be told.'

My ears closed, I wanted to go home to watch the waves creep up the strand from my bedroom window.

'Are you listening? It's important you understand no one should know anything, for all our sakes. But most of all yours.'

Mammy sounded adamant and stern as the train made its way, passing green fields full of cows and sheep, then peat bogs where carts waited attached to dozing donkeys to be loaded by men working the land.

'I hear you, Mammy,' when what I wanted to know was what lay ahead for me. Of course I understood university would not be happening soon, but wanted to know if, when this was all over, would I still get a chance to study in Dublin or Cork?

The convent was a huge ugly building. Mammy had to stand on her toes and stretch up to ring the doorbell. It reminded me of a picture I saw once in a book of a hospital. An elderly nun opened the door and bid us to come inside and leave the sunshine behind. A damp, musty smell followed us through the cloisters, and then mixed with wax polish and soap as we entered the main hallway. I feel sick now remembering the smells. Sick to the pit of my stomach.

Mammy was giving her daughter to the nuns, but she never thought to tell me. It was worse than leaving an infant at the door. Time came for Mammy to leave and she hugged me so tight, I didn't want to let her go. I think she still loved me and blamed Da for making her take me to that place. He could not have loved me really, it's horrible to think someone you trusted with all your heart could betray you if it suited them. The real shame should have been the fact they could not listen to their daughter, I should have been able to tell them what happened and be heard instead of being turned into something I was never, and am still not. They should not have been ashamed of me, disowned me and inflicted a life sentence on me the way they did. All because society and most of all the church hissed and tutted because a baby was to be born. What a mess.

'Now Biddy, you be a good girl, and write to us about cousin Orla.' The last words I ever heard my mammy say to me.

I stood with tears choking me and waved until she was out of sight.

Sunday

Is Mrs Morriarty still in the village, I wonder? What did Mammy tell them and did they believe her? That wonderful clever daughter of hers never to be seen again. Did they think I had gone to Dublin and become too grand for the likes of them?

My daddy was the man I thought best in the whole world and my mammy was someone who loved her good girl but they threw away their bad girl.

I wasn't a bad girl, even if the nuns said 'bad and evil with the devil in her soul'. I was Satan's work and the child in my womb his spawn. The likes of me had to be hidden away because we were a temptation to men. Temptation, huh, men just help themselves then blame, shame and rename their acts on us girls. My name is Biddy Duffy. Not Carmel of Magdalene or number 56 or any of the other things the nuns thought suited us better. I think some poor girls nearly forgot who they really were and became a number. Not me, I was always Biddy inside.

Sunday night

'When are you due, then?' said a tall nun with large masculine hands.

'January I think.'

'You think?' she growled. 'Have you not seen a doctor?'

'I have and he told me the end of January.'

'That's good.' She looked me up and down. 'Yes, there's plenty of work in you yet. God's work, that's what we do here.'

I had to strip off my clothes, standing naked while scissors clicked round my ears and all my long hair fell to the ground in clumps.

My first long night there tears flowed alongside those shed by other girls in that hell hole. My life as I knew it was over.

Monday

My best friend at school was a girl called Carla, and her with a mop of red curls. When she was very young she wore glasses with a patch over one lens to mend a squint. She could always make me laugh being so full of mischief. One day I spotted her about to tie Patrick's shoe laces together. Patrick was a clever quiet boy and the envy of all because he could afford to have smart lace-up shoes and buy a comic each week. He lived in the biggest house in the village, the one with a great view out over the strand. He was absorbed in reading his comic and had no idea what Carla was thinking of doing. I liked him and at that moment hated her for wanting to humiliate him just to make everyone laugh.

'Carla, quick, over here,' I shouted.

She left him to his reading and ran across to where I stood staring at a bare piece of ground.

'Sorry, the frog has gone. You were too slow.' I couldn't look at her.

'Frog?' she shouted. 'I see no frog.'

'It was a speedy sort of frog,' says I.

'Biddy Duffy, you'll have to go to confession on Saturday now cos you got a big whopper of a sin to tell.'

We laughed, friends again as we skipped across the play-ground to join the other girls.

Carla never thought to come and find me. Probably she was one of those to believe I had grown too grand for her and home. And Patrick, where would he be now? I wonder who he ended up married to or maybe he became a priest. I hope he found some nice girl who would look after him well.

Tuesday

It was Tuesday today. All day. I hate Tuesdays. He came today and sat with me for a while. He visits once a week, reminds me of Father McInally. I don't like men as a rule but he's an elderly man, kind and gentle. He never gets cross or says horrible things.

Today he said nothing when I spilled out a sorry tale. Well nothing of any use to me. Write it down, he said again. Write it down, write, write, for what good it might do I have no idea.

Apparently I suffer from anxiety and am depressed. I do feel anxious and sometimes confused. Not totally round the bend as Mrs Morriarty would say, just on my way to who knows where.

A nice girl comes and teaches us how to make baskets, another has us knitting squares to make a big blanket for people who need a warm blanket or two. We drink lots of tea and always there's someone chattering on about something or other in the community centre. There's a priest comes on a Friday and tries too hard to be funny. Some of the others laugh. He doesn't seem to mind that I don't want to pray. No one seems bothered.

Wednesday

Yesterday I spoke about it out loud for the first time ever. The right words don't exist to tell of it, I struggled. No one is clever enough to invent vocabulary adequate to describe it. I certainly am not that clever even if I was supposed to go to university.

I feel better today for letting it out. It's been locked away for too long. Then at the end of it he says write it down. Maybe it was because while we talked we sat in the sunshine out on the balcony. The skyline reminded me of home and in the distance I could hear the distinctive cry of an oystercatcher. But when I talked I felt sick.

I remembered music on the night air from another time, holding a dark-haired boy as we danced. Watching him as he weaved his way through the crowd to get us lemonade, content with the knowledge that he would return to me. It made me happy seeing other girls look longingly in his direction. Before the dance I indulged a fantasy he might lean forward gently, brushing his lips on mine and tried to imagine what it might feel like. I felt pretty that night; alive, optimistic. I remembered a young girl walking hand in hand with her dark-haired, blue-eyed boy laughing. The girl at the dance with Joseph, who was the envy of all the other girls. It was so romantic feeling his fingertips holding mine. It felt safe and I wished he could hold my hand like that forever as he walked me home, leaving the dance, the noise, the giggles behind. The sweet air of a May night was on the breeze.

There was something of the same on the breeze yesterday.

'Come, Biddy, let me show you a secret of mine I keep in old Wattie's shed.'

In my naivety, curious, laughing and carefree I followed him. There was a musty smell mingled with the scent of pinewood. It was not a black night for the moon was high and bright in a clear sky.

Suddenly his mouth pressed on mine, not soft and romantic as imagined, but rough and hard. He pushed me away from the door kicking it closed with his foot. My body clattered against the wall.

'No. No, stop.'

He pinned me down. The length of his body lay on mine. My heart thumped and I tried to scream. His hand pressed over my mouth so hard it hurt.

'No one will hear you, Biddy. Come on, you know you want to, all you girls want to even when you say no.'

Babylorn

Afterwards, crumpled in a corner I became aware of Joseph holding out a handkerchief.

'Here, take this. Put it in your knickers. You're bleeding.'

I took the handkerchief in a trance.

'Come on; I'll take you home,' he said.

'I can get myself home,' I whimpered.

'No, I insist; no one is going to say Joseph wasn't a gentleman seeing his girl safe home.'

I walked by his side, unable to feel any more, just numb.

We got to the gate and all lights in our cottage were out. How could I face Mammy?

'Now, Biddy, good night to you.' Joseph leaned forward making me flinch. He didn't try to kiss just hissed in my ear, 'Don't worry, it gets better, your secret is safe with me, I never blab and neither will you.'

Without uttering a word I left him to enter our cottage and climbed the stairs, quietly lifting the latch of my bedroom door.

'Biddy, is that you?' Mammy said.

'Yes.'

'Did you have a good time? Will you come in here and tell me about it now?'

I found strength somehow and tried to sound as if all was well.

'Grand, Mammy, but I'm done in. Can we speak in the morning?'

'Alright so, night, night and sleep well, pet.'

That poor girl curled up on her bed and cried copious silent tears so her Mammy wouldn't hear. She could tell no one or else be branded a slut and a whore like the cheap girls she heard ridiculed. Joseph would say nothing; she was probably not the first girl to fall prey to his charms.

When the house was quiet, and making sure Mammy's bedroom light wasn't on, I crept downstairs to the kitchen, filling the kettle with water and putting it on the stove to boil. Gradually I filled the deep white kitchen sink with warm soapy water.

Undressing, with the moonlight silhouetting my slender body, I stood on a wooden kitchen chair and turned to sit in the water. I washed, again and again and again.

Standing up and stepping from the chair to the floor, I dried the moisture from my body with a towel. My clothes lay in a heap on the floor. I put them into the soapy water to be scrubbed and scrubbed.

Had I stopped bleeding? I wondered. I tore a rag from an old sheet which was kept for the purpose and lined my clean pants. Putting on my nightdress I reached for the salt cellar and a cup from the cupboard. Running the cold tap, I filled the cup and put a generous amount of salt in, stirring it with a spoon before lifting it to my lips. I filled my mouth, swirling the potion into every crevice then, spat into the sink. Time after time I did this until my mouth felt numb. I took the wet clothes to my room to dry, having climbed the stairs as silently as they were descended, then curled up on my bed.

There were no more tears, I could find no more.

'It's over, it's over.' I prayed God would give me strength to remain undetected, by those who knew me, in my state of sin. I resolved that not even the confessional box would hear of this. God would help me, for I wasn't a bad girl.

But, I was a bad girl, wasn't I? They all told me I was bad and God never listened to my pleading with Him to take me home again when I was there.

'How do you feel today?' he asked me. I have no idea but want to believe I feel better. He actually asked the question like it mattered. 'Perhaps a bit,' says I. 'Facing my demons' as he called it, should help me work through the things that have troubled me most over the years.

I asked him if he was telling me to forget. No, says he, you will never forget. But let's aim to get these demons in a place they don't hurt so much.

Then he says maybe a prayer would help.

This time I did scream. Honestly, I screamed. 'Why would I want to pray; no one has ever listened before.'

He says nothing, just nods knowingly. He does a lot of the nodding knowingly thing, not letting on what he's thinking. I don't really care what he thinks. It's of no consequence to me.

So how am I feeling today? Angry. Yes, that's it. Extremely angry.

Sunday

I've calmed down a bit now. Was not good for me, all the anger. It gave me palpitations. Martha knew something was up but I wasn't for telling her. She's a good friend all the same.

Maybe he was right when he said to face my demons would help. Anyway, I do feel calmer today. Last night I dreamt of my baby. There she was cooing and smiling up at me the way she used to. She won't be a baby now but a grown woman.

My baby Lorna a grown woman, imagine that. I called her Lorna because one of the other girls in the laundry was Lorna and it cheered her up no end, for a day or two at least, to know my baby had been called after her. Her baby died, broke her heart and then she was moved somewhere else. Someone mentioned Tipperary and another said Cork. The child, dead and buried in the convent grounds, and her not allowed to be near and it not given a decent headstone nor nothing but there was to be no getting away from the nuns for her all the same. She got shifted to another laundry. I asked about her but those nuns wouldn't tell me anything.

Thursday

It is some time since I've written in this book. He tells me it's alright and natural enough, my need for it is perhaps coming to an end.

We still meet from time to time but not every week and yes I do feel better. Time helps and life here is alright.

Today

Dear Lorna,

I have taken out this book again. Before giving it to the nun who is coming to visit me who says she knows you. I am glad to know you are well and have had a good life with good parents.

I cannot meet you, please forgive me. I am sorry for that. I beg you to respect my wishes. Read my book and try to understand.

Be sure I shall never forget my baby Lorna.

And most of all be happy.

From your Irish Mammy.

Kirsty became completely convinced it had been Biddy who visited her in a dream but couldn't be sure where the fairground fitted in to it all.

*

The following Monday she had an extra-long session with Mr Maloney. It was getting to a point where a substantial slice of her weekly wage was being handed over to gain the advantage of his listening ear and his wisdom. She took Biddy's book with her. He could not read it all but saw and heard enough to know his client was experiencing profound feelings of loss and rejection. He encouraged her to hold on to the hope that maybe one day Biddy would feel able to meet her daughter.

Chapter 23

Visit

Kirsty sang to herself as she worked, fitting the words to the tune of 'Frere Jacques'.

'Sam is coming,
Sam is coming,
Going to a concert,
Going to a concert.
A little walk along the strand
A little walk along the strand
Sam's here today.'

The skittish mood became heightened with music blaring from the car radio on her way to the station. By the time she stood waiting for his train to arrive a semblance of calm had returned. No nerves, no more over excitement, just a contented acceptance of spending time together.

That afternoon she showed him the strand and they enjoyed a long walk. 'Race you, ready, steady, go!' he shouted when they turned back having reached the ice cream van. They ran headlong into the wind until both became flushed and breathless, laughing together.

'Would you believe I have been in Eastbourne four times

since the funeral and taken Aunt Maud out for tea?' he said once they'd got their breath back.

'So you see, Mr Modesty, you are a hero after all,' Kirsty teased.

'I think I could get used to being promoted to the ranks of hero,' said Sam, playfully ruffling her hair.

A short time later they relaxed, sitting outside the hotel enjoying a coffee. Kirsty reached into her bag, lifting out an envelope. She placed it on the table in front of Sam.

'What's this?' he asked.

'Aunt Cressida's letter. I want you to read it.'

'Sure?' He looked serious.

'Yep, very sure.'

He read then sat back, saying nothing before lifting it again to read it a second time.

'I often wondered. Something my mother said years ago when I was only a smout.'

'Really? What did she say?'

'Not sure I can remember exactly.'

She didn't want to feel impatient with him. 'Try, please, I'd be interested to know.'

'Something about Marie, a baby and Philippa. I was young, didn't understand but what I remember is her sudden awareness I was in the room, like it was supposed to be a secret, so she quickly distracted my attention by giving me a biscuit from the tin.'

Kirsty wondered what sort of age he would have been then but didn't ask.

'Mmm, babes do have ears,' she said, remembering Aunt Maud saying this once to Philippa, wondering if it was a connection.

'How do you feel about it all now?' Sam asked but she didn't hear him, lost in thoughts of the adult world she had viewed through the eyes of a child. He repeated the question.

'Oh, sorry. It explains a lot,' she spoke slowly. 'Huge amounts, in fact.'

There was a short silence before she added, 'I have curiosity, of course, which I suppose is only natural. Roots, origins, biological connections and all that.'

'Absolutely. I find it hard to imagine what it must be like for you.'

'I've done a bit of searching, in among the myriad other things which have been going on.'

'Oh?' Sam sat up and looked extremely interested.

'Yes, there is something else I want to show you, but later.'

The hotel bar was completely different at night. The drab grey atmosphere steeped in the stench of stale beer apparent during daylight hours became redundant. A renewed vigour filtered through every crevice. Two musicians, a male and female, entertained with piano, guitar and songs. The queue for drinks never abated, with pints of Guinness constantly lined up along the bar to settle. Later in the evening, much later, nearing midnight, an open mic session found no shortage of volunteers. Kirsty shrunk back in horror at the thought of 'doing a turn', but they both enjoyed the talent on display, agreeing Brendan, a lecturer from Oxford University, was a star. His song of setting off the atom bomb with 'an accidental nudge from his arse as he walked past' made everyone laugh. Miles, a local fisherman, gave a heartfelt rendition of 'My Only Son Was Shot in Dublin', then got upset because three large ladies talked throughout his next contribution, 'Danny Boy'. But, for them both, the absolute highlight of the evening was a man who told the story of Peeping Slooty and the Pransome Hince, turning all the words inside out until the entire audience laughed so much their ribs ached.

Sam was Sam. That's what she always said in the past. Just Sam, with a charming smile. Kirsty found herself looking at him regularly throughout the evening. The boyish quality of his laugh, his tanned arms and deep blue eyes found her identify a feeling of being drawn to him in a way she was not altogether sure she should be.

When he went to queue at the bar she liked the way his blonde hair rested on his blue shirt collar, the flexing muscles in his arms, and good hands with long fingers, those of a piano player. She guessed he was just under six foot and had to admit he was rather a perfect specimen physically. The thing she liked most was what she'd become particularly aware of recently, and grown to appreciate, was his good heart.

The following afternoon they drove to find the cottage where Matthew and Marie used to live nestling high in the Kerry Mountains. The road climbed steadily, white sheep dotted the green hillsides as the car ascended higher and higher until it became no more than a grassy rutted track. Finally, they arrived at a broken wooden gate which needed to be lifted in its entirety, requiring one of them at each end, before they could enter the cottage's grounds. Lichen crept over stones and dense weeds eradicated the residue of a gravel driveway.

'September light.'

Sam nodded suggesting he knew exactly what she meant. A spectacular view over Kerry and down to the coast stretched out before them for miles. They stood side by side at the doorway of a decaying cottage agreeing it would be great to enjoy the stunning view daily through each season.

'Oh Lordy, I feel his pain,' said Sam quite unexpectedly.

She quelled the urge to reach out and touch his arm, unconfident he would welcome the gesture. She was no longer sure how to know what was true, the scars of a failed marriage remained. Our minds tell us what love should be like but our hearts lead us astray and con us into false places, she thought. They moved towards a broken wall, sitting side by side. Sam told her he'd at one time been engaged to an ambitious girl named Sarah.

'It would have been a disaster. I see that now, although my heart felt broken at the time.' Then he turned and looked at her. 'Do you feel a sense of liberation, without Toby?'

'Yes, oh yes, deffo,' she responded in a way intended to deter any further dialogue on this topic.

Sam raised his arm and flung the small stone he had been flicking back and forth from one hand to the other. It landed with a faint rustling sound in the long grass.

Kirsty tried to remember what her mother said, there was a vague recollection of someone 'ditching' him.

She regretted the lack of contact within their family over the years. Now it felt good to be able to provide space affording him the same compliment of listening and validating his experience as he'd readily extended to her.

Sam intimated he held no bitterness over the absence of a father during his teenage years.

'My dad and Marie got it about right. They cared not one bit what anyone thought or said about their relationship. Good on them. That's what I say.'

*

'I do like that young man,' Mrs Devlin said later, catching Kirsty alone before she and Sam went to a concert in Killarney. 'There's something captivating about him.'

Mrs Devlin kissed each of them on the cheek saying to Sam, 'Look after her and have a lovely evening.'

They found their seats amid the throng of people filling a large circus tent. Wisps of smoke puffed up to the roof, eventually forming a shroud beneath the greying canvas ceiling which separated them from the starlit sky. Three men and a woman became enveloped in the mist belching from beneath the perimeter of the ring. A spate of coughing among the audience harmonised with strumming guitars and Irish songs. When the music stopped a well-known author read a short story illustrating the passion and resilience of an Irish spirit.

A bud deeply rooted in the pit of Kirsty's stomach started to grow, the truth of her own Irishness. Such a strange sensation to acknowledge this as something which was never alien.

While she listened her eyes scanned along the rows of people and back again, repeated several times. Her people, but would they ever recognise her as one of their lost? That night she found the same purity held in single malt, the irrefutable legitimacy of her Irish identity predestined to be cupped, sipped and savoured.

She wanted to share, but was unsure how to. Sam's smile insinuated he understood.

It brought no joy to think of him departing again. The train was due to leave at two o'clock on the Sunday. Lunch first, Sam insisted, somewhere in Killarney would be best and he wanted it to be his treat as a thank you to the 'bestess hostess'. Having looked on the internet she suggested a venue not far from the station which would avoid any last minute pressure to be there in time for the train's departure. They sat together in the plush boutique surroundings of the Ross Hotel. Kirsty fidgeted and fussed with her napkin, her bag, the tablecloth until Sam asked, 'What's up?'

'Did you bring your sketch book or any poetry?'

'I did,' he replied. 'Would you want to see some?

Extracting a leather-bound book from the zipped pocket of his canvas bag, he slipped it modestly across the table and enquired, 'And what was the other thing you wanted to show me?'

She tried to smile. 'I hadn't forgotten. Just worried you might think differently of me after reading it.'

'Not at all.' She felt he dismissed her concerns rather too flippantly. Releasing the book his discerning fingers touched her hand gently.

'Nothing will change the way I think of you, you are Kirsty.'

Her trust restored she suggested, 'I'll leave you alone to read my book, the one I'll give you in a moment, and take yours through to the lounge.' Looking at her watch she suggested ten minutes, fifteen at the most. Biddy's book, contained in its original brown envelope, was then tentatively placed on the table. Leaving him alone she made her way to find a quiet corner.

The previous night as they walked from the concert to the car, she had shared, with difficulty, further details of her relationship with Toby. The only man with whom she'd shared physical intimacy, but made no mention of that to Sam. Lately she had begun to accept what her imagination suggested, that tenderness between a man and a woman should surely be better than her experiences.

Exactly fifteen minutes later she approached the table observing him with head bowed reading intently. The concentrated countenance remained and he was completely oblivious to her. Seeing him wipe a tear from his cheek brought her to a complete standstill. Inside she felt a tightening and sadness combined with excited anxiousness. It was nothing she could find a name for but a weird jumble of everything tussling inside her for supremacy. She remained absolutely still until the pressure of time forced her interruption.

'I took the liberty of copying out one of your poems,' she said and sat down opposite him at the table.

A crumpled handkerchief fished out of his pocket hid his face as he blew his nose.

'Is thatokay? You don't mind? Me copying a poem, I mean.'

'Of course not.' Sam closed Biddy's book slowly.

'Thank you, Kirsty. Thank you for sharing.'

The depth of his emotional response and the expression of compassion in his eyes, not pity, touched her profoundly.

'Be very sure it does not change even a tiny bit about the way I think of you.' Sam looked directly at her.

'Your poems are impressive. Love them. But, if you want my honest opinion I think your genius is in the art work. Some of these sketches are just wonderful. You deffo have a talent.'

Sam tried to laugh saying, 'Flattery will get you everywhere.'

'I like this one,' she said flicking the book open at a page.

'Oh that's one of the ancient oaks in the New forest,' he said.

'And I really like this one; in truth I think they are all good.' She turned the page to show a quaint cottage nestling among trees.

'That's my cottage, the one I rent. You must come and see it for real sometime.'

'I'd like that,' she said, smiling.

Then standing and pushing the chair to the table he said, 'Come on, or I'll miss my train, get me to the station.'

'Right, let's go. I've settled the bill - my treat.'

'It was supposed to be me who was treating you,' he protested.

'Next time,' she smiled, 'because I hope there will be another opportunity.'

During the short walk to the station Kirsty explained how she came to be in possession of Biddy's book. As they waited on the platform she managed to suppress an urge to kiss him. It was during these final minutes before his departure that Sam announced he had been shortlisted for a job interview that held the potential for a move to Canada. Dismay caught her from behind, delivering a body blow. She weakly responded, 'Great. I am pleased for you. They'd be mad to turn you down.'

Sam didn't appear to notice her distress as he said, 'Such a fantastic opportunity. Scared, I suppose, in case fate conspires to deprive me.'

The imminence of the train's departure forced them to exchange a friendly hug and promises of keeping in touch.

Watching the train disappear from view, Kirsty knew it had been a good weekend, the best for a long time.

Chapter 24

Party

Just over a week later the Flannigan cottage was pristine and the copious amounts of alcohol purchased in Killarney were set out in readiness with back-up supplies in the hall cupboard. Sister Mary Cecelia was anxious everything should be just right to guarantee Callum could relish every moment of his special evening. Kirsty was deployed to help during the preparations. The two women enjoyed the company, sharing a few giggles.

'Oh Lordy,' the nun exclaimed as a scorched cake emerged from the oven. 'I wonder, let me think. No, t'wouldn't work, not a hope of saving it. Oh dearie me, such a pity.' Her head tilted to one side examining Kirsty's baking effort.

'When they are drunk enough no one will ever notice,' protested its creator.

'Drunk! I do hope not.' Then giggled nervously at her own dismay. 'I really don't suppose we can hope the evening will be one of sobriety. Silly thought!'

Heaps of sandwiches, baked sponges and scones waited on plates. Kirsty then returned briefly to make sure all was well with Mrs Devlin who objected, saying she was no longer an invalid and quite able to make her own tea. 'I'm regaining my independence, let me enjoy it,' she protested. 'You should be where you are most needed and know where you are not needed,' her playful tone was at the same time discernibly serious.

Kirsty meandered back to the cottage on the hill to find Sister Mary Cecelia talking to herself. 'Dear God, what have I done with my glasses now? Praise be to the Lord, those sandwiches look delicious. Well done, girls, you triumphed.'

During the interim period, Kirsty noticed the hallway had been adorned with flowers from the garden forming a stunning arrangement of white and yellow lilies adding the final touch.

'What time are they due to arrive?'

'Arrive? Oh from seven thirty onwards. If I were a betting person, which I assure you I'm not, my money would be on the doctor being first.'

Kirsty found this continual borderline hysteria becoming irksome. 'Look, why don't you have a seat and relax? Surely we're all sorted now?'

The nun surrendered. 'Oh dearie me, you're right, of course. Be an angel and put the kettle on while I quickly check on Callum.' Sister Mary Cecelia disappeared for a very long 'quick check'.

On her eventual return, she grinned, saying, 'Isn't God great? My brother is so happy.'

'You look nice,' said Kirsty, noticing the nun now wore a neatly pressed brown habit which did not have the same dreary saggy look to it.

'Can't have me looking like a poor lost waif with guests arriving, can we?'

She then added a compliment on the flower arrangements, referring to them as the jewels in the crown for a perfect evening.

Doctor Hanlon, as predicted, arrived first, soon followed by Father Carlin. All effort and attention to detail were not wasted on the good doctor.

'Well now, Sister, who's been a busy little bee?' he said, peeping round the kitchen door.

'Not only me. I have a marvellous assistant and, God willing, everything will taste as good as it looks.'

He laughed. 'I'm glad to hear my stubborn friend is finally prepared to accept support when it's offered.'

Kirsty liked the doctor, who bore his sixty years with distinction. Painstakingly smart at all times, on this occasion he wore a well-cut jacket, neatly pressed shirt, red tie and grey flannel trousers all of which complemented his fine military figure, crowned with groomed white hair. He exuded genuine care within his unfailing affable manner.

When Father Carlin arrived he shook Kirsty by the hand. 'How are you?'

'Good, thank you. And you?' she responded affectionately.

'Grand indeed, thanks be to God.' He patted her hand twice.

'And Mrs Connor?' she smiled.

'As always, God love her.'

Mrs Connor, the priest's housekeeper, was a slightly tragic person who retained her job more out of pity from the cleric than any aptitude for the task. She lurched continually from one crisis to another. A burst pipe, the fridge not working, her car rattling or giving off fumes. She certainly kept the local tradesmen employed and often baffled.

Derek, who owned the local butcher's shop, and Mattie arrived together. The noise of male chatter and laughter grew louder, echoing throughout the little white cottage on the hill. Derek was a jolly, round man with a liking for rich cuisine who reminded Kirsty of a Toby jug. When greeting these two she consciously set her focus on him rather than Mattie. The butcher bordered on flamboyant, sporting a yellow silk bow tie speckled with blue spots. At one time a rumour circulated in the village that he frequented a drag club in Killarney, but only on a Monday night! Some wag got hold of the theory and let it flow for a while.

All the men arrived on foot, ready to indulge the supplies of Irish whiskey and selection of beers they'd anticipated would be on offer. No one would be disappointed, as a variety of glasses waited in serried ranks ready to take their fill. Callum emerged appearing relaxed and refreshed after a long afternoon sleep, which did not belie his gaunt features and sunken eyes. A baggy blue shirt denied defiance of the skeletal frame resulting from the ravages of his illness.

The two ladies opted to wait in the kitchen for nine o'clock, the time designated by the nun, to fulfil their hostess catering duties. They both laughed hearing Derek being shouted down by the others for daring to talk about the weather.

Sister Mary Cecelia shook her head and smiled. 'Dearie me, poor man, he's always fancied himself as our local weather expert, habitually reporting on conditions throughout Kerry. He told me that when he feels full of devilment he suggests diverse elements to each person he meets just to see what response he gets. To Jack or Fred: Cold today, isn't it? Then to Joseph or Declan or whoever: Warm today, isn't it? Apparently they most often agree. But, I do swear he could name every weather presenter that's ever been on television, or radio for that matter.'

Kirsty removed a bottle of Chardonnay from the fridge, decanting some of the contents between two glasses. The faint protest from the nun that she ought to go and say some evening prayers was ignored.

'Dear God,' she exclaimed in acknowledgement of the full glass handed to her. 'I only need to smell alcohol and my cheeks flush. If I drink that lot I'll end up under the table!'

Kirsty laughed. 'Only drink as much as you want. I'll not take any offence, promise.'

'Oh, I know you're too nice to be offended by a silly nun who can't take a drink.'

'What about the altar wine? What table does that have you under?'

'One little sip is alright. Besides, I never think of that as alcohol. It's the blood of Christ.'

'I see,' Kirsty raised her glass. 'Cheers. Here's to Callum having a great night with the boys.'

'Cheers. I have to drink to that now, don't I?'

Male voices were beginning to loosen with the consumption of alcohol, steadily becoming louder and interspersed with hearty laughter. Sister Mary Cecelia took several sips from her glass saying, 'I'm off the notion altogether of climbing stairs to pray. God will forgive me tonight.' She was clearly starting to enjoy the taste of wine.

'Gracious, will you just listen to them laugh. You know, I think we could be missing out so. The *craic* is ninety, what do you say we tune in a while?'

Kirsty raised her glass and nodded.

'Do you remember Sean Fallon?' said Father Carlin.

'I do, vaguely. Is he dead now?' asked Callum.

'No, no, not dead, just not as obvious these days. Has a bad leg or some such thing and can't get about the same. It's curbed his volunteering spirit.'

Callum laughed. 'Yes, he would be one of those "I'll do it" types. Someone needs a job done, he was there in a blink saying, "I'll do it, I'll do it".'

'How right you are. Well, it would be about eight years ago now when Willie Connor died,' Father Carlin continued. 'Big long, tall man. Died in his bed and the widow and his two sisters were looking for someone to move the body in order to have the wake in their sitting room.'

'Aye, he was too,' said Derek. 'Very long and very, very tall.'

'Paddy the undertaker was supposed to call that same afternoon with someone to help. He had already popped by in the morning and left the coffin downstairs ready but couldn't stay to finish the job, Matt Docherty had also died.'

Derek interrupted again. 'Yes, I do recall. 'Twas a terrible week for deaths and no mistake.'

Father Carlin continued, 'Yer quite right. Paddy and his man had been detained at Martha Doherty's house with all the funeral arrangements to go on there. One of the Doherty daughters who live in England these many years was late arriving and held up everyone's day. This meant the undertaker was not able to be at the Connors until the daughter arrived at the Doherty's. Of course, the Connors could only hope it would be before the guests might start arriving at their house for the wake.'

Callum guessed the next bit of the story, saying, 'Of course, James gets wind of it, so takes himself off to see the widow and the sister full of his "I'll do it".'

'Got it in one,' said the priest. 'With no sign of the daughter and a wake due to be starting at the Connor's house; the widow agreed that James would bring the body down to the waiting coffin. There they were, the widow and the sisters, all dressed for the occasion. Yer man, I heard it said had rigor mortis, so was difficult to move. Anyway, James with his "I'll do it, I'll do it" gives no thought to such matters. Off he goes upstairs and somehow he gets to carry the corpse on his shoulder with a few fecks thrown about. There he is all of a teeter under the strain, swaying this way on the stairs, him struggling all the while and the sisters looking on. Then all of a sudden, does the corpse not break wind, two of the biggest farts the ladies ever heard.' The priest was on a roll now, pleased with the hearty laughter from his companions, so gave the punch line. '"Jeez" says James, flushed and sweating, "if ye can fecking fart ye can fecking walk".'

'Well Father, you can still tell a story,' said Callum. 'Where's my handkerchief? I have tears with all this laughing.'

'The widow, bless her, said she had not had a laugh like it for many a year.'

What followed was starting to resemble a storytelling competition to see who might be awarded the loudest laugh.

'Now my turn,' said Doctor Hanlon. 'Mrs Dempsey, you all

know her I'm sure, stays in the cottage beside the post office, a fine woman.'

Clearing his throat he continued, 'One day I had reason to go to the house, not to see her and no one was ill, it was on another matter I needed to speak to her man. A knock on the door brings no answer, so I opens it, sticks me head round to give a bit of a shout, hoping to find someone at home. What do I see? Mrs Dempsey, and you have to agree she is large, a rotund woman altogether, running at great speed down the hall with an aerosol can in her hand spewing out its contents with a great deal of force the length of their newly decorated hall. Cursing she was, under her breath, "Myra and her fecking bargains. I'll be after fecking killing her. Oh, hello Doc, open the fecking door, quick open wide," she shouts. I had to move fast and was just about bowled over in the rush to get the spewing article out of her neat little house. She told me, Myra picked up six cans of furniture spray at a bargain price followed, with "I'll fecking bargain her".'

'Indeed a grand old bargain that was,' said Father Carlin. 'Imagine the clean-up.'

'My own dear wife was less than impressed by my messy suit, but it was worth it for the laugh. Molly Dempsey was some sight to behold in full flight.'

The women giggled along with the men as their stories became increasingly ridiculous, until Sister Mary Cecelia decided it was near enough nine and time to deliver refreshments. She led the way and entered the sitting room first, saying, 'It's great to hear you enjoying yourselves. I thought it would be good to have a sandwich or two to soak up the alcohol, followed by a nice cuppa and cake before you head home.'

Mattie stood up taking the tray and acknowledging her efforts with a wink.

Kirsty noticed but was more concerned seeing Callum smiling and flushed with a watery glaze in his eyes. She found it moving to see him so happy and relaxed.

'Mattie, perhaps you would be good enough to hand out the plates and napkins?' said Sister Mary Cecelia rather formally.

'Thank you, I shall be delighted to, my dear, and will give you a nod when we're done. You're a good woman, the best.'

'She is that,' agreed Callum.

'Yes, thank you, ladies,' the other men chorused.

Leaving them to it, they could hear their animated chatting resume. After nearly an hour had passed Sister Mary Cecelia became irritated, hissing through clenched teeth, 'Why don't they leave now? Excuse me, Kirsty, but I need to go outside for a breath of air. Let me know if you hear them starting to move.'

It was Callum's turn to clear his throat in readiness to speak. 'Now, gentlemen,' he started, with a distinct slur and mispronunciation to his words. 'We are all gathered together in an attempt to cheer me up. That is my understanding of the general plan for this evening. Am I right, Father, you get the credit for being the brains behind it and Mattie, my dear friend, the brawn and generous provider? Well now it is time to declare that I am happy and pronounce I be duly and ab-sooolutely cheered. Suitably entrancimicated even.'

'He's drunk too much,' said his sister, standing silhouetted in the back doorway.

He continued, 'Consider your goal achieved, 'tis done, and a fine job. But, I must say to each and all that my wake, yes my wake, has to be accelerabration, in the same way, for I'll be there too. No weeping, wailing or gnoshering of teeth permitted under any circumstoneris. In fact, if anyone wants to sing 'Mellow Yellow' I'd appreciate it. 'Tis my theme tune cos I be turning yellow. So let's raise a glass… to a merry wake.'

'To a merry wake,' the gathering chorused.

'For he's a jolly good fellow,' said Mattie and led the others as they sang to their friend, followed by three raucous cheers.

'Bags I tie the thread to the fingers and have first twitch,' shouted Derek.

Kirsty smiled, as she recalled being told by a work colleague the mischief children would be up to at an Irish wake, tying thread to the fingers of a corpse. Then crouching quietly until an unsuspecting mourner approached to pay their last respects then tweaking the thread from their hiding place under the table causing minor, or sometimes major, distress to the innocent victim.

'Me for second twitch,' said Doctor Hanlon.

'I shall refrain from twitching, as I am at all times completely celibate,' said Father Carlin.

'Ah go on, Father. One little twitch never hurt anyone,' laughed Callum.

It was a good hour or more after Callum's speech before a lot of bumps and bangs could be heard and the whiskey drinkers started to move. Kirsty nipped to the back door and, looking out, could see Sister Mary Cecelia sitting upright on the wooden bench beside the cottage wall radiating an air of irritated tension.

'They're going.'

'At long last, thank God.'

The two women moved and observed a clutter of men at the front door. 'Feck, what the… aw jeez, I just stood on a frog,' Derek the butcher sounded distraught.

'A frog?' said Mattie. 'Aw poor thing, now it's got a headache, I'd say.' He bent down peering at the ground. 'It's alright. You haven't squashed it.'

'Doc, quick, get yer medic bag. There's a frog here in need of emergency treatment on the front step,' said Callum.

'Nee naw nee naw, make way, make way,' said Doctor Hanlon.

'Would you know? I'll go now and get me sister to kiss the fecking thing and transform it turn into a prince to whisk her away,' giggled Callum.

'Sister Mary Cecelia's prince is the Lord. She has no need for another,' said Father Carlin, sounding as serious as he was able under the circumstances.

'Aw dry up, Father, will ye. Callum, your sister is a woman and a beautiful one. Who knows, a prince might be the making of her, nun or no nun.'

'I think, Mattie Devlin, you may have had a little too much to drink to say such a thing. So I shall choose to ignore that statement,' reprimanded the nun approaching the congregation gathered at the door. However, the sudden flush of colour to her cheeks was not wasted on Kirsty.

'I will maintain a dignified silence on that one, Mattie Devlin,' responded Father Carlin, stumbling over his words and nodding at Sister Mary Cecelia. 'I think it best if I too be pretending I heard nothing, maybe you should do the same.'

'Hear not, see not or something like that,' slurred Callum.

'That's the one,' said the priest.

'I have me diagnosis,' said the doctor. 'We have a frog suffering from a severe headache. So I'd say any hopeful princess may get no response from this poor prince. Good night to you all. I have no doubt we'll sleep soundly.'

'But Doc, wait, see you are wrong. The frog is gone, it has vanished,' shouted Derek delightedly.

'You are a tonic and no mistake, each and every one of you,' declared Callum.

'Good night and thanks, ladies; you did us proud,' Mattie slurred.

Each gentleman in turn bid their thanks and good night.

'You are a tonic and no mistake,' Callum kept repeating shaking them by the hand one by one.

When they were all gone he closed the door with a loud bang which shook the fabric of the cottage. He requested he be left to sit alone for five minutes, insisting the ladies retire to bed.

Kirsty squeezed into her makeshift sleeping accommodation which was really no more than a large cupboard, but did have a small window. A short time later she heard Callum hum 'The Mountains of Mourne' followed by 'Danny Boy', his feet thumping on the stairs. After a short time lapse Sister Mary Cecelia tapped on his door.

'You alright, Callum?'

'Yes indeedy.'

'Night, night, sleep well. See you in the morning.'

'Indeedy, night, night.'

Chapter 25

Sickroom

Early the next morning, Kirsty went to Callum's room to find him lying on the bed fully clothed, snoring loudly. It had been agreed she would stay overnight at the Flannigan cottage, as increasingly her time could become shared between the two houses. Mrs Devlin insisted she 'would have it no other way'. Today the plan was to provide opportunity for Sister Mary Cecelia to rest longer in bed.

Immediately evident was the smell of vomit, she hurried to the bed where it was visible on the bedding, blankets and floor. Callum breathed heavily, totally unaware of her presence. She nudged him gently, whereupon he groaned loudly, opening his eyes.

'God, Mary, I feel rough.'

'You've been sick,' she said, softly resting her hand on his shoulder. 'It's not Sister Mary Cecelia, it's me, Kirsty.'

'Sick, yes I feel sick,' moaned Callum.

'Just relax. I'll be back in a moment,' she left the room briefly, returning with a basin of warm soapy water and a bucket. Walking past Sister Mary Cecelia's room she wondered if she should knock, but decided not to disturb her for the time being at least.

'Here, I've brought this just in case. I'll put it by the side of the bed,' she said. Callum groaned and rolled over to the edge of the bed, vomiting again.

Gently she rubbed his back as he retched. 'Poor Callum,' she murmured, 'all you wanted was a good night's *craic* with your friends.'

He collapsed back in the bed, his face ashen. Handing him a tissue to wipe his mouth she squeezed a sponge in the basin and wiped his face, dabbing it dry with a towel. Then she sat on a chair beside the bed, allowing him time to recover.

'When you feel up to it, you can sit in the chair and let me sort the bed.'

Eventually he was ready. 'Okay, go for it.'

It took a huge effort, but Callum managed to sit in the armchair and Kirsty started the clean-up operation, stripping the bed, replacing with fresh sheets. She washed and changed him then ensured he was settled comfortably in bed with the bucket emptied and cleaned, before going downstairs to soak the sheets.

Now she felt it was time to knock on Sister Mary Cecelia's door. The nun was clearly already awake, judging by her quick response.

'Oh dearie me, not good?' she said when Kirsty explained, and went immediately to her brother and became distressed finding him so poorly. 'I'm going to call Doctor Hanlon.'

'It's too early,' groaned Callum.

'I don't agree. Besides, how often has he said to him to call him any time?'

Having left a message with Mrs Hanlon, Sister Mary Cecelia returned to sit with her brother. Tilting her head, in her own peculiar way, to the right she dismissed Kirsty to attend to some domestic chores.

There were several more episodes of vomiting before the doctor arrived mid-morning.

'Poor Callum is not a well man at all today,' she said opening the door to the doctor who made his way upstairs to see the patient.

A short time later she overheard the doctor chastise himself for not closely monitoring his friend's alcohol consumption. His belief was that the effect was enhanced because Callum's metabolism inevitably had become dysfunctional. He suggested trying to persuade him to take sips of water, little and often. If this induced vomiting, he was to try an ice cube wrapped in a little gauze to moisten his mouth every fifteen minutes. 'Sister Mary Cecelia, if there is no improvement or you feel concerned about anything I want you to contact me any time, day or night, do you hear?'

'I hear. Thank you, Doctor, and praise God we have you to help.'

Before leaving the doctor said, 'If the alcohol has made him toxic let's take the view it is better out than in. Remember to call me at seven tonight, or before if you feel the need. I fear the possibility of a couple of days in hospital cannot be ruled out.'

Sister Mary Cecelia spent most of the day next to her brother, snuggled on a chair with a blanket over her. Only once did she request her companion take over for twenty minutes.

Kirsty, meanwhile, busied herself with household chores. Then at noon she walked the mile to Mrs Devlin's to give her lunch and update her on the situation. The elderly lady was rarely alone for long, with a continual stream of friends from the village dropping by to chat. All that was needed was to ensure a plentiful supply of tea, coffee, milk and cake.

Mrs Devlin surprised Kirsty with news about Mattie. He had set off for Dublin soon after breakfast. 'He's promised he'll be back before we have time to notice he is away.' As if her words carried a conviction to ensure his swift return having become informed how poorly Callum had become.

Doctor Hanlon was phoned at seven that evening and was pleased to hear the sickness had subsided and fluid intake was progressing. He visited again the following morning but emerged from the room even more serious. The night had not been a good one for the patient. In spite of Sister Mary Cecelia's determination that he was improved, everyone was aware the patient's rapid decline was not purely alcohol related. The doctor announced he could feel Callum's liver was enlarged and the patient complained of a new pain in his right shoulder saying this could be suggestive of the cancer having spread. He shook his head, determining the celebratory evening symptomatically accelerated what would have happened in the near future. No sign of comfort could be found in the doctor's grave expression.

'You should seriously think about using additional help over the coming days. I know you have Kirsty but I could also arrange for a nurse to visit and allow you both to have some time to rest.'

'I see. I see. Yes, I do see. Oh dearie me.' The nun pretended to be strong, with only a small slither of steel apparent in her voice, which she obviously dug deep to find. 'What's your prognosis, Doctor? Days, hours, weeks?'

'Difficult to say precisely at the moment. He could rally from this episode and have ten days or even a fortnight, alternatively all this upset could have weakened his resources and we'll witness a rapid decline. The next twenty-four hours will tell.' The doctor sighed deeply. 'Where's Mattie? Why not get him to come and sit with you a while?'

Kirsty found herself answering the question. 'Mattie will be back on Friday. He had to return to Dublin.' She turned to Sister Mary Cecelia. 'I'm sorry, meant to say, Mrs Devlin told me. It was urgent, apparently.' She felt desperately sorry for the nun, who sat with head bowed, tugging at the dowdy brown sleeve of her habit.

Doctor Hanlon looked at his watch. 'Remember, you must not neglect yourselves in all this. I have to say, Sister, you look pretty awful today. Please consider another nurse? I must go now, there is another call waiting for me.'

Sister Mary Cecelia managed the glimmer of a smile. 'Thank you.' Her head tilted to the right so she avoided direct eye contact. 'I'll think, I promise, about your suggestion.'

*

Visiting Mrs Devlin to make sure she was settled for the night provided Kirsty with a brief escape from the intensity of the Flannigan cottage. Time there became a blur, with alarm clocks set irregularly to facilitate sleep between shared nursing care. On the Friday, forty-eight hours after the initial finding, Kirsty entered Callum's bedroom early in the morning, he was asleep and snoring gently.

The smell of approaching death clawed into her nostrils. It was a new experience for her and seemed to leave a taste in her mouth even when she was absent from the cottage.

'He need not be disturbed yet, his medication is due at seven, I'll be in my room if you need me,' said Sister Mary Cecelia who'd been sitting with him all night.

'Go and get some rest,' said Kirsty. 'I'll call you if there's the slightest need.'

As the sun rose it indicated another warm day and the bedroom already felt stuffy. Drawing back the curtains, she opened the window as wide as possible so air might circulate. Her movements disturbed Callum who became restless. He woke, saying he felt nauseous. His face contorted, shunning efforts to get him to sip water from a spoon, before he lapsed back into slumber.

Sometimes his sonorous breathing became interrupted with groans as he clutched his stomach with pain. On one occasion he said, 'If only I could have a good long fart like that old corpse.'

Unexpectedly a swallow suddenly flew through the open

window into the room. It was closely followed by a second of its kind. Kirsty watched the birds circling and diving, and dared not move fearing it would cause them to panic. As suddenly as they'd entered, they exited and were gone. She was left bemused, wondering if it had actually happened.

'Swallows,' said Callum quietly.

'How strange,' she said.

'No,' he croaked. 'Not strange at all.'

She took hold of his hand. 'You are a good man, Callum Flannigan. Truly a good man.'

A faint smile traced his lips and he nodded, answering in a hoarse whisper, 'Absolutely.'

Doctor Hanlon arrived at ten o'clock. He looked sad hearing of the increasing severity of his patient's colicky pains, saying he would increase the dosage of morphine to ease his discomfort. 'His liver is failing to cope at all. Fluid intake is crucial so I will insert a drip to flush out some of the toxins which will, I hope, help him feel less nauseous.'

'Oh, dearie, dearie me,' said Sister Mary Cecelia when both the ladies went downstairs leaving the doctor with Callum.

'Three days ago I felt there was time for us to talk, and now there's only a vague promise of snatched moments with my dear brother.' The nun's eyes filled with tears as she desperately searched for a handkerchief in the sleeve of her brown habit.

Kirsty wanted to reach out and give her a hug, and found herself saying, 'Mattie will be here soon. That'll help. You know how both of you enjoy him and his silly chat.'

Sister Mary Cecelia's head tilted acutely to the right. 'Yes, and we could give you a night off to stay with Mrs Devlin. An opportunity to have an uninterrupted sleep.'

'As you wish,' responded Kirsty, unable to disguise the unexpected irritation rising in her.

As a result of increased doses of morphine, Callum slept much of the time. When he woke later it was Kirsty who sat with him. Instantly he appeared much improved although his voice was still weak and she had to bend close to hear his words. 'How about a shave? I must look like the old man of Borneo.'

She gladly propped him up with pillows and ran to fetch the necessaries. His bony hand reached out and picked up the mirror. 'Bloody hell,' he croaked at the reflection which greeted him. 'Well, I'd have to say this handsome prince can search no more for any beautiful princess.' Straining to smile he added, 'You know, when we were all young bucks we used to say a shit, a shower and a shave was all that was needed to be ready for the most beautiful girl in the world.'

A frantic charade ensued, of plumping up his pillow, afraid he would notice the tears in her eyes.

'But,' he continued, weakly nodding, 'perhaps the princess can still have her prince.' She felt colour rise in her cheeks. 'Where is my friend Mattie these days? Your friend too, I think.'

'He'll be here this afternoon, or before if he can manage.'

Callum endeavoured to sound as upbeat as possible. 'Good, look forward to seeing him. Can I tell you something?'

She nodded.

'That injection the old doc gave me was pure magic, I declare myself a pain-free zone.'

Lifting the mirror again, he added, 'I do think you should all start calling me mellow yellow.'

She stroked his arm, promising to find Donovan's version of the song for him on YouTube so he could sing along.

'Yes, you look him up. I'd like that.'

At this point Kirsty felt she had to pretend it would be best to have two towels as an excuse to leave the room and regain her composure. When she returned she shaved Callum gently, changed his pyjamas and rearranged his pillows, striving to make him as comfortable as possible. By the time she had finished he looked tired.

'Excuse me,' he said, having broken wind.

'Shhh. No worries, not a problem. Hope it helps.'

'Would you say yes to a night at the flicks with this poor critter?' he yawned.

'Of course, and I bet many a girl was charmed by you. Now rest. I'll sit with you a while.'

He slept almost immediately. She quietly watched his laboured breathing and could not help thinking it would be kinder if one of these breaths was his last. Switching her phone onto silent mode she sent a text to Sam.

Kirsty - HELLO SAM HAVE A FAVOUR TO ASK

Sam - ASK AWAY

Kirsty - U KNOW THE POEM I SAID I COPIED FROM YOUR BOOK

Sam - YES SORT OF ... U NEVER SAID WHICH

Kirsty - THE GATE. WD YOU BE OK IF IT WAS READ AT A FUNERAL

Sam - WHOSE?

Kirsty - CALLUM'S

Sam - I WD TAKE IT AS A COMPLIMENT. HOWS U?

Kirsty - BARING UP ... JUST ABOUT ANYWAYS

Sam - HOW IS HE?

Kirsty - NOT GOOD. IN FACT GRIM

Sam - SORRY TO HEAR

Kirsty - ME V SORRY TOO. NOT FAIR. HE'S A GOOD MAN

Sam - CALL ANYTIME IF U NEED TO TALK

Kirsty - OK AND THANKS FOR THE POEM SPEAK SOON

Chapter 26

Death

A woman stared at Kirsty from a silver frame on the bedside cabinet. A rather sad-looking dark-haired man stood behind her resting his hand on the woman's shoulder. Although he smiled his eyes appeared distant. He had the same dark hair, receding hairline and stature as Callum. Her gaze diverted from the photograph to scrutinise the dresser, there was a small angel with one wing missing. Beside the angel, a wooden-backed hairbrush with chipped varnish and a scarcity of bristles. A colourful assortment of ties draped through a loop hung on the left-hand side of the mirror and on the chair a neatly folded pair of grey trousers. Several indents visible on the black leather belt marked the progressive weight loss of its owner.

She gently stroked Callum's face and tried to pat down a wayward tuft of hair standing upright on his head. Still he snored. 'You are a good man, Callum Flannigan, one of the best. I want to find someone like you,' she whispered. Yawning she closed her eyes and dozed on the bedside chair.

'I gave him a shave and change, then he slept,' she blurted, stirring from semi-consciousness disturbed when Sister Mary Cecelia entered the room.

'Good, thank you. I'm glad to hear it, he'll feel better for that I'm sure. There's a piece of salmon and some salad downstairs in the fridge for you. We must eat. Callum loved, I mean loves… Oh God have mercy on us - no I suppose I have to say loved to eat fish.' The nun's chatter sounded nervous. 'I remember the day he and Da arrived home with the young boy's first salmon caught out on Caragh. So happy, both of them, such a proud father he was delighting in his only son's achievement.'

'Is it lunch time?' Kirsty asked. 'I barely know what day of the week it is. Any sign or any sort of contact from Mattie?'

'Call it brunch time,' Sister Mary Cecelia smiled. 'Any time now, yes, very soon Mattie will be here.'

Leaving the nun alone with her brother, Kirsty made herself coffee and toast. She had no notion to eat salmon. Mrs Devlin had a friend visiting so no need to worry about going to see her, which meant there was time to have a nap. The days had developed a shape of their own, which involved waiting and caring. Waiting, but knowing that once the wait was over it would not make things better. Sitting in a chair she dozed for an hour or so, then returned to the sick room to see what else she could do to be helpful.

'Do you know the thing I would like most of all at this moment?' said Sister Mary Cecelia. 'I would like, yes indeed, how good it would be, oh dearie me, I would just love to be able to walk along the strand with Callum, chatting and laughing at nothing in particular.'

Kirsty, without hesitation, handed the nun her mobile phone, accompanying the gesture with a solemn promise that should there be any change at all, no matter how slight, she would call. Sister Mary Cecelia should have her walk, even though it would have to be alone. It came as a surprise when the nun agreed, saying she would not wander far from the cottage.

Callum is the only person who could ever question his sister's motives for sacrificing her life to a religious order, thought Kirsty as the nun departed. Floral curtains remained drawn across the window excluding the outside world. It was somehow abstruse why she felt peculiarly safe being alone beside a dying man.

It was not long before her moment of contemplation was irritatingly disturbed by the phone ringing downstairs, reluctantly she went to answer it, picking up with a resentful, 'Hello.'

'Hello. Mattie here. No need to eat me, Kirsty dear. Sorry I've not been in touch for a couple of days but it's been ridiculously busy here. Getting on top of things now; Mattie the fixer is nearly done fixing. How is Callum?'

'He's not good. You need to be here. The doctor does not have hope he'll be with us for more than another couple of days.'

'Jeez… Maureen, Fiona, what is it they call you again?'

'Kirsty,' she said frostily, in that moment hating him.

'I plan to be back in Balvohan later, probably early evening some time. Tell Sister Mary Cecelia. If there is any change I'll phone. Alright, dear?'

'I will, but I think she's expecting you sooner.'

'Really? Will see what I can do then. Tell me this,' he said, lowering his voice to a husky seductive tone. 'Have you missed me at all?'

She tensed. 'I'll pass on your message to Sister Mary Cecelia and Callum.'

'You're a good woman. See you, pet,' adding in a flirtatious tone. 'I know when I am not wanted.'

Kirsty laughed, not that it amused her but because everything he was saying sounded so ridiculous and totally out of context.

'One thing I can always do is make you laugh. Byeeeee.' Then he was gone.

Returning upstairs, she became frightened by Callum's breathing. It would stop for a few seconds and when her heart beat fast, fearing he might be dead, he took a huge gasp, bringing himself back from the edge. She knew he was still aware of her presence because when she tried to speak comfortingly he sometimes lightly squeezed her fingers.

When his sister returned from her walk and had been updated on Mattie's predicted arrival time, Kirsty left to make a brief visit to Mrs Devlin. The old lady was saddened to hear of Callum's critical condition. She repeated her insistence that Kirsty should be where she was needed most. Arriving back at the cottage on the hill within an hour, Sister Mary Cecelia told her that Doctor Hanlon, having visited again, had suggested calling Father Carlin. The priest, she said, was on his way. At this moment Kirsty found God in His mercy very difficult to understand. 'Do you want to wait downstairs for him and I'll go and sit with Callum until he arrives?' said Kirsty.

When she re-entered Callum's room, the sickly smell of death caught the back of her throat making her retch. She appreciated these moments alone with him, understanding it would probably be the last. There were things she wanted to share, to let him know how much he'd helped her, how kind he'd been and she was desperately sad he had to die like this. Taking his hand in hers she sat in silence beside the bed until Father Carlin arrived and he alone administered the last rites.

When he had finished, wearily, with leaden feet, she climbed the stairs again, leaving Sister Mary Cecelia to talk with the priest. Hearing the cottage door close when the priest left, she then heard the sister's voice gaining volume saying, 'Feck it, feck it, feck it, feck the whole bloody mess.'

Mattie was visibly shocked by the sight of his dying friend. His last memory would be sharing stories at the drinks evening, nothing like the fading man who now lay in bed. He sat down beside his dear friend, opposite Sister Mary Cecelia. Kirsty made sure the nightlight was lit, fetched more blankets and supplied sandwiches and hot drinks. The nun, she knew, was teetering on a tightrope, it worried her that Sister Mary Cecelia might be unaware how her state of mind and the fragility of her emotions could lead her into becoming overly reliant on Mattie.

Around midnight, unable to sleep, Kirsty returned to the sick room, carrying a hard wooden dining chair and tapped lightly on the door.

'Come,' said Mattie.

He nodded approving her unspoken suggestion, so she sat discreetly in the corner. These hours became a time to remember – Sister Mary Cecelia, Callum and Mattie in different ways for a variety of reasons. The atmosphere was palpable, each one of them inhabiting a place where no words were spoken.

After a time of collective contemplation Callum stirred and groaned. His sister sat slumped awkwardly, dozing, a blanket draped carelessly over her for warmth. Mattie remained awake and Kirsty observed as he leant forward, placing his ear close to Callum's mouth.

The dying man whispered something she was unable hear. Mattie recoiled momentarily but then patted his friend's hand and leant forward to whisper some inaudible words of his own. There was a frustration in being unable to hear the content of the exchange. Soon after, his breathing became harsh and rasping, and with wide eyes he stared straight ahead. Mattie shook Sister Mary Cecelia gently who woke immediately and sat up rubbing her eyes.

'I'm here, Callum. I'm here, have no fear,' his sister spoke gently. She moved to sit on the bed and held her brother's left hand while Mattie took hold of his right. Kirsty could only observe, with an amalgam of sadness and fear. The gasping breaths settled again to what outwardly appeared a normal sleep. Then rising forward, Callum's face lit up, as if seeing someone he wanted to be with. He remained upright for several seconds, before slumping back into the soft white pillows letting out a long deep sigh, breathing his last.

No more harsh sounds emanated from his ravaged frame.

His face changed from the look of a man who'd endured torture to one of calm. A new peace reflected by the faint smile on his lips.

Callum was gone.

'Goodbye, my dearest brother,' whispered his sister over and over.

Mattie tenderly closed his friend's eyelids and sat down again.

Chapter 27

Wake

Sister Mary Cecelia handed Callum's best suit to the undertaker. Jack Darcy expressed his sorrow for her troubles before proceeding to prepare the body. The open coffin was, at the nun's request, positioned near the sitting room window so her beloved brother could have his favourite view out to the Atlantic Ocean. Kirsty manipulated her moment alone with the cream, silk-lined mahogany casket. Callum lay at peace, pale and handsome. She placed a red silk handkerchief, bought specially in Killarney, into the top pocket of his jacket.

'It's wild out there today,' she told him as rain pelted noisily against the window. 'Although that's nothing to deter your friends from coming to see you. It would take more than a drop of rain. Are you in heaven, Callum?'

'Yes, he lives with Our Lord now,' said a voice from the doorway. Sister Mary Cecelia paused for a moment before continuing, 'And what's more, I look forward to seeing him again someday alongside Mammy and Daddy.'

Kirsty quelled the urge to question her belief, and just nodded. In spite of her best efforts she was unable to stifle three big yawns in quick succession.

'Rest a while, you look exhausted, I'll sit here and read,' suggested the nun.

Sleep did not come but she sank into the armchair in a mournful haze, subconsciously studying the neatness of the nun's brown-laced shoes with dark-brown nylon pushed into them, gathered in wrinkles at her ankles. The dowdiness of the brown well-worn habit struck her as a crime when worn by a beautiful woman. The alternative hung upstairs in a wardrobe, sponged and pressed in readiness for the funeral. Modern nuns more often wore casual clothes with perhaps only a crucifix to denote their religious vocation. Was this a particular rule of her order or a personal statement of some kind? Kirsty wondered.

Sister Mary Cecelia could easily be mistaken as considerably younger than her years. Translucent skin, wide brown eyes, a decent figure, combined in an attractiveness she would never have admitted. Amid her slightly chaotic ways she exuded mystery and goodness which was captivating. Her mother, father and brother all gone, her vulnerability had become palpable.

Father Carlin was the first person to disturb the Flannigan cottage that evening. He arrived anxious to deliver assurances all was in place for the funeral, scheduled for mid-morning on Wednesday and hoping Sister Mary Cecelia did not mind, but he had taken responsibility for speaking to the undertaker to arrange an announcement in the local newspaper. With his cooing and well-practised sympathies, for the first time he annoyed Kirsty.

Mattie arrived soon after the priest had departed, declaring his mother was bearing up, although he had left her with a promise he'd send Kirsty to provide companionship. This instruction was acknowledged by his employee with a forced glimmer of a smile.

'We're all tired,' he said as he escorted her to the door around six o'clock. 'Here, take my umbrella. It's still wet and I noticed your car is at the foot of the hill.'

She thanked him, hesitating for a moment because of an impression he wanted to say more.

'Mammy's looking forward to having you all to herself for a while.'

She took the umbrella and walked away feeling irked, mostly with herself.

Mrs Devlin commented that Kirsty looked tired, insisting in a motherly way an early night was needed. Accepting this excuse Kirsty retired. The old lady said she was content just having company in the house, and could not stop thinking about Callum or the pain his sister would be experiencing.

Chapter 28

Controversy

Mattie, meanwhile, planned to use this contrived time with Sister Mary Cecelia. 'I'm glad to be alone with you,' he said, then quickly added, 'with both of you.' He moved towards the window where she sat beside her brother and stared out into the darkness of the rain-sodden night.

'I don't think either of us is in any mood for small talk with the villagers tonight. No doubt they will arrive in droves tomorrow. Callum was always popular and well respected.'

The nun observed his stocky figure standing in front of her.

'Come stand closer by me a moment please, my friend.' He held his hand outstretched. 'Let's view the wild night from the window together and know we are fortunate to be cosy behind closed doors. That is, unless you are about to send me away to battle with the elements.'

Slowly his request was obeyed and she stood beside him saying, 'Such a night. It's as if the anger in the wind, laments the loss of a good man from our world.'

Mattie wrapped a comforting arm round her shoulder drawing her closer and whispered, 'He loved you a great deal, you know, very much indeed.'

'I know,' she replied, 'and he loved you.'

'I think you need a proper hug,' said Mattie. Tensing his arm and giving her shoulders a gentle squeeze, then bending forward pressed his lips onto her brow. 'Yesterday I made a promise to the best friend anyone could ever have, which I intend to keep.'

The nun tilted her head, resting it on Mattie's shoulder. 'Thank you. Thank you for everything, you've been a great support. Oh dearie, dearie me, let us pray he is at peace.'

She paused and tried to extract herself from his grip. 'I also think it would be best if you go now, I'd like some time alone with my brother.'

Reluctantly he obeyed her request. Having pressed his lips to her brow a second time, he stepped out into the wild dark night.

There was no period in his life when the name Flannigan had not gained admiration from him. As someone who had become accustomed to commanding respect this made them all the more unique. Callum was gone, Mattie missed him desperately, having to accept his wise counsel could only live on now in the hearts and minds of those he left behind. Over the years his best friend's sister had presented him with a challenge. Lively and pretty as a child, she had become a beautiful woman both inside and out. God was being greedy by claiming exclusivity of her attention.

Chapter 29

Day

Calm followed the storm, bringing clear, crisp early autumn sunshine. From mid-morning a continual stream of people made their way to and from the little white cottage on the hill. Kirsty returned after lunch to assist Mattie and Sister Mary Cecelia. She moved among the guests, chatting easily offering refreshments. Most of the men wore suits. The few who did not sported a shirt and tie as a show of respect and attempted to offer comfort.

'I am sorry for your trouble.'

'Callum was a good man.'

'He will be sorely missed in the village.'

'One of the best.'

Mrs Morriarty determinedly manipulated Kirsty into a corner almost pinning her against the wall. The postmistress was on a mission to gain information, in a state of desperation she relentlessly pursued any small detail to dispatch from behind her shop counter.

'Did he go peacefully? Was Sister Mary Cecelia with him? When does Sister Mary Cecelia return to Dublin?'

This woman and her stream of premeditated questions, quickly became irksome. It seemed she expected to be privy to every minute detail of Callum's demise. Finding her selected captive was not forthcoming, her questions turned instead to the funeral saying Father Carlin always gave folks a beautiful send off.

'Will Callum to be buried up in the cemetery with his mammy and daddy? I did wonder might he have his own grave beside them? Would Mrs Devlin be fit enough to attend? Would anyone be staying onto deal with the house? Did she know if it would be sold or kept?'

Feeling exasperated and having revealed nothing, Kirsty managed to escape with the excuse she was needed to make more tea. Mrs Moriarty's disappointment was obvious when abandoned, bereft of any answers which could be repeated to local customers.

Sister Mary Cecelia's countenance carried a deep despondency as she politely engaged in conversation. Mattie was haggard and grey. He still managed to move in an effortless way among the gathered mourners, his well-practised charm in automatic mode. Observing him from a distance, he became alarmingly reminiscent of the husband Kirsty longed to forget. Mattie, she believed, hid his emotion behind an ability to make people laugh, being gifted with an amusing comment for just about anything.

Father Carlin arrived to be warmly greeted by Mattie who handed the priest a large measure of Paddy's whiskey which was gratefully accepted. The two men became engaged in deep conversation. She observed them and wondered what it was they discussed so earnestly.

Sister Mary Cecelia drifted from person to person, in a daze, holding a plate containing lemon sponge which provided an excuse not have to tarry with any guest.

Mattie then moved away from the priest to converse with Sam Dillon and his ruddy-complexioned wife. Father Carlin took the opportunity to approach Kirsty. The priest appeared happy to talk over the funeral arrangements in minute detail, as if working through a check list. Callum had provided most of the content, he told her, having been quite particular in his wishes. While he talked she watched his mouth move and became distracted by a small area of stubble on his cheek until it became hypnotic and she had an urge to count the exact number of hairs. Nodding occasionally and shifting the weight from one leg to the other and saying at intervals, 'Oh really' or 'mmmmm' as the priest talked.

Then quite unexpectedly, he said, 'How are you, Kirsty? I mean really how are *you* within yourself?'

'I'm alright thank you, Father.' She did feel gratitude, after all, he'd been the first person to give her a sense of belonging, but at this moment preferred to shy away from convoluted discussion on her issues. 'I should be aware, Father, but can't think what colour of vestment will you wear to conduct the funeral?'

'Purple,' he responded, giving her a formal explanation. 'Prior to Vatican II the tradition was to wear black for a requiem, but it became believed to have negative connotations, suggesting utter destruction and oblivion. So purple became the alternative. It's connected in Catholic culture to the process of salvation, as opposed to white which signifies the conclusion of salvation.'

Then he said, 'You didn't ever answer the question who should read the poem as you agreed with Callum. Who was it written by?'

'I would like you to read it, Father. It was written by a good friend of mine.'

'I will be glad to, no indeed, would be honoured. Delighted we have that sorted. Can you excuse me a moment. I've just remembered something else.'

He moved across to where Mattie was speaking with a tall, thin, craggy-faced man. She noticed the interruption was greeted enthusiastically providing an excuse to terminate his current conversation. After only a brief exchange Mattie edged away from the priest and paused briefly to whisper to Kirsty, 'The poor bugger's befuddled,' before going to speak to an elderly gentleman saying, 'Walter, good man. How are you?'

She felt annoyed. Father Carlin, the man, was in mourning too. He'd lost a good friend and all his talk about Callum being with God in Heaven was his comfort zone. A woman approached who she remembered having been introduced to earlier as Martha Doherty's daughter. She could only think of the aerosol incident as she shook hands, smiling broadly when really she wanted to giggle.

'How are you doing?' she whispered to Sister Mary Cecelia as she passed by with a plate containing a cake. 'Can I do anything for you?'

'No thank you. I hope they'll start going soon,' she grimaced. Taking this as her cue Kirsty, made her excuses to the Doherty woman and started to gather plates and cups.

'I am glad I found you. A little treasure,' Mattie whispered noticing her efforts. She felt colour burn in her cheeks, and hated the fact. 'Watch me, I intend to chase this lot away home to their beds.' He winked at her.

Mrs Morriarty, true to form, was the last to leave. Mattie deftly edged her towards the door, but doggedly she refused to be defeated. 'Mattie, you'll be able to tell me. Did he go peacefully to meet his maker? And when is it Sister Mary Cecelia would be planning to go back to Dublin?'

'Goodnight to you, Mrs Morriarty.'

'Will you be going back up country too or staying a while longer with us in the village?'

'Goodnight, Mrs Morriarty, thank you for coming. I'm sure Callum would be appreciative.'

'Is your mother going to manage to go to the funeral?'

The doorstep had been reached.

'Yes, of course Mammy will be there. Goodnight, Mrs Morriarty. Sleep well.'

Having virtually pushed her outside Mattie shut the door,

hissing beneath his breath. 'Jeez. If she had a brain she could be dangerous.'

Chapter 30

Funeral

Sun filtered into Kirsty's bedroom through flimsy floral curtains. It had been arranged for her to be with Sister Mary Cecelia on the morning of the funeral and Mattie with his mother. Flicking on the radio she listened to the weather forecast. Blustery showers would be moving inland from the Atlantic. Forcing herself onto the edge of the bed and pushing her legs to stand, she became overwhelmed by a dizzy sensation, forcing her to sit again.

After a few moments she felt able to pick up her toilet bag, only to find the bathroom occupied. She returned to her room and waited until hearing the door open and the nun return to her room.

She feared her plan to be first downstairs was stymied. A navy suit and cream blouse waited on a hanger. Finally, having showered, she was ready and pinned a Claddagh brooch to her left lapel. The mirror reflected back her pale cheeks in spite of rouge, gleaming hair, mascara, lipstick, with no obvious smudges, and with concluding liberal spray of perfume said, 'I suppose that'll have to do.'

'Breakfast in ten minutes,' she called, hearing Sister Mary Cecelia was still moving about in her room.

'Thank you. Oh dearie me, what a day.'

Kirsty glimpsed the nun delicately tucking her hair beneath a pristine wimple.

Breakfast was simple: tea and toast. Sister Mary Cecelia ate little and talked in a whisper.

'You know, I can see him sitting opposite me at this table right now and even hear his voice. It's as if I could reach over to touch his arm. I can smell him, that same horrible smell of illness. But look, he smiles at me, his lovely smile.' She stood up, turning her back to the table, and moved to the window.

'The tide is out, Callum, the sea is calm, gentle, no longer wild and hungry. Remember when you were a boy wearing short trousers, dodging and weaving to avoid being "it" in our game of tag on the golden strand. Oh Dear Lord, I pray look after my dear departed brother for me.'

Kirsty felt like an intruder and said, 'I'll go and sort my room.'

She tried to relax on the bed until hearing the nun call, 'Will you get the door please? I'm in the bathroom. Tell them I'll be down in a minute.'

A gentleman dressed in a black suit stood at the front door. Beyond him she saw the hearse waiting at the gate. A second sombre man in an immaculate black suit approached with slow, funereal steps. Callum was about to leave his home for the last time.

The first man requested permission from Sister Mary Cecelia to close the coffin before they gently carried the casket, slipping it expertly into the unappealing chasm of the car. The two ladies walked side by side behind the hearse on its creeping decent to the foot of the hill. Their route flanked by the remnants of fuchsia hedges battered by the storm. Rich velvet autumnal scents of vegetation and residual fruits mingled with sea air to ease Kirsty's headache. Who might feel able to give her a hug, she wondered, looking at the nun who walked beside her with head bowed.

Sister Mary Cecelia had insisted Kirsty travel to the chapel with her, although strictly speaking not one of the chief mourners, the security of her friendship aided her strength to face the day. They had formed an affectionate bond in a short time and to be seen to lean on Mattie could be misguidedly interpreted by some as inappropriate for a bride of Christ. A second black limousine waited to transport them to the chapel, Mattie and Mrs Devlin already occupied the back seat. The driver stood respectfully, holding the door open.

'Good morning, Sister Mary Cecelia. How are you, ladies?' said Mattie.

'Good morning, Mattie. Good morning, Mrs Devlin. I am bearing up.' The nun sighed. Kirsty also greeted each of them solemnly.

'Not a bad day weather-wise,' Mrs Devlin said with satisfaction.

'Yes indeed, the sun can stay, it does make the autumn colours so beautiful,' said the nun quietly.

With the topic of weather exhausted, silence took over, interrupted only by the smooth purr of the car engine as it manoeuvred through the village towards the chapel. Numerous cars waited in side roads and pulled out to follow behind the black limousine, forming a procession which eventually bore resemblance to a black-headed multi-coloured snake. The mourners arriving on foot stood still as the hearse passed, blessing themselves with the sign of the cross. Elderly men with weather beaten faces removed cloth caps from their head and small children stared.

The procession halted at a farm gate a short distance downhill on the opposite side of the road from the church. One by one the cars were parked and a crowd quickly gathered to walk behind the hearse for the last steps to the church. Mrs Devlin was determined she could manage with the aid of a walking stick and Kirsty's arm to hold.

Derek, Mattie, Dr Hanlon, Declan, Jack and Peter, the

bearers requested by Callum, raised the coffin shoulder high, leading the way to the chapel. Sister Mary Cecelia walked alone, directly behind her brother, with Kirsty and Mrs Devlin following. Audible shuffling footsteps brought the throng to Father Carlin waiting to welcome the body into the church. The bearers bowed their heads as the priest recited prayers and sprinkled holy water from the aspergillum.

Aspergesme, demesne hyssop, et mundabor, avabis me. May dues exsectata vos suus regnum.

Farmers, traders, publicans and their families filled the church to capacity. Callum was then carried to the altar and placed with tender respect upon a waiting stand. Each bearer bowed to the altar before turning to find his place in a pew.

'In the name of the Father, the Son, and the Holy Spirit.'

United voices recited the requiem mass responses. Callum's chosen hymns echoed out onto streets, over the mountains and down to the sea. After the Gospel readings Angela Murphy sang 'Ave Maria' as collection baskets passed from row to row. Kirsty's thoughts were with Biddy seeing the raven haired lady with an abundance of jewellery. She recalled her mother's wish that she had listened to this woman when as a girl she'd given a warning that Joseph Meechan was not so sweet or innocent. By the time the collection baskets had gone all the way around the church they brimmed full with ten and twenty euro notes, donations to a cancer charity.

Before the consecration prayers, Mattie walked onto the altar. His black tie slightly askew. Kirsty felt an urge to set it straight.

Squaring his shoulders, and with his eyes fixed on some distant point, he sang 'Panis Angelicas'. An exquisite resonant tenor voice captured the collective emotion and made every hair on the back of her neck bristle and many tears within the congregation demand release. A deafening hush descended when he finished, broken only by rustling handkerchiefs and nose blowing.

Father Joe Carlin stepped up to the lectern and read.
The Gate
Please, accompany me to the gate?
But no further, not today, you still have
Years ahead, I pray, to share and enjoy.
Happy am I to pass through on my own,
With the knowledge that at some later date,
We can share things as we used to do,
Laugh together as we wonder at 'why'?
It seems so foolish today anyone should cry.
Celebrate my life, rejoice, sing and dance,
And know I am with you not just by chance,
I shall listen, content, to hear each word you speak,
Ever there, to help you find the things you seek,
Always remember, separated only by a small gate,
I remain close to you, only now dwell in another state.

In spite of her recent disillusionment at how easily some members of the Church could tell lies and play with people's lives, Kirsty found the format of the requiem soothing in its progression from consecration to communion. She made a silent act of contrition before joining the slow procession to receive. If God is to be found anywhere, she thought, it has to be in the mountains and coastline of Kerry. God renounced Lucifer, so He would surely do the same to those whose sin is the theft of a childhood. The accounts of child abuse which tainted the Church, a sickness hidden behind false good.

She felt a certain gratitude for not being left behind the walls of an institution where mental tortures gnawed inside those who became Ireland's lost and forsaken through no fault of their own. Receiving the host and returning to her pew, she became dismayed to find the wafer stuck to the roof of her mouth, loathe to shift, impossible to swallow.

Father Carlin blessed the congregation, 'Go in peace to love and serve the Lord. The Mass has ended.'

'Amen,' replied the congregation and stood for the final hymn.

A grey-haired lady at the organ played 'Give Me Joy' as the bearers stepped forward and carried Callum from the chapel into the cemetery beyond to his prepared grave. The mourners walked behind the coffin as large globs of rain spat intermittently, dropping from a thundery black cloud before increasing to a drenching deluge. Father Carlin recited prayers with droplets forming on the end of his nose, splashing onto his open prayer book. Mattie was the first to lift a handful of sodden earth, dropping it into the grave where it landed with a dull thud on the coffin lid. Several more people followed, faced with difficulty to be rid of mud wedged between their fingers. Then the cloud moved westward leaving a vivid rainbow arched over the craggy mountain.

Mrs Devlin, mercifully persuaded by her son to wait in the car, cooed sympathetically as they rejoined her. 'There is sure to be a long old queue at the toilets when we reach the hotel. Look at the state of you.' Mattie held up his hands to display mud-smeared fingers.

'Yes,' said Kirsty feeling able to join the conversation, 'but bags me first for the ladies,' she smiled at Mrs Devlin who reciprocated.

Sister Mary Cecelia suddenly gave her nose a good long blow and resurfacing from behind a large handkerchief, declared, 'Oh dearie me, what weather. I am grateful that I don't ever wear mascara for it would have been a black river down my cheeks.' Tucking the handkerchief up her sleeve she continued, 'Right, everyone, we've shed our tears and now it's time to celebrate Callum's life. As of now there is a ban on having gloomy faces.' Then looking directly at Mattie she added, 'You know better than anyone how my brother enjoyed a good party.'

Mrs Devlin offered distraction, saying, 'Wouldn't Callum have been so flattered and pleased how many people came to see him off. I can't remember when I last saw such a crowd at a funeral in our chapel.'

Mattie responded, exuding importance, 'We can be safe with the knowledge our friend has no more pain and hope he's in a better place.'

'Mattie Devlin, are you forgetting you are in the company of one of Christ's brides and you say such a thing,' exclaimed his mother.

'Oh dearie me, don't you be worrying. I know where Callum is and will be forevermore. Nothing that anyone says will change that.'

He looked at the nun in a way Kirsty recognised; he wanted to kiss her.

The steady stream of cars made slow progress to the hotel. Mrs Devlin seized her opportunity. 'I wonder if I might change the subject?' she said. 'What are your plans, Sister Mary Cecelia? I don't mean to appear forward and certainly don't want an absolute answer immediately, but perhaps by mentioning it now I can give you the opportunity to consider. I appreciate you've been unable to think about much beyond today. Oh to hang,' she drew breath and blurted, 'I was wondering what you plan to do with your cottage.'

With no appearance of being in the least bit offended the nun responded, 'I'm not sure. Callum and I did talk of selling it.'

'I wondered if that might be the case and have been thinking,' Mrs Devlin lifted the handbag from her lap before firmly forcing it back down again with black gloved hands. 'I was wondering,' she hesitated, 'Sister Mary Cecelia, please permit me to ask with the clear understanding there's absolutely no rush to answer.'

'Mammy, for goodness' sake, just get on with it,' said Mattie.

His mother glowered at him and then turned back to the nun. 'Would you be prepared to sell the cottage or rent it to me? It would be great when the family come and visit. Who knows, Mattie might even find a new wife in the future and I'm sure you're aware Peter has promised to visit regularly.'

Sister Mary Cecelia looked thoughtful. 'Yes indeed, I do see possibilities.'

Mrs Devlin, clearly encouraged, said, 'It would make sense to have somewhere for them to stay so we wouldn't be falling over each other in my little house.' She glanced in Mattie's direction, but his eyes were still fixed on the nun. 'I am a creature of routine, as I am sure Mattie and Kirsty can vouch.' She waved a hand at her son, but failed to gain his attention.

Sister Mary Cecelia, as far as Kirsty could see, appeared oblivious to Mattie and his gaze.

'Let me think about it. I would like to chat things through with Dan Keane, our solicitor.'

'Perfect, take as long as you need,' Mrs Devlin said, peering out of the car window to observe who else was already there, as they stopped outside the hotel.

Kirsty reached for the door handle, desperate to satisfy a need for fresh air and visit the ladies powder room.

Before joining everyone in the bar she sent Sam a text.

YOUR POEM GREAT TY
BIG CROWD HERE
V. SAD

Chapter 31

Aftermath

During the days following the funeral, Mattie appeared restless. Kirsty gladly agreed to his request to stay on with Mrs Devlin, not so much as a care giver but more of a companion, for a further few weeks. Sister Mary Cecelia had decided to delay her return to convent life in Dublin remaining in Balvohan for another two weeks to tie up legal matters.

Mrs Devlin confided one day with great delight that it had been agreed she was to rent the cottage on the hill for six months initially, with a possibility of a purchase in the future. The rental income was to be paid into the convent funds. Mattie was apparently disappointed that it would not be received into a personal bank account. She said he'd failed to persuade the nun to have an account in Sister Mary Cecelia's real name, Mary Flannigan.

Nocturnal hours were worst, elongated with conflicting dilemmas competing for Kirsty's attention. Sometimes the worry was eased by getting up to make a hot milky drink. One night when on walkabout Kirsty was surprised to find Mattie sitting at the kitchen table.

'Are you alright?' she asked.

'Fecking sure I am.'

'You don't look alright.'

'Dublin is giving me a headache, but nothing I can't sort. Come sit with me, my dear.'

She shivered. 'It's cold in here. Would you mind if I put the heater on?'

He appeared sober and there was no hint of alcohol.

Mattie explained he needed to go to Dublin the following day. Then said something she did not fully understand regarding being worried about losing his integrity. She nudged a packet of biscuits towards him, which he ignored.

'I have to take decisive action,' he said. 'No one will be permitted to trample over me and get away with it.'

Unsure what to say, she pulled her dressing gown tighter round and flicked the heater to a higher level.

'I'm not always a good man, Kirsty. Not all bad either. I do try, I believe, to be fair-minded.' He sighed. 'Perhaps it is easy to share with you because soon you will disappear back to wherever you came from. I've a sense you don't do much of the sharing thing either. Am I right?'

He didn't acknowledge her non response and continued to talk about how he experienced lust with ease, he loved sex, but surely there had to be more to it. Sex without a bit of something else was destructive, not worth having. He had screwed around and part of him hated the mindlessness of it all. He became incoherent, rambling about love as opposed to loving, perfect love, ideal love. But she did understand when he told her he liked a challenge and was not deluded enough to imagine any of this was about her.

'An older woman who is a virgin, now that has to be the ultimate challenge to a man like me.' Silence dominated, until he shook himself free of troubled thoughts, saying, 'You're a good woman, Kirsty. I like you. We can laugh together, share as friends are supposed to. I've made you laugh, haven't I?'

She nodded.

'You know something else I'm wondering?'

She shrugged her shoulders.

'This love malarkey probably doesn't exist. It's a figment of our active imaginations created to fool us.'

She was beginning to wonder about his state of mind, and having enough thoughts of her own to contend with stood up, pushing the chair under the table, saying she needed to sleep.

'I do like you, truly,' he winked. 'You're a valued friend of this Blip.'

Snuggling into bed alone and grateful to be so, she lifted her MP3 player from the bedside cabinet using music to effectively shut out the world until sleep took over. In the morning she found a scribbled note on her bedside table.

Gone to Dublin back ASAP.

M

So he'd been in her room while she slept. What was that all about? she wondered. Had he hoped she would be awake and welcome him? Perhaps she needed to be clearer that anything happening between them was totally out of the question.

*

Mattie returned to Balvohan three days later. He laughed a lot, talked a great deal and even confided some of his Dublin dilemmas to Kirsty. Much of his angst, he intimated, was caused by his eldest son, Declan, whose behaviour was a disappointment having become belligerent and greedy. Several times he mentioned retirement, complaining he was too tired to continue living in the fast lane. 'Perhaps now the time had come to let others take over.'

She listened and carefully scrutinized him, wondering what she knew about the real Mattie and the other world he lived in. Who was the person hidden from public view? Long ago she became convinced there was absolutely no physical attraction, although could not deny a growing fondness for this quirky character. Certainly he was nothing like Toby, but she recognised he was suspect and self-serving.

Sister Mary Cecelia called at the Devlin house most afternoons, having first spent time in the chapel. Mattie was easily coaxed to walk on the strand with her, after which they both joined his mother for a chat. At other times he might be found tending to the garden at the Flannigan cottage.

'Like brother and sister,' said Mrs Devlin one day, watching Mattie and Sister Mary Cecelia leave her cottage together.

Who is she trying to reassure? Kirsty wondered.

Chapter 32

Surprise

'So I've been allocated the Thursday night slot?' Kirsty teased Sam who'd started to phone regularly each week. These conversations were something she looked forward to. Canada had not been mentioned recently so in essence she'd chosen to forget the possibility.

Mrs Devlin, who became increasingly determined to prove renewed independence, suggested her carer could also be used to help Sister Mary Cecelia clear the cottage on the hill. A big final clean was needed before the nun returned to her convent.

Kirsty assigned several days to the Flannigan cottage working through a long list of tasks as each one was presented to her by the nun.

'Would you be an angel and give the bathroom a clean? It's been on my to-do list for days, but oh dearie me, where does time go?'

As she bent over the bath with a sponge and cleaning fluid, weary of kitchens, bathrooms, cups of tea, endless food interspersed with tipples of whiskey, she thought: Good old Kirsty, isn't she an angel? Nope, she decided.

'Hello. Anyone about?' Hearing Mattie's voice, she chose not answer.

'Yes, in here,' replied Sister Mary Cecelia from the sitting room.

Kirsty heard them talking but at first paid little attention. It was only when the words, 'I think I have fallen in with love you,' seemed magnified among the others that she stepped quietly onto the upstairs landing.

Silence.

It was frustrating not being able to see the nun's reaction.

'You have become precious to me. I hope I'm right in thinking you are at least fond of me?'

Oh yuk! What a scumbag!

'Dearie me, this is quite a shock.' The tone of panic in the response was not wasted on Kirsty. 'Of course I'm fond of you.'

Mattie responded sarcastically, 'So I'm the same as a cream cake or a bar of chocolate. Or something else of that ilk you might say you were fond of?'

Serves you right, what's with this trying to seduce a nun, jeez.

Sister Mary Cecelia backtracked. 'You must know how much I've appreciated your help during these difficult weeks and I do enjoy the time we spend together but please stop this.'

Kirsty imagined the wringing of hands in that peculiar way the nun did when agitated. Although maybe not, she longed to see the body language. Still no 'oh dearie me'. On the contrary, the voice to be heard sounded firm and self-assured. 'Mattie, you know we should not be having this sort of conversation. I'm not available and never shall be.'

'Don't be scared of me please,' he pleaded.

His tone easily recognizable to one who knew, she could see it all just as plain as if it was she who stood in front of him. A finger tenderly tracing from brow to chin, before leaning forward to kiss her forehead. Curiosity to know just how well his practised seduction technique was succeeding became overwhelming. On tiptoe she started to make her way downstairs, but then suddenly they were all disturbed by a loud knocking on the front door, followed soon after by the door latch clicking open.

'Hello, Sister. Are you there?' Father Carlin's voice drifted into the hallway.

Sister Mary Cecelia had already hastily retreated to the kitchen. It seemed Kirsty was invisible from her position on the stairs to the priest as he stepped inside saying with obvious surprise, 'Mattie! It was Sister Mary Cecelia I hoped to see. Would she be about?'

'She is, Father. Although I believe is outside feeding the hens. Did you not see her on your way in?'

'No. I thought you'd returned to Dublin. What is it, I wonder, that holds you in Kerry? Your mother is well enough I hope?'

'She is, thank you Father.'

'And still has Kirsty caring for her, I think.'

'Yes Father, she has.'

There was an awkward pause before Mattie continued, 'I sometimes pop by to see if Sister Mary Cecelia needs any help. Mammy likes me to help out, since it will be her who takes on the cottage when the good Sister returns to the convent.'

'How thoughtful! I am sure your kindness is appreciated. Would you be good enough to fetch Sister for me?'

'I will certainly, then if you'll excuse me, I must press on. Work to do for Mammy.'

Kirsty decided she resembled tired old wallpaper that becomes no longer noticed. Once the two religious figures became engrossed in conversation, she too left the cottage, without saying anything, making a detour along the strand on her way back to Mrs Devlin.

*

Father Carlin recited Mass mechanically and skipped giving a sermon. Delivering a mumbled excuse about there being a funeral during the main mid-morning Mass. Kirsty stared blankly at the altar, unsure why she was in there at all.

'Any good *craic* at church today?' asked Mrs Devlin.

'Somebody called Moira Kelly's funeral is at eleven o'clock Mass. She lived in a new-build at the top of the hill. Anyway, how do you know I've been to Mass?'

'Moira Kelly would be what we call a blow in,' Mrs Devlin avoided answering the question. 'Poor lamb. Had been ill this last six months but that's her with her maker now, eighty something I believe. Might be me next.'

Then she tapped the side of her nose, her brown eyes dancing with mischief. 'See no evil, speak no evil and hear no evil.' Picking up the teaspoon she smacked the top of her boiled egg saying, 'Now leave me in peace, I'm going to enjoy this.'

Mrs Devlin was to spend Sunday with a friend and stay overnight. Mattie was glad, claiming he needed to talk to Kirsty. She shrugged, inclined to say 'whatever' but couldn't deny her inquisitiveness to know what his latest agenda might be.

At 11.45 precisely his mother was escorted to the red Jaguar for her planned arrival as Mrs Dempsey's guest prompt at noon. At 12.30 Kirsty was irritated by the arrival of a text.

PLEASE BRING MAMMY'S OVERNIGHT BAG. FORGOT!

'There we are, all sorted,' said Mrs Devlin when her bag was duly delivered a short time later.

'Don't you be getting up to mischief now; alone in the house with my Mattie.' She laughed.

'I won't,' Kirsty smiled, but felt irked she'd laughed rather too much at the old lady's comment.

Around two o'clock Mattie suggested a walk along the strand. They had not gone very far when he insisted they should sit on the sand dunes to watch the tide coming in.

'Sister Mary Cecelia...' he started to say, shifting position to stretch his short chunky legs straight out in front of him. Kirsty wondered momentarily if he had become confused as to who actually sat beside him until he continued, 'Would you be prepared to take her back to Dublin next Wednesday?'

'Yes of course, I thought that had already been arranged by your mother. She felt it would be a nice gesture to have a friendly travelling companion. As I've already confirmed with her, I'm more than happy to be that person.'

He wriggled around on the sand removing one of his shoes to shake out a quantity of golden grains. 'This fecking business of mine in Dublin has me demented. I'll have to go back up country on Monday.' He reached for his foot awkwardly, making grunting noises in a contorted manoeuvre, managing to replace the shoe on his foot. 'My dear, tell me this, do you see our favourite nun settling easily to back into convent life?'

'Might take a little while, but I'm confident she will.'

'More to the point, do you suppose she wants to settle back into the religious life?'

'Yes, I believe so.'

'There is an available alternative, you know.' He observed her reaction which involved squirming uncomfortably, shifting the sand beneath her, before commenting glibly it was surprising how hard it could feel considering it was so soft.

Turning his head to stare wide-eyed into the distance he totally disregarded her claim to discomfort. 'I kissed her. I kissed a fecking nun.' Then with his finger he gouged the sand to form the outline of a face. Kirsty could visualize quite clearly in her mind his sensuous delivery of a well-practised, lingering kiss.

Marram grass rustled as a breeze lifted sand particles, causing her to turn her head and close her eyes. A cloud drifted across the sun, delivering a sudden chill causing an involuntary shiver. Mattie lurched on with his eulogy of how good life could be if you found perfect love. 'It might mean a move from Balvohan to stop people talking. A neat little garden and a well-furnished house with lots of new friends who are ignorant of our past.

Kirsty started to speak. 'But…'

'Shhh, my dear, let me finish. I appreciate it would not be straightforward but she would not be the first nun to leave the religious life. When the dust settled we could get married. I have my annulment and what a wonderful thing too, it means in the eyes of her God I've never been married at all. It could even be a white wedding.'

Gulls flew overhead, their angry squawking dominated the rolling surf, until they moved along to disturb families picnicking near the café. A small tortoiseshell butterfly settled on her leg and spread its wings, exhibiting perfect symmetry within its vibrant colours. She'd retreated to a safer place as Mattie's monologue became progressively more strange and fantastic. He touched her arm to remind her, undivided attention was his preference.

'So do you know what she comes out with, she feels there is no hope of us finding a lasting peace together.' Throwing his head back with mocking laughter, his short chubby figure vibrating on the sand dune. 'I cannot see it in that way. I felt a passion rise in her every bit as much as it did in me. I do know women.'

Relief in never permitting him near her bed translated in her thoughts to: what a load of twaddle he spouts. Her hand dug into the sand, tugging at a grass root then clawed deeper in an effort to free it, golden grains ran through her fingers during repeated futile attempts.

'I want to walk with my best friend's sister to the gate, and pass through it together when our time comes.'

Her distaste accelerated into anger hearing the reference to Sam's poem, bringing her dangerously close to saying something she would regret. It was the clincher prompting her to terminate this ridiculous dialogue.

'Come, the tide is on the turn, we've been here long enough. I want to go.'

Scrambling awkwardly to his feet he managed to catch up with his companion who'd set off at a brisk pace.

Silence conquered the walk as Kirsty thought of Biddy.

'You go on ahead. I want to visit the chapel.'

He looked surprised but didn't comment as he re-entered the house alone.

Kirsty didn't see Mattie again until late evening. She'd been feeling apprehensive regarding Sister Mary Cecelia's ability to counterattack Mattie's charm offensive. Her conjecture as to how aware the nun might be of some male motives, or what drove certain types of men, ended by arriving at the conclusion, it was not really any of her business what the pair of them did.

As she sat idly flicking through television channels Mattie appeared at the door to say he was going for a bath but needed to talk to her again and she was to go nowhere in the meantime. Her heart sank.

Half an hour later he waddled like a duck across the room and lay on the sofa with only a very large white towel wrapped around his body. This persona was perturbing and found her hoping he did not have plans for anything other than talking. Such ridiculousness induced the urge to giggle helplessly or seek out a dummy to put in the mouth of the oversized nappy-clad baby.

On route to the sofa he'd placed a small rectangular card on the table in front of her. 'I go to Dublin tomorrow. Do you know where my office is?'

She shook her head.

'The address is on that card,' he pointed to the table. 'Now, this is the part I need you to pay attention to. I anticipate there will be no need for your involvement, but if for some reason I'm unable to collect items from the safe in my office, someone implicitly trustworthy will be required to do so. And you, Kirsty, my dear, are the only person for that job.'

Without committing herself she responded brusquely, 'Continue, I'm intrigued.'

'As you enter the building, my office is on the ground floor and first door on the left. The safe is hidden inside a large bookcase on the left-hand wall. Go to the top shelf, where you will find two large hardback books, *The Irish Tax System* and *Business Accounting*, and what a load of shite they are too. Remove them both and behind looks just like the wall, but if you prod around the bottom right corner it should move enough to lift up and underneath you will find the safe. Now commit this combination number to memory, 99723497.'

'Mattie, stop! You're starting to frighten me.'

He repeated the number three times before insisting she repeat it aloud. The towel had fallen loose and barely covered him, his bulky belly and chunky short legs, ridiculous yet intriguing and beguiling.

'It's not money but a large brown envelope that contains important papers which has to be collected. These are vital.' His voice sounding irritated. 'Kirsty, I need you to listen carefully and to take this seriously.'

Still remaining hesitant to agree to any of it she stood up, turning her back on Mattie and walked to the window. A full moon shone brightly, illuminating the outside world. There followed a long silence. 'You ask a lot of me,' she eventually said returning to the armchair and the view of his physique languishing on the sofa.

Comprehending she was not an eager participant, he struggled to appeal, wide-eyed and smiling, using his, as he believed, irresistible assets. He persisted in giving assurances it was unlikely she would be needed; any potential involvement in this was merely a remote back-up plan.

'Must I?' she said with a sigh.

'No, I don't suppose any of us must do anything we don't want to. I'm sorry. I'll not mention it again. Be an angel and pour me a drop of Irish?'

The intensity in his tone dissipated unexpectedly, becoming casual and jaunty, as if nothing else had preceded and he was making a normal request. Kirsty obediently handed him a generous Paddy's whiskey and as she did so, discerned tension in his white knuckles combined with the rigid set of his jaw. Time to think alone was needed, so she excused herself, to visit the bathroom promising to be back in a minute.

Her previous existence was so far removed from anything like this. Curiosity had her in its grasp, so to simply walk away no longer remained an attractive option. Feeling she knew Mattie well enough to be confident her compliance would not hold any dire personal consequence, her decision was made.

Re-entering the sitting room, she said, 'Mattie, can I talk and you actually listen?'

He gave a 'tut' and rolled his eyes heavenwards, although her subsequent enquiry was not one he'd expected.

'Over the last few weeks, when Callum was ill, did he ever,' she paused, 'say anything to you about me? Perhaps large doses of morphine caused him to speak incoherently or say things to make you wonder.'

'He liked you,' said Mattie. 'Even tried to match-make, reckoned you would be good for me.'

'Mattie, please! I'm being serious.'

'I know, sorry. I'm trying to relax. Feel very tense tonight.' He rearranged the towel. 'You are a strange one sometimes, and no, he never did share any personal things about you. So what exactly is it you're not telling me?' He gazed at her expecting a response but, not receiving any, said, 'Callum did want me to promise to look after his sister, that's an easy one to keep.' Adopting a smug, self-satisfied look he added extra emphasis on the word you. '*You* made a bad choice, rejecting the best man ever likely to cross your path.'

Kirsty ignored him and persevered, 'So he said nothing?'

'Nothing, but you have me wondering.'

There was a long pause, as he waited patiently for her answer regarding the collection request. She appreciated this silence, aware he didn't want to risk an outright refusal.

Eventually he said, 'Perhaps you should get yourself a habit.' He laughed and winked. 'Sometimes a habit makes things possible where they otherwise seem impossible.'

What this meant she had no idea but relented to his mischievous grin.

'Why me and what is it exactly might have to be collected?'

'You for two reasons. First and foremost, I was hoping you would be willing to bring my car back to Kerry, so it will be safe here at the house.'

'And the second reason is?' she asked.

'The papers stored in the safe will only be needed if I decide to go abroad for a while.'

'Oh! Pray tell more?'

'Retirement will only happen if I manage to get the business sorted out. Also, as you know, I have, or maybe should say had, hope of a future containing Sister Mary Cecelia and myself sharing life together. The latter, me thinks, is a nonstarter; regrettably that convent of hers dominates everything.

'So why abroad?'

'Jeez, you ask a lot of questions, but 'tis Okay, don't mind telling you. My office safe contains important documentation enabling access to my money if I leave the country. The taxman and I are not on friendly terms; need I say more? There is absolutely nothing iffy or anything which could pose a risk to you. Just don't want anyone in my family knowing all of this. Less they know, for now at least, the better. Surely you can trust me as much as I trust you?'

'Alright, you can rely on me. And I'll make sure your car gets safely back to Kerry.'

'Also, if there is any chance of me not taking the papers with me I don't want Peter to see them. It's private for my eyes only. So can I ask you to burn the envelope in the unlikely event that it is not safe in my hands.'

She nodded saying, 'Yes I understand.'

'That's a relief. Now take this,' he held his hand outstretched, 'it's a separate phone which can be used for me to contact you or vice versa. Keep it charged and carry it with you at all times.'

For the next hour they sat in quiet companionship both absorbed in their own world. She would have liked to talk to Sam but felt it was too late to call.

Chapter 33

Dublin

Kirsty arrived at the cottage to collect Sister Mary Cecelia on a crisp, bright October morning. Giving each other a warm embrace she said, 'Good morning. Let me have a last check round the house and I'll be right with you.'

'There's no rush. We've oodles of time, I'll wait outside.' Kirsty lifted the small leather suitcase placing it on the back seat of her car. She sat in the driver's seat with the engine running. Looking in the mirror, she noted the person who stared back was barely recognizable, thinner faced and desperately needing her hair cut.

Sister Mary Cecelia carefully locked the cottage door pausing to fasten the bolt on the wooden gate. Just as they were about to drive away, Jack Delaney, the postman, approached waving a letter in his raised hand. Disengaging the gear lever, Kirsty lowered the window.

'Phew, glad I didn't miss you. Good morning all. Sister, there's a letter for you.'

He handed an envelope through the open window. 'Good luck to you, Sister,' he spoke across to the passenger. 'We'll miss having you in the village.'

'May God bless you and your family, and good luck to you too.'

With a brief perusal of the envelope's exterior and a shrug of her shoulders, the nun placed the letter in her bag saying, 'Right, let's be on our way.' Her eyes focused straight ahead with no final sideways glance at the cottage. There was no knowing when she might return to her Kerry home, overlooking the Atlantic, if ever. No attempt was made by either of them to force conversation about weather or mundane matters. The nun's gaze remained fixed on the road ahead, without any glance at the strand, the church, hotel, and post office. Only as they passed the cemetery gates did she turn her head and make the sign of the cross.

'When he was alive, we talked of this moment. Oh dearie, dearie me. Our little home and the sound of ocean waves. How everything has changed.'

Once the car had been parked at Killarney station Kirsty placed the keys under the mudguard on top of the front tyre, as instructed by Mattie. It had been arranged that it would be collected later by a friend and returned to Mrs Devlin's house.

On the train they sat facing each other with a table between them. Church bells chimed noon but any potential to say the Angelus prayer was interrupted by a loud, shrill whistle compelling the train to creak and sway as it moved out of the station. Quickly it gathered momentum, taking the ladies from Killarney on their way to Dublin.

Biddy, Mattie and Callum occupied Kirsty's head, and there would still be barely half a day pass without Toby briefly squeezing into her thoughts. The management of him had become easier.

'I imagine you'll be glad to get back to the convent,' Kirsty said, monitoring the nun's face for any flicker to betray their journey could be a facade. Every time she mentioned or heard the word convent it reminded her of Biddy and the hideous crimes.

'Certainly. I have missed it, particularly Sister Christina, my dearest friend.' She paused before adding, 'I hope you know everything you have done is appreciated. My plan was to write to you on my return to the convent because I never feel adequate having this sort of conversation. Some things are easier to express in a letter. I would like us to remain in contact.'

Kirsty felt a pang of guilt, nonchalantly saying, 'Mattie seems to like you, anyway.' As the words left her mouth she wished they hadn't.

'Mattie is very good at charming everyone,' responded the nun.

Feeling relief, she continued the campaign saying, 'Men only cause problems, as far as I see it.'

Sister Mary Cecelia giggled, 'You could have a point.' But then she looked serious. 'I suppose being a nun does have its drawbacks, expectation to be continually devout lest it be thought we're not doing our job.' She glanced at her watch before asking, 'Kirsty, would you say I'm very serious?'

'Actually no, you have great humour. And, if I may say, are a little dippy from time to time, which is endearing.'

'I hope we can remain friends, exchange letters? It would probably be beneficial for both of us.' Sister Mary Cecelia clasped the bag on her lap tightly with both hands and Kirsty remembered the arrival of a letter that morning.

'How are you with the Biddy, for want of a better word, business?'

'I've had some guidance and help from a psychotherapist in Killarney. I've never mentioned it before but have been seeing a counsellor regularly. Not sure exactly how it works, but I freely admit he's been a great help.'

'Good, glad to hear it. If there is ever anything else you think I could do, please don't hesitate to say. My order of nuns had no connection with laundries or mother and baby homes. We're similar to Carmelites; although the vow of silence is not so strictly observed we still would be more contemplative be-lieving our prayer and petitioning the Lord brings help where needed. But, as you know sometimes we can communicate with other orders. So if ever you wish me to make another approach on your behalf, please ask.'

'Thank you, much appreciated.'

Kirsty preferred to pretend she was dozing for the next hour as they continued to make rapid progress towards the city.

'Kirsty, Kirsty dear, wake up, we've arrived.'

Having gathered their cases, they stepped onto the station platform and Sister Mary Cecelia said, 'I think you would enjoy a city tour on the open-topped bus. It leaves from O'Connell Street, which is no distance from here. I shall be absolutely fine making my own way back to the convent.'

'No, absolutely not,' protested Kirsty. 'I promised Mrs Devlin and Mattie to accompany you safely all the way to the convent door.'

'Oh my dear. Not at all, they are fussing rather too much. It would be simple for me to get a taxi and you could head straight into town.'

Her face flushed while procrastinating about what her companion should do. 'You know, when I think about it, the better option would be to go straight to Trinity College and see the Book of Kells. There would still be time after that for a wander around the shops before they close. Be sure, I won't be telling anyone.'

Reluctantly defeat was accepted. 'Oh alright, but let me at least see you safely into a taxi.'

The taxi rank was easy to find. Sister Mary Cecelia held out her arms to hug her friend, insisting there was no need to wait. Kirsty grudgingly obeyed, but on reaching the station exit, doubled back, discreetly positioning herself behind a pillar to see Sister Mary Cecelia standing outside Butler's Chocolate Café. A young couple near the nun embraced as they greeted each other and a youth dashing to catch a train bumped into her. 'Sorry, Sister, you alright?' but didn't tarry long enough to hear an answer.

Taking great care to remain concealed, Kirsty witnessed what became apparent as an agonizing waiting time for Sister Mary Cecelia. Seconds became minutes and as the minutes grew in number, she appeared to become more confused and despondent. The brown clad woman paced up and down then circled the neat leather suitcase, all the while tugging at her crucifix. It was pathetically painful to watch. Finally, in the same way an eagle swoops to snatch its prey, the nun grabbed her suitcase and set off with long strides in the direction of the taxi rank. Obliviously unaware of being followed she stopped briefly reaching into her shoulder bag, taking out a different letter, one smaller than received earlier in Balvohan. This previously unseen envelope was then released into a green post box. The slight delay meant Kirsty was able to reach the taxi rank first.

'Whatever are you doing here?' exclaimed Sister Mary Cecelia.

'Caffeine fix required, and the thought of a crowded bus held no appeal so I decided to treat myself to a taxi into town.'

Without indulging an outright lie the nun made her excuses. 'I've been observing. Yes, people-watching, with renewed fascination. Seldom do I see such crowds.' Gesticulating defensively, she said, 'Do you ever try and guess what someone's occupation might be?'

'St Ursula's convent, please.' Kirsty bent forward to speak to a taxi driver before turning to Sister Mary Cecelia. 'Now us meeting up again has me totally convinced I am destined to see you safely back to the convent.'

There was no further argument as both ladies climbed into the stationary cab, sitting side by side on the back seat. The driver talked to them by looking into his mirror when they stopped at traffic lights, apologising that they were about to experience rush hour in Dublin. He was in his fifties, with thinning hair and a man who obviously wanted to chat, so they let him articulate his opinion of the economy and how slow his own business was with fewer American visitors. He informed them their journey to St Ursula's would normally be about forty minutes, but at this time of day it was anybody's guess how long it would take. An air of resignation draped itself over the three occupants of the vehicle.

Much of the time they hardly moved at all. Eventually, tired of the lack of response from his passengers the chatter ceased. Kirsty's head ached. She believed Mattie had obviously not been where promised, and she was supposed to trust him. Searching out two Anadin tablets from her handbag she gulped them down with the last of the water in a bottle bought in Killarney.

They had not moved an inch for the last five minutes. Straining to see the road ahead, the railings of St Stephens Green were barely visible in the distance. The driver drummed his fingers impatiently on the steering wheel.

'Sure it just gets worse and worse trying to drive anywhere in this city. It's no way to make a living.' Another five minutes passed and still they didn't move. 'What the fff... is going on?' He managed to stop himself swearing.

Opening his door he stepped out to get a better view. Then getting back in, said, 'Not sure what's going on at all. Certainly not doing much for my earning capacity, all this going nowhere.'

Kirsty experienced a strong urge to reach out to Sister Mary Cecelia with reassurance Mattie was not worth it.

'I was waiting for someone,' said the Sister, as if by telepathy she felt the need to answer the unasked question. 'Someone I would have preferred to speak to in person, but it was not, it seems, to be granted. They will know soon enough as a letter will do just as well. I get the impression you feel there's a need to protect me.'

'Maybe so,' responded Kirsty carefully.

'I do know Mattie, better than you think. Nor am I as gullible as I might appear. He will soon forget, if he has not done so already.'

I should never have doubted her, thought Kirsty reaching over to squeeze her companion's hand.

Gradually they started to move and picked up speed, finally making progress through the city. Heading north along the coast road to Clontarf and on to Malahide, past Portmarnock until the driver signalled he was turning left and steered the taxi between two large, maroon, metal gates. The car snaked up a steep driveway, lined with ancient trees until reaching a flat area of gravel in front of a large sandstone building.

'Well, here we are.' The driver turned to look at his passengers. 'Glad we made it in the end, my apologies, ladies, for the delay.'

Sister Mary Cecelia insisted on paying for this journey before they both got out. The driver retrieved the small leather suitcase from the boot. Without saying anything they hugged. 'Who needs words anyway?' smiled Kirsty.

'Oh dearie me, it has been quite a time, altogether. Now off you go and look at those shops. We can talk again on the phone in a couple of days. Alright?'

Kirsty got back into the taxi and as it drove away she turned and peered out of the back window to see another nun silhouetted in the open doorway with outstretched welcoming arms. She certainly had to agree it had been 'quite a time altogether'.

'Could I go to O'Connell Street, please?' She requested. Then said, 'Please excuse me, suddenly I feel very tired.' She slumped in the seat closing her eyes.

But it was not over yet.

Chapter 34

Strange

Beep. Beep.

The noise roused Kirsty from a state of semi-sleep. It took her a moment to work out where it came from. Her phone revealed nothing then she remembered the other mobile she'd been given by Mattie and found a text.

PLEASE COME TO THE OFFICE NOW.

She responded saying she was in a taxi and would be there as soon as possible before updating the cab driver. 'Sorry, but I need to change the plan.

St Clément's Street, please.'

'Not O'Connell Street?' responded the driver.

'No, St Clément's thanks.'

Beep. Beep.

GET THE TAXI TO DROP YOU AT THE FOOT OF DALY HILL WHERE IT MEETS AUG. ST AND LOOK FOR MY CAR.

She informed the driver of another change.

'No problem. We could think of it as third time lucky, eh?' he smiled trying to engage with her in the mirror.

Remarkably quickly, they arrived at the designated spot and she paid a further twenty-five euros, which to her seemed excessive. Nevertheless, she added another five as a tip for his trouble.

'Here, let me give you a card, it has my mobile number on it. Don't be stuck, do you hear? I am on until eleven tonight.'

Kirsty thanked him and watched the taxi become absorbed into the constant stream of traffic. She walked to the corner and within minutes spotted a familiar red Jaguar emerge from the early evening greyness. As it drew to a halt in front of her she leant forward to open the passenger door.

'Hello. How are you doing?' said Peter.

Gradually the significance of this made perfect sense. She sat beside him, neither of them talked while she discreetly observed curls, less grey than Mattie's, resting on a white shirt draped over narrower shoulders.

The car travelled at speed through dank north Dublin streets. There was a scarcity of people on the pavements. Those observed were predominantly scruffy men or youths. Some of the shop windows had been boarded over and displayed assorted and sometimes elaborate graffiti. The Jaguar started to climb a steep hill, a myriad of street lights flickering and dancing below, in the sprawl of a city she hardly knew.

Peter halted the car outside a building and looked at her with raised eyebrows.

'Why am I here?' she asked, tired of prolonged non-communication.

'All Mattie said was for me to bring you to the office and you would know what to do. So here we are, and I'm waiting. Try not to be too long with whatever it is.'

Having searched out Mattie's key from her purse, fuelled with a steely determination to get the job done quickly, rapid steps propelled her towards the building. Tantalising thoughts of being able relax in a comfortable hotel room brought a determined effort to get this over with quickly. The key slipped into the lock and she entered the unfamiliar hallway, following Mattie's instructions to locate his office. Instinctively she checked behind the door before dragging a chair across to the bookcase, and clambering up managed to reach the top shelf. The two large books mentioned were removed and dropped noisily to the floor. Sweat trickled down her face as she tapped frantically at the bottom right corner, feeling a surge of panic when nothing happened. She tried again, and this time met with success, the safe door became evident. As soon as she typed in the number, it opened, permitting her to reach inside and lift out the solitary large brown envelope. Tucking this under her arm, she closed the safe and before leaving carefully replaced the books and chair. It all felt like a dream.

Peter's bulky profile stood blocking the doorway.

'Is that you finished then?'

'Yes.'

The phone in her pocket bleeped.

I AM ON THE ROOF BRING THE ENVELOPE

'Now Mattie tells me he's on the roof and expects me to deliver this envelope. Frankly, I fail to understand why I'm here at all.'

'That thought occurred to me too,' responded Peter, clearly disgruntled. 'Come, follow me.'

He led the way along a narrow corridor to the rear of the building before proceeding to climb a dimly lit stairway.

'Well Da, is it then?' she heard as Peter nudged open the door to reveal the scene. Declan stood tall, with a superior smirk conveying some kind of perverse pleasure he really knew his father better than Mattie had ever given him credit for.

'Declan, for goodness' sake, what the hell are you on about now?' responded Mattie, from where he was seated on a concrete ledge.

'That's right, Da, you get cross.'

'For the love of God, what do you expect?' his father said with obvious exasperation.

'Yeah, suppose I might get a bit tetchy an' all if I knew my fucking time as Lord of the Manor was up.'

Peter appeared perturbed and whispered they'd better not interrupt. Gesturing with his hand implying Kirsty should remain behind him.

'Really, Da, you have me all wrong, you don't think I am about to give up on this one do you? I have the respect of all those out there who can make sure you do not operate any more as the boss.'

'Come on, Declan. It is time to talk, really talk.'

'Talk,' Declan snorted. 'When did you ever talk to me?' His manic eyes conveyed venom towards a man he obviously despised. 'You paid for my education and thought that was enough. Threatening me with all sorts if I ever hinted Francis might learn things about your business, or buying my silence with fancy cars and the like. But talk you did not. Even now you still want to tell me what I should do.'

Declan spat as he spoke, drops of poisonous saliva visibly sprayed on to the chilled air of an autumn night.

'Let me tell you, I will run this business far better than you or that old fart Rafferty with your mixed morals.'

'I promise this time I'm listening,' pleaded Mattie. 'I hear your anger and please believe me, I am truly sorry if I am responsible for making you hurt so much. Can we please try and talk now, father to son?'

Declan scoffed again, 'I should tell you, Da, no amount of your shite speeches will do you any good now. You always believed you have a way with words, eh? I'm sure the gift of the gab dug you out of a few tight corners.'

Mattie did not reply, but taking a phone from his pocket started typing a text. Peter looked at Kirsty, who knew instinctively to switch the phone onto silent immediately or their eavesdropping would be revealed.

She whispered, 'He says, "Where the hell are you?"'

'So when did "Mr Morality" and "Mr I" just get others to do my dirty work for me change?' sneered Declan.

'That matters not,' said his father wearily.

'There we are. You're not communicating with me at all,' shouted the son. The aura of menace emanating from the young man was becoming frightening. Declan squared his shoulders to look taller. 'I have respect,' he gestured with a wave of his arm towards the city lights stretching out as far as the eye could see. 'All of them. No one, absolutely no one, would dare to mess with me.'

'Was I really such a bad father to you?'

'Worse, you were no father at all.'

'I'm sorry.'

'Didn't hear.'

'I'm sorry, so sorry. I am begging you that we try and get this mess sorted once and for all. Please can we go inside now and draw up a proper agreement. Take time to communicate and find something which is mutually suitable. Then I can retire, move away and leave you to get on with a good share in the business. Alternatively, I'll hand it all over to Peter, for now at least.'

The son laughed. 'Don't stop. Beg some more, come on, grovel, you bastard, grovel.'

'Okay. I'm begging, can we talk? Ultimately the choice of outcome is yours.'

'Naw.'

'Come on, for pity's sake, Declan.' Mattie was trying his persuasive soothing tone. His son turned, hearing a different but familiar voice, and saw Peter standing in the doorway.

'Holy shite, what now?' he shouted, wiping his brow and stuttering. 'Where the hell did he come from?'

Peter took a few steps forward. 'Interesting conversation,' he said. His soft-soled shoes inaudible on the flat roof surface. Kirsty stayed behind, remaining an observer.

'How long have you been there?' Declan demanded.

'Long enough,' Peter stepped closer until face to face with his nephew. You certainly get a great view of the city from here. And you, Declan, seem to think you are Lord of the Manor, overseeing all that is laid out before us.'

'Yer, right,' responded the youth, defiantly grinning broadly. 'Lord of all I survey.' He glanced at Mattie and laughed, then turning back to Peter he said, 'Look at the two of you, Tweedledum and Tweedledee. I'm better than both of you put together, or just that sad old bastard. It should by rights be the eldest son who inherits the entire business, not a brother.'

Mattie looked at Peter. 'Who's the sad old bastard?'

'Well, I'd say he thinks you are,' Peter smiled calmly. 'Dear sweet Declan,' his comment loaded with sarcasm. 'How very wrong you are. It's me and the sad bastard that remain united and you are nothing more than a spoilt brat.'

Kirsty clutched the brown envelope. Increasingly tempted to leave it on the ground by the door and creep away.

The youth's piercing blue eyes radiated blatant defiance. 'My da and my uncle, fine men. Oh how the mighty can fall.'

'For pity's sake, will you just shut up,' said Mattie.

Peter stepped closer to Declan and spat impatiently into his face, 'You are a worm, an insidious little worm. Do you hear? Your da wants to give you another chance. I don't agree with him. You must come on side if we are to work together.'

'Now it's you who needs to shut the fuck up,' said Declan.

'I take it that's a no?' said Mattie.

'Fecking sure it is.'

Peter, without warning, cracked his head hard into his nephew's face. Blood flowed copiously and the younger man fell to the ground in a crumpled heap. He cried out in pain, as he lay splayed out between the brothers' feet.

'My nose, it's busted, I'm bleeding.'

'Might knock some sense into you,' smirked his uncle.

Declan groaned. Mattie turned him gently onto his side. 'Yep, definitely temporarily incapacitated, but not about to lose his life.'

Mattie drew a handkerchief from his pocket and held it to his son's nose, asking, 'Is Kirsty here and did she get the envelope?'

'Yes, she's here, and by the way, you do know how to make an exit with high drama.'

Declan tried to get to his feet, his father and uncle helped him then the three of them walked slowly towards the door. Kirsty was amazed at how casual they had all suddenly become. Even Declan, whose mumblings through the handkerchief pressed to his nose, displayed humility.

'Uncle Pete, did you really have to do that?'

When they saw how startled and upset Kirsty was, Peter suggested it was probably a good plan to say the young man had slipped on the stairs causing an injury to his nose. The entire group moved downstairs and sat on wooden chairs at the reception desk.

Peter nonchalantly said to Mattie, 'The car will be waiting in the yard at seven in the morning with the driver you requested. I also have the plane tickets and passport. Tam the Forge has done a good job.'

'Grand,' said his brother.

'You have a UK passport in the name of Tom Turner. Not very imaginative, but the taxman's never heard of Mr Turner.'

'Excellent.'

Mattie, turning to Kirsty, started to talk casually as if they were back in Kerry.

'Did Sister Mary Cecelia make it to the convent alright?'

'Yes she did and I have the envelope for you.'

'Good girl,' he looked straight at her with wide eyes, adding, 'You really saw nothing.'

'Absolutely nothing,' she nodded. 'I'd like to go now. I'll call a taxi.'

Mattie pretended he hadn't heard and carried on talking. 'I am glad you'll be able take the Jaguar back to Kerry for me. The driver Peter has organised would not be so trustworthy. Besides, he has to be dropped off at some point. My faithful car will be much safer parked at home.'

'What time would you like me to return tomorrow morning? I'll find a hotel room in the city.'

'No, not at all, I insist you stay here. There is ample accommodation, Peter and Declan are going anyway and there are two bedrooms. Make things much easier for you.'

Kirsty's amazement became complete when Peter and Declan left together with no obvious ill will between them. She knew well enough from her teaching experience that the dynamics within some families could be challenging to understand.

'They'll be alright,' smiled Mattie. 'Spats between us are nothing new but this time my son took things too far and needs to learn how to accept what's on offer, not be a plonker.'

She handed him the envelope.

'Thank you. I wonder did you notice if Sister Mary Cecelia got any post today.'

'Yes she did, one letter arrived just as we were about to leave. Lucky the postman caught her.'

She paused before asking, 'One thing puzzles me.'

'Go on,' he said

'Why could you not collect the envelope? I don't get why you needed me to do it.'

'Two reasons, one is I needed you to be here, my car has to go back to Kerry.'

'And the second?'

'Maybe I needed to test you in some way. Not fair I know but let's not over analyse, you are here and that's what matters.'

Mattie showed her to a room at the far end of the building. He was pleased his plan to lure her to the office had worked as he handed her a list of local takeaway restaurants and left her saying, 'Sleep well. Just knock on the door at the end of this corridor if you need anything.'

She found the room was pleasantly equipped with a bed, en suite facilities, TV and a small fridge. Strangely, she did not feel at all nervous or upset. She ordered a Chinese carry out and set the alarm on her phone for 7 a.m. as Mattie said they needed to be away by nine to get to the airport.

Peter returned early the following morning and declared Declan would be absolutely fine. The knock apparently appeared to have calmed him down enough to listen regarding the future of the business. As he assured his brother all would be well, he took hold of his hand pulling him closer embracing him saying, 'We'll keep in touch.'

Mattie put his hand on Peter's shoulder and sounding serious said, 'Just one thing I ask. Please, don't go head butting my son every time he argues with you.'

Peter smiled. 'I won't, promise. Seemed to do the trick though, we can hope he'll have better manners from now on. I am sorry.'

'Time we were off, keep in touch.'

Mattie held the back door of the car open, indicating Kirsty should get in. She sank easily into the soft leather seat. The driver was a dark-haired man; she guessed he was about fifty. His arms rested on the steering wheel, he wore dark glasses, and a dark stubble shadow gave him a grubby appearance. Mattie seated himself beside the driver and tapping his hand twice on the dashboard said, 'Okay. Let's go.' The Jaguar navigated smoothly out of the gate to start its route downhill to the main road.

'You drive safe remember, no smart moves. Nice and sedate, nothing at all to have the Garda alerted.'

'You can count on me, sir. I need the work.'

'Good, glad we have an understanding,' said Mattie turning casually requesting Kirsty pass him *The Irish Independent* newspaper lying beside her on the back seat. Idly he turned the pages, scanning the headlines as the car progressed through Dublin following signs to the airport. Quite soon the last page of the newspaper had been perused with little sign of interest. Folding it roughly and squashing it down beside his feet he said, 'How about we listen to the radio?'

'Aye, aye, Captain.'

She noticed how Mattie's shoulders tensed as the driver's

hand reached forward to click on RTE1. They found themselves listening to an elderly gentleman with a strong Cork accent share his experience of visiting Little Nelly's grave in the grounds of a former Good Shepherd convent. Kirsty, who was glad of the distraction, listened with interest to the story. It gave reasons why a group of people were petitioning to save the child's grave for posterity. The convent had recently been purchased by a property developer, causing fear Little Nelly's resting place would become lost forever. The gentleman caller insisted she was 'a frightful holy child' who died at the age of five having lived all her life in the convent with her unmarried mother. Several more callers supported the campaign saying they'd prayed at Little Nelly's grave and believed miracles ensued as the result of their entreaties. The discussion then turned to whether or not this child should be a candidate for canonization. Kirsty was intrigued, becoming oblivious to Mattie's bulk occupying the passenger seat and the stranger who drove.

Once they were on the M50 the car became almost static, creeping along in a queue of slow-moving traffic. Mattie drummed his fingers impatiently. 'I want you to turn off at the next junction and we'll take the back road.'

'Aye, aye, sir.'

'What a smartarse we have here,' Mattie said with a smile, turning to look at Kirsty. As if the Jaguar felt relief gaining liberation from slow traffic, it willingly accelerated away from the motorway, eating up the country roads with ease.

'Now take a left at the T-junction.'

'But the airport is right, sir.'

'Take a left.'

'Yes sir, left it is.'

'Now a mile up here we come to a crossroads, I want you to turn right.'

Kirsty peered earnestly from the window, wondering where the airport was and why the detour.

'Now I want you to stop in the lay-by just ahead of us on the left.'

She could only see an area of wasteland dotted with old fridges dumped to rust and decay alongside two burnt-out cars abandoned by joy riders.

'Turn off the engine,' Mattie demanded.

'Why?'

'Just do it.'

The car became silent and the puzzled driver asked, 'You got another pick-up or what?'

'Shut it,' Mattie responded with disdain. 'Now I want you to get out of the car and go stand over there by that empty oil canister. Kirsty, come and sit in the driver's seat.'

What's he up to now? she thought, stepping out from the rear of the car.

Mattie snarled at the driver, 'Oh, and take off those ridiculous sunglasses. Anyone would think you were trying to hide something.'

The stranger revealed his icy grey eyes.

'That's better. Now go and stand beside the canister as I told you.'

The driver muttered, 'If it's a square go you want I'll have the better of you.'

She was painfully aware there was little possibility of her escape so moved without protest to sit in the driver's seat. She could see the stranger who dutifully waited taking a packet of cigarettes from his pocket, and lighting one inhaled deeply.

Mattie leant forward, with one hand slipped under his jacket he revealed a gun. 'I have my trusty friend with me. See, a good old 9mm Browning. But don't you go worrying that pretty little head. You are perfectly safe. I do care about you, even if you don't seem willing to believe it,' he winked.

Such flippancy irritated Kirsty, who was by now visibly trembling.

'No. Wait,' she hissed at him. 'You can't–'

He didn't let her finish. Bending even closer, he whispered in her ear. 'For pity's sake, it's a fake, but yer man over there needs to feel what it's like to experience blind terror. Just trust me.'

She felt only slightly relieved, still far from comfortable with the situation, but nodded to indicate a glimmer of insight.

'Can you be ready to move the car as soon as I say the word?' he said and started walking to where the driver lingered. The two men stood facing each other. Mattie stared into the piercing blue eyes as if seeking something. 'That's better,' he said. 'I want to examine your soul. I believe we have someone in common.'

'Do we?' The driver looked mystified. 'Peter, your brother?'

'No, try again, loser.'

An arm flailed in a futile attempt to strike out at Mattie, who in the same split second, stood pointing the gun held with both hands at his opponent. His feet slightly apart as he stood firmly on the ground, in total control, aiming the weapon at his victim.

Thunder rumbled in the distance. A sudden gust of wind lifted an empty polystyrene container, carrying it several metres. She shivered, fondling the key which dangled tantalisingly in the ignition. How easy for her to be gone from here, following the skein of Brent geese calling out as they flew overhead. 'Declan?' whimpered the driver.

'Nope. Still the loser. Try again?'

'Sam Dillon?'

'Sam Dillon. Doubt it. He has more sense than to use the likes of you. You ever stopped to wonder why you get little or no work. Eh?' Mattie sneered as distinct fear overtook the previous cocky demeanour of the driver. 'You've never been anything more than a wannabe. Some stupid notion you could impress by sorting out a few bad uns with a baseball bat, and we would think you were a main man. Well you're not, neither could you ever be clean. You're capable of nothing more than wrecking the life of a sweet girl with a pathetic act of self-gratification.'

'I don't know what you are on about,' stammered the driver.

'Your name is Joseph Meechan, is it not?'

'Yes.'

Hardly believing what she'd heard, Kirsty frowned. The man who stood with shoulders hunched, pathetically grovelling, was her father. She fought back a sudden urge to cry out his name shouting that he had raped her mother. Instead, a mishmash of words tumbled uselessly until she managed to say, 'Mattie, I need to speak to you.'

He shouted. 'Be quiet. Stay over there in the car out of the way.'

Then he prodded Joseph in the chest, making him flinch. 'Think again. Who in this world might you have deeply offended?'

'I've no idea.' Joseph appeared genuinely flummoxed.

Contempt etched into Mattie's features, as he spat, 'Right then, let me inform you. Biddy Duffy.'

'Who?'

Intensely irritated, the gun in his hands jerked twice in an upward motion. 'Come on, man, stop these games, you're no fecking good at them. You,' he yelled, 'raped a young girl on the threshold of adulthood robbing her of a promising future. Biddy Duffy, now does that name ring any bells?'

With renewed defiance Joseph smirked as if to say was that all? 'Oh her, yeah I remember, a frigid cow.'

Gripping the steering wheel tightly until her hands hurt she clenched her teeth so her jaw ached. Kirsty imagined running over and screaming at him, how dare he speak of her mother in that way when he should be overwhelmed with remorse.

Mattie contemptuously looked his victim up and down. 'You're a cool customer, have to give credit for that. Most men with no certainty what I might do next would at the very least, shake a bit.'

'Maybe. But, I know you won't kill me,' sneered Joseph.

'Won't I?' Mattie yelled. 'You ruined her life.'

Shaken by the eruption of such ferocity, Joseph's expression reverted to pathetic, his efforts at defiance evaporated.

'You raped her and got her pregnant. She was dumped at a Magdalene Laundry to have the child.'

'A child?' Joseph mumbled with disbelief.

With no warning, Mattie's right foot kicked Joseph with considerable force in the groin. He sank to his knees doubled up in pain.

'Yes, a child. Even you with limited intellectual resources must know what that is.'

Joseph spluttered and groaned.

'Sad her father was such a bastard.' Mattie spat on the ground in front of his victim. 'Let's see if I can make you sweat a bit more. Just for another moment or two, savour your fear, then I'll shoot to kill, because I need to be somewhere else.'

The firearm remained pointing straight at Joseph. The accused started to weep uncontrollably, reduced to a defenceless wreck. In this displayed vulnerability, Kirsty examined her father. It distressed her to think she was in any way connected to this pathetic specimen of a man. Her head throbbed, searing jabs of pain induced by efforts to search for any hint of compassion or repentance. She should tell the snivelling wretch who she was and he was a repulsive disappointment and beat her fists on his body. But, her white-knuckled, aching hands couldn't let go of the steering wheel. Black cawing birds circled overhead, like vultures.

'You have no idea the pleasure it gives me to see you so terrified, begging for mercy,' Mattie spoke with contempt. 'Any second now, when this gun fires, it will be straight into your heart. Bang. My redundant wedding ring shall be placed on your finger before I pour petrol all over you and then finally torch your wretched carcass. With luck the Garda will think the burnt to a crisp corpse is me. At least until all their fangled

DNA tests prove different, but by that time I will be long gone from Irish shores. You deserve to die for what you did, although Biddy will never have the satisfaction of knowing any of this.'

Joseph lay on the ground, in a pool of his own vomit, pleading for his life.

'Ready, steady, go,' said Mattie, elongating the three words. Joseph curled into a tight ball with his arms clasped over his head.

Kirsty too shook with fear, as a loud crack echoed in her ears, swiftly followed by a second. It's a cap gun, a cap gun, caps, not real.

He's not dead! Then she heard the accuser say, 'Normally I wouldn't stoop so low as to kick a man when he is down but in your case I make an exception.' He lashed out with his right foot, aiming a second time at Joseph's groin. Leaving him groaning.

'Go, Kirsty,' he said, landing with a thump on the passenger seat beside her.

Sparking the engine and engaging first gear, she rapidly drove away. Mattie shouted out of the open window to the crumpled specimen still lying on the ground, 'I'll make sure you never get any work in Dublin. Good luck trying to get back to wherever it is you would rather be.'

Large droplets of rain plopped onto the windscreen and thunder clapped directly overhead, causing Mattie to jump.

'Left,' he said as they approached the main road. Then laughed saying, 'It's a long old walk back to Dublin. There's a lay-by a bit further up, I want you to stop. Here, stop here. Feck this rain. Look at the state of me.'

Kirsty screwed her nose but was starting to feel secretly relieved that Joseph had been punished for his crime.

'Need to get rid of this, can't imagine strolling through airport security with it in my pocket. A toy pistol, but a bloody good imitation. 'Twas a birthday present years ago.'

'Certainly had me fooled,' she said.

He walked to the edge of an old water-filled quarry with green algae floating on the surface. Giving the pistol a last wistful look he hurled it into the quarry where it landed with a dull plop and sank into the murky depths. The boot of the car was raised, blocking Kirsty's rear-view mirror. When he lowered it again it was evident he had changed into a clean shirt, beige trousers and smart cream jacket. Methodically he poured soapy water from a container and washed his hands several times. The dirty clothes were bundled carelessly into a black plastic bag and tossed into the boot. Then he returned to the passenger seat saying, 'I hope you know me well enough not to have doubted me for a single moment?'

Kirsty said nothing.

'I wanted to make him sweat a bit.'

She remained mute having no notion what to say. He'd scared her, she felt used. If she started to speak, those pent-up feelings would escape in a tirade of words which could prove unwise.

Instead she remained silent, wondering why she was there at all with a man called Mattie Devlin on an area of wasteland somewhere in Ireland. Slow rain droplets suddenly became a torrent, battering the car, making visibility difficult.

'Before we head to the airport, how about a hug.' He reached across awkwardly, to embrace Kirsty.

'No, I don't feel that well, my head hurts,' she responded pushing him away.

'Take two of these and you'll be right as rain, scuseee the pun!' He produced a strip of analgesic tablets from his pocket holding it her direction. His voice adopted the practised sexy tone, 'Could we make time for a quickie before I go?' which he seemed to find hilarious.

No appropriate riposte to express her disgust sprung to mind.

'Please yourself. You won't get a better offer today. Anyways, just messing, trying to get a smile out of you. Come on, take me to the airport.' He pulled the seat belt across his rotund waistline, clicking it into place and tapped his hand twice on the dashboard. 'The airport is signposted from the next junction.'

Kirsty found her voice, 'Just before we go,' she said. 'Can I ask you something?'

'You've changed your mind about the quickie?' he laughed.

She ignored him and carried on, 'How did you know about Biddy Duffy being raped by that man?'

'Callum.'

'Callum! What did he say?'

'He said Joseph Meechan had raped a girl he'd once been very fond of. She was only sixteen at the time and ended up pregnant. Bad news, it ruined her life as her parents abandoned her forevermore leaving her to rot in a Magdalene Laundry.'

'Is that all?'

'Yes that's all. Is that not enough? Why do you want to know?'

'Just wondered.'

'I was only doing a favour for my best friend,' said Mattie. 'I hope Callum was watching. Apparently, the same Joseph Meechan went off with the fairground crowd later that year after they pitched up in Killarney. Vanished from Kerry but at some point popped up in Dublin. That's where I remember him from, as one to be avoided. No good by all accounts, and clumsy. Not to be trusted at all.'

The fairground! Kirsty repeated silently connecting with her dream.

'Now come on, let's be gone. I need to be at the airport.' He tapped on the dashboard again.

Eager to bring the ordeal to an end, she selected first gear and drove. Mattie took a canister of aftershave from the glove compartment, spraying it liberally on his face, neck and hair, causing her to cough and open the window.

'Glad I can rely on you to get my car back to Balvohan.'

'I will.'

'You're a good girl and who knows, had we met under different circumstances…'

His patronising tone annoyed her intensely as images loomed in her mind of Joseph, quivering with fear and Sister Mary Cecelia stepping through the cavernous door of the convent. A faceless pretty young girl suffering torment at the hands of nuns forced unnecessarily to be a slave in a steamy laundry. Then Mattie in all his guises, Mrs Devlin, Father Carlin, Mr Maloney's wisdom, and Toby, yes, he was still there. The tablets had not yet touched the intensity of her throbbing headache.

'A good girl, I am not,' she muttered.

He talked on, words she didn't hear.

'My head hurts,' she mumbled.

Having signalled, she accelerated rapidly to overtake three slow-moving lorries. 'Slow down, for the love of God. You'll have a Garda car after us.'

'Doing anything for the love of God makes it alright, I suppose?' she snarled.

Amid the windscreen wipers pounding back and forth incessantly, she could see them all standing drenched at the graveside. She wanted to see Biddy's face, Callum's face, Sam's face in the globules of water, blurring together becoming rivulets presenting a challenge to the wipers. Just as quickly as it had started, the rain stopped abruptly as they progressed onto dry roads with water dripping from the car.

'At last,' she muttered, negotiating the final roundabout, following signs to reach the drop-off area at the front of the airport terminal. Breaking harder than was necessary she looked at Mattie willing him to be gone.

'Thanks, Kirsty, you're a star.' He leant across as if to kiss her cheek, but she recoiled.

'I want to ask something of you,' she said.

'Go on, try me?' he smirked.

'Please don't ever contact me again.'

'Do you really hate me?' he looked hurt and puzzled.

'No, I don't hate you but–'

'Fair enough.' He shrugged, not letting her finish and got out of the car. Slamming the door, he walked away and she noted his confident swagger was still intact as the stocky figure disappeared into the departure terminal.

Kirsty drove to the short-stay car park, painfully aware how much her hand shook reaching to take a ticket at the entrance barrier. Having parked, she wrapped her arms around the steering wheel and bent forward to rest her head. Tears of relief, shame, loss, longing and disillusionment merged to become one large tear of hope.

Eventually she felt able to resume her life and directed the car to Kerry.

Chapter 35

Peace

Driving through the outskirts of Dublin, a double rainbow arched in splendour above the Jaguar effortlessly carving out its route. A weight had been lifted from Kirsty. To be able to put a face to a faceless man, instead of making her feel worthless and despondent, buoyed her up. She could not pretend to understand what made someone like Joseph the way he was, but actually seeing him brought closure of a kind which became renewed optimism for the future. Why worry that he was part of her, plenty of people shared precarious relationships with their parents, she felt more secure now in her own identity. A wish that Biddy's life had been different would always remain. It brought sadness to think her conception was responsible for snatching another life with a bright future. One day, Biddy might feel able to meet her daughter.

Before leaving Dublin she'd determined staying at the B & B in Killaloe found on her original journey to Kerry would be good. That evening she sent a simple text to Sam.

HELLO HOW R U?

No immediate response was forthcoming so she lay on the bed and stared up at the white ceiling, examining a frail cobweb dangling from the light. The blank television screen served to validate silence as her friend, until disturbed by the sound of her phone ringing just after midnight.

'Hello, Kirsty. Are you alright? I only found your text now. Were you asleep?'

'Yes, I am alright, and no, I wasn't asleep.'

She delighted in letting Sam be Sam, enjoying the comforting familiarity of his voice until he asked, 'So what's new with you?'

'I'm on my way back to Kerry.'

He asked from where, and heard a sterile version of taking Sister Mary Cecelia back to the convent, and returning Mattie's car to Kerry.

'Great,' he said. 'A little adventure for you to visit the big city, although no doubt you'll be pleased to get back to home comforts.'

Their conversation ended with a promise to talk again soon. She switched off the light, although emotionally and physically exhausted, she was remarkably content and slept.

Next day she boarded the Kilmuir Ferry crossing the Shannon to be back in County Kerry. Hopes of seeing dolphins at play alongside the boat were not fulfilled. Mrs Devlin was delighted to receive an update on progress, insisting there was no need to hurry. 'Why not take the opportunity to enjoy some of our beautiful scenery?' she said offering no room for argument.

Kirsty drove via Kenmare, remembering Callum's suggestion it was worth a visit. As promised it was picturesque but she preferred Killarney with its bustle and colour. In the fading twilight, she drove on without further dalliance, to arrive late evening at the Devlin house. Tiptoeing upstairs, with relief she sank onto the familiar bed still fully clothed. She slept soundly until woken by the radio alarm. 'Good morning, welcome to RTE1, the time is seven o'clock as we go across to the news desk.'

The perfect power shower blasted away lathered soap, dislodging residue of city grime from every pore. Feeling refreshed and awake, straightaway Kirsty settled back to the domestic routine of preparing breakfast.

'Don't get a fright,' she said tapping on the elderly lady's bedroom door, 'the wanderer returns.'

Mrs Devlin beamed, stipulating the breakfast tray be put to the side and to give her a hug. 'It's lovely to have you back. I want to hear all about your trip.'

'I boiled you an egg just the way you like it,' said Kirsty.

'Lovely. I shall miss you when you leave, but no need to get depressed about that quite yet.'

'When do you leave Balvohan?' asked Mrs Morriarty later that morning, as always overtly to the point.

'Three weeks tomorrow, the ferry is booked.'

The shopkeeper reached into a drawer to get a book of stamps, having previously slammed the cereal box ungraciously on the counter. 'Well, it's been nice having you here, God's speed be with you for a safe trip home.' It would have been difficult to sound less sincere.

'Thank you. Could I also have another book of four stamps for myself, please?'

With everything paid for, Kirsty lingered near the door pretending to peruse a rack of greetings cards, anxious to commit every detail of this shambolic shop to memory. She loved the merging of old and new in a way which made it unique. Even the postmistress had developed bizarrely attractive qualities. The half-empty selves Mrs Morriarty would defiantly insist were half-full.

'I'll miss this village,' she said.

'And the village will miss you. A bit of foreign blood about the place does well,' said Dan Boyle as he entered the shop, 'to know life exists outside this old County of ours.'

Kirsty chuckled.

'Good luck to you.' He shook her hand. 'And haste ye back. Is that not what they say in your part of the world?'

'Isn't it great to be great but better still to be grand?' said Matt Daley to no one in particular as he too entered the shop and stood beside them.

She smiled knowing it was the people more than the shop she would miss.

Later the same evening she sent a text to Sam.

FERRY BOOKED – THREE WEEKS TOMORROW CHAT SOON TO FIRM UP ON TIMINGS

Sam had suggested it would be great if a visit to the New Forest could be possible before returning to Scotland. His invitation had been graciously accepted. The thought of spending time with him came wrapped in an element of elation she chose not to over analyse.

*

'Could we go to the Flannigan Cottage today? I would like to make sure there's enough bedding and have a final tidy before Peter's comes next weekend,' Mrs Devlin asked. The first of her younger sons promised visits was about to occur.

Placing the key in the lock, Kirsty took a few minutes to gain enough courage to turn it enter the white cottage on the hill. Her worst fear instantly confirmed, it was still there, perhaps not as obvious, but the smell lingered in spite of their giving it a thorough cleaning. Mrs Devlin didn't seem to notice, or passed no comment and sat at the table to methodically compile a list of items to be purchased in Killarney. Cutlery, tea towels, bedding, light bulbs, and muttering how something important would surely be forgotten. Meanwhile Kirsty opened every window and placed a scented cone in each room. Nothing was the same, she thought, how foolish to imagine that it could be.

There were personal reasons to celebrate the passage of time, a summer season ended which left her feeling calmer and more confident than ever before. Nothing could be gained from remaining static. She missed Callum, Sister Mary Cecelia and of course Mattie. They had all been an important part of her coming home.

*

'How is Declan?' was her first question to Peter when he arrived late on Friday evening.

'He's grand. Come to his senses at last,' he laughed, displaying the same insolence as his brother in a less appealing way.

'Have you heard from Mattie at all?' he asked.

'No. Why would I?' She was surprised he expected she might be a point of contact.

It was Mrs Devlin who answered. 'My lovely son is in a warmer climate. Wise man.' Her eyes glistened. 'I do miss him so much.'

'Of course you do, but I'm here, Mammy.' Peter gave her a hug.

'Don't you be fretting. You'll be seeing a lot more of me and the family. I promise.'

Kirsty's observation of the visit as she viewed the body language on show gave her a sense it was not a resounding success. At the time of his departure two days later the younger son repeated these assurances saying he would visit again in three weeks and bring the children.

*

Tring, tring, tring, tring.

His name lit up the caller panel on her mobile phone.

'Hello, Sam...'

'Great. That all sounds possible,' he said having listened to Kirsty explain her arrangements and predicted timings for her journey.

'It'll be great to meet up again. I've several touristy things lined up this end for us to do.'

'All sounds good to me. Looking forward to it as a welcome interlude before facing the reality of trying find a job.'

'Where do you plan looking?'

'Edinburgh, Diane has kindly offered me accommodation again.'

Sam ended their conversation reiterating how much he'd enjoyed the visit to Ireland, and hoped he could make the New Forest as exciting. 'Call me sometime before you leave Kerry. Or anytime, for that matter. Alright?'

'Great, see you soon, bye for now.'

Mrs Devlin smiled with raised eyebrows and a quizzical expression.

'You were listening?' Kirsty laughed.

'Maybe,' her large brown eyes sparkled with mischief. 'Oh, I am so pleased. Sam is such a nice young man.'

Kirsty sank back, on the sofa, and noticed the room was not looking quite as polished as usual.

'I'll just take five minutes, to give the place the once over with a duster.'

'Stop trying to change the subject,' chuckled Mrs Devlin.

'When I'm done we can watch *Mastermind*.'

'Forget the polish and duster. It can keep until tomorrow. Why not just bring the box of chocolates from the kitchen? I could do with a strawberry cream.'

They munched chocolates and giggled like schoolgirls despairing at how few of the quiz questions they could answer.

Evenings during Kirsty's final days in Balvohan were generally spent nestled in floral armchairs beside turf aglow in the Kerry stone hearth. The two ladies enjoyed each other, sharing comfortable companionship as they watched TV or chatted about all sorts of things. Peter phoned alternate evenings precisely at six o'clock taking his new role very seriously. Kirsty's heart melted every time when seeing the gratitude in her companion's wide eyes. If Mattie achieved one deed of greatness, this had to be it.

Daytime duties were not onerous as Mrs Devlin became determined in doing most things herself, because soon there would be no alternative.

Kirsty was pleased when she overheard her say to one of the many visitors she felt ready to live alone again, although had greatly appreciated having companionship.

'Lucky to find such a nice girl.'

Her time in Balvohan was drawing to a natural conclusion, but first she wanted to say farewell to those who had become special. Of course Father Carlin was at the top of her list for a final visit. As she rang the doorbell of the parochial house she vividly recollected how much had happened since the first time she called. The priest was slow to answer, 'Kirsty, how nice, please do come in.'

She followed the him into the sitting room.

'Horse racing,' he said silencing the television. Initially their conversation was about Hurley and Gaelic football. The parochial house felt cold and pictures of the Sacred Heart and Our Lady stared from each wall with unforgiving eyes. Kirsty thought, how lonely life is for a priest. This man has to be confidant, advisor, and give absolution, no matter how he's feeling. Who is there for him?

It wasn't until they were about to part company she got to the main reason for her visit, which was a desire to say a sincere thank you for the freely given information and his empathy. Father Carlin was anxious to know if his input had been helpful. She reassured him adding how truly grateful she remained and always would, suggesting they could keep in contact by email. The priest readily agreed saying that would be great and should she need any further assistance in searching for family material then she should never be afraid to ask. If he didn't know the answer he might well know someone who could help.

'This country of ours has been through some very dark times. I believe a day of reckoning will come for some of our compatriots who ignored humanity. Please, whatever you hear, remember that not all of us are tarred with the same brush.'

She smiled at him, unsure exactly what he meant, but felt she had a good idea and appreciated the sincerity in his voice. She supposed he was referring to the recent evidence of abuse to children inflicted by members of the Catholic clergy. The involvement she would personally have in any future revelations was at this time unknown to her. There was no lengthy confession or divulging of sins, but before leaving, she knelt before him to receive absolution and a blessing.

'I shall keep you in my prayers, and perhaps you could say one for this old priest in Kerry from time to time.'

*

The three weeks flew by in a way that Kirsty found hard to accept. She felt increasingly that to depart from Balvohan was also to leave Biddy. Mr Maloney shook her hand warmly wishing her well. Their last official session consisted of trying to formulate a fitting résumé of all the issues which had been explored over the preceding months. He reinforced previous validation of her feelings adding a warning not to become complacent regarding the power Toby could exert if she saw or spoke to him again. His parting comment was, 'Mobile phones are a wonderful invention, if used with prudence.'

Both of them were relaxed enough to smile, recollecting a midnight moment on the strand. Her ultimate walk beside the Atlantic surf was unhurriedly indulged leaving transient footprints perfectly sculpted on golden grains. Cold sand compressed between her bare toes as she memorized the sensation alongside all the other precious moments. These treasures stored so they could be indulged at will when parted from her beloved Ireland. Pressing hard with her left foot saying aloud, 'The day Cressida wrote a letter,' right foot, 'the day I left Toby,' left foot, 'Biddy's book,' right foot, 'Mrs Devlin's wisdom,' left foot, 'the swallows flying in Callum's room.' So deeply engrossed did she become the biting wind nipping her ears was superfluous.

Turning at the far end near the ice cream kiosk, she imprinted her reversed footprints retracing her steps exactly. This time saying, 'Mattie, manipulative and charming.' Like an onion with layers peeled back to expose another dimension of his personality. 'Toby, and his mask of sanity. He wore it well. She pressed her foot harder, to squash the negatives, frustrated by her compliance within their union.

Then treading softly said, 'Sister Mary Cecelia, a genuine friend, Mrs Devlin, a dear lady, Callum, a good man, Father Carlin, lost in a world I do not understand, Diane, my caring and loyal friend.' The penultimate step was for Sam, 'A very special friend'. So too was the ultimate imprint for 'Sam, who was Sam.'

Returning to the pebbled track, she managed to squash her feet back into cold shoes. Turning to look back in order to absorb a final impression of the strand with its slithering, shifting dunes, azure rock pools, distant ripples and rolling waves. Following the path passing by the house and through the village, because there was someone else she wanted to visit. The cemetery gates creaked begging for oil. Callum should know all was well in Balvohan. Turning up the collar of her jacket to shield against the nip of the wind she sat by his grave.

'Hello, Callum. It's me, Kirsty. Your sister is safe in Dublin and tomorrow I leave the village. I miss you; thank you for treating me with kindness. To use your phrase, I do believe "all shall be well".'

Twilight gathered on top of the Kerry Mountains, before forming a shroud over the village as she finally arrived back at a unique elderly lady's haven of security.

In the morning they both shed a tear, and exchanged promises to keep in touch.

Chapter 36

Return

Kirsty booked into a hotel in Dalkey for her last night on Irish shores. Taking only enough from the car to cater for the night she marvelled when escorted to a particularly luxurious bedroom. Its corner position overlooked trees, their last hints of autumnal mellowness in shades of brown meandering to greet winter. Ferry lights could be seen from the front window moving out of the harbour, heading across the Irish Sea to Wales, until gently fading over the horizon

The brown hues led her to think about logs on the fire, or turf cut from an Irish bog, squelching mud on a country walk, or a glass of ale, a rustic fence, an angry sea with cream-crested waves, a river in-spate, church pews, wooden floors, steaming coffee. The list seemed endless. Each with its aroma, turf differs from logs as it burns. Creosote to protect wooden posts, salt-laden wind, beeswax polish, and the tantalizing aroma of steaming coffee. That evening it became a colour more varied in its moods than any other. It brought her comfort in a cooked fillet steak, browned onions and mushrooms on a plate sitting beside a turf fire in the hotel hearth.

Once aboard the ferry she knew well enough how to get to the rear platform and feel the sea air. The engines droned beneath her feet as the boat withdrew from Dun Laoghaire. With wind in her face, she stood watching the Irish coastline shrink to the point any detail of houses could no longer be seen, but instead observed a view greater in compass as the vistas entirety emerged.

A sweet Irish girl named Biddy Duffy committed no crime. She was incarcerated behind high walls. Innocent but forced to endure a vicious punishment, never afforded the luxury of choice. There were probably countless others who, finding themselves pregnant out of wedlock stood on a boat watching their homeland become distant. Contemplative and scared embarking on a voyage arranged by the parish priest and sanctioned by their family, to deal with their problem. Or some would have told no one and lived these moments alone and scared. To travel as foot passengers would make it more epic because there would be need to find a bus or train before finally reaching the address scrawled on a piece of paper. Unaccompanied, so very much alone, with no one back home willing to acknowledge, the truth of their disappearance.

Forgiveness is easier when you understand.

'Be happy, Biddy,' said Kirsty out loud.

Suddenly a piercing bleep radiated from her handbag to disturb these thoughts. No unread message on her phone found her momentarily puzzled until remembering the other phone. In the midst of her preparations to leave Balvohan, she had placed it on the charger, with the intention of giving it to Peter but had completely forgotten. She read the new text from Mattie.

MISSION ACCOMPLISHED. PICKED UP A GOLDMINE HERE. SHAPELY AND BLONDE WITH ROSY RED LIPS TO KEEP ME WARM AT NIGHT. SEE YA LITTLE BRO.

Laughing out loud caused two fellow passengers to turn and view her with curiosity. Then with a casual flick Mattie's phone was tossed into the Irish Sea.

Chapter 37

New Forest

Sam lived in Lyndhurst, a small village at the heart of the New Forest. It took her a little over five hours driving from Holyhead to reach its centre. She parked near a newsagent's, having seen several flower-filled buckets with a notice saying 'pick and mix'. Carefully selecting an attractive mixture of sunflowers, holly with berries and some fronds of fern she congratulated herself on her originality. Already in the car was a Kerry hamper containing a Barry's Fruit Cake, Cloudberry Brownies, Sea Spaghetti, Dovinia Chocolates, Dingle Chocolate Fudge, Glór Peanut Butter and Harty's Char Grilled Pepper Jelly, as a treat for Sam.

The accommodation which he had booked, in advance of her arrival, was easy to find. It turned out to be a quaint house with a thatched roof. The proprietor was considerably older than she wanted to appear, being rather overdone with perm and paint.

Anxious not to arrive early at Sam's, Kirsty retrieved the smaller suitcase from among all the clutter collected in Kerry and returned to her pink frilly bedroom. Waves of sadness washed over her in the shower.

'Nothing to keep me in Britain,' he'd told her two days earlier on the phone. She was experiencing a new level of hatred for this potential job in Canada.

An hour later, hoping she looked as good as possible, she lifted the latch to the door, and set off in search of Sam. The former woodcutter's cottage was easy to find following his directions. It nestled among a distinguished stand of mature beech trees. From the gate a brick path led, between flower beds, to the front door. Pine wood scents drifted from the chimney, carried in curls of smoke rising heavenwards. To the left of the front door a gnarled tree shivered releasing the last of its autumn leaves gently to the ground.

'Come on in, welcome. It's great to see you,' Sam said promptly responding to the knock on his door.

Inside was pleasingly attractive, with subtle lighting and a wood-burning stove glowing in a charming red brick fire-place. Above it a timber ledge exhibited a chaotic collection of pictures, and ornaments, mostly owls.

'Pity it's not daylight,' he commented. 'Still never mind, I can give you the grand tour tomorrow. Plenty of time.'

Kirsty sank into the soft sofa which was not modern or pristine, but more like something found in a second-hand auction. She liked it.

Sam's boyish enthusiasm could not be disguised. 'I thought we could dine at The Oak, a good pub just a short walk from here. And before we go, I insist it's to be my treat.'

'What's that?' she asked, noticing a picture on the coffee table.

'Oh, that's for you. I had a copy framed specially as a keepsake.'

She lifted the picture. 'Thank you. It's lovely.'

'A property developer bought the house,' he said. 'I meant to tell you before, but we always seemed to have other things to talk about and it slipped my mind.'

'They don't look that much different?' Kirsty voiced her inner thoughts as she sat, allowing the photograph to rest on her lap. Six pairs of eyes stared at her from a significant moment in time long ago. Mother, father and four children.

Maud with extravagant ringlets, Cressida's hand resting on her father's arm, Matthew with blonde hair parted and flattened to his skull. Each of them looked so innocent and naive in the ways of the world. She had no memory of their father but recalled the only grandmother she had ever known as a kind lady. Plump Philippa, her mother, looked so solemn. A girl who had grown into womanhood with expectation of conceiving her own child but nature's cruelty was to deprive her of such fulfilment. So many things left unsaid. Experiencing a moment of profound sadness released a slow tear.

Sam spoke quietly, 'Is there not a quote somewhere which claims mothers are angels who teach their children to fly?'

'A noble sentiment.'

'Still, we should agree our mothers and fathers have to take credit for quite a lot.' He smiled. 'After all, we didn't turn out too badly, did we?'

Unsure what exactly she expected from their evening together, it turned out to be disappointingly uneventful. They slotted into each other's company in a comfortable way, like brother and sister, she had to admit. Any secret hopes he would announce a change of heart regarding Canada did not materialise.

Having mentioned how she missed being able to feel wet sand squash between her toes, laughing and saying it was better therapy than any expensive massage, then believed it sounded a bit pathetic. She chattered incessantly about mundane things to the point where a small voice in her head suggested perhaps it was time to shut up. This state of mind began to disturb her. She felt powerless and suddenly very lonely in Sam's company. The onus on conversation deftly redistributed, she sat back encouraging her companion to speak.

At around half past ten she tried to smile at one of Sam's stories but her body did nothing to disguise the fact she felt emotionally drained and physically fatigued. The cumulative effects of a frantic week.

Sam was sensitive enough to notice, saying, 'Time to get you back to Meadow Cottage and a good night's sleep.'

Before they parted company outside her B & B accommodation he suggested they meet up again, in the morning. 'Come to my place around ten-ish for coffee, thereafter I shall transport you to visit some superlative local treasures.' He accentuated the word superlative and laughed adding, 'I'll turn you into a proper tourist.'

Breakfast was not up to a great standard but feeling refreshed and ready to go, Kirsty retraced her steps to arrive again at Sam's cottage. This time it was bathed in sunlight. A dove cooed, while at the same time, acting in contrast to a rook which cawed loudly from a distant location. She was surprised to notice his roof was thatched, which had not been obvious to her the previous evening. A wonderful smell of ground coffee greeted when the front door opened.

'Mmm, smells good.'

'Yep, all ready and waiting.' Soon he was handing her a pottery mug decorated with a pretty blue and yellow glaze brimming with coffee. Sitting down on the same faded sofa she sipped the contents while he related some of the places she would visit on her grand tour of the New Forest.

'A famous witch known as Sybil Leek lived not so far away in Burley. Long ago she was known as a gifted psychic, astrologer and author.'

'Pity she's not still around,' said Kirsty. 'It would be good to know what the future holds,' then after a moment's thought added, 'There again, maybe not.'

They left the cottage beside Swan Green and walked along a path Sam said was called the Cut Walk. It led them through magnificent, unenclosed woodlands, past the tiny hamlet of Alum Green, and on to a Roman bridge across the water. Then they turned back to collect the car. Sam drove slowly constantly pointing out landmarks but Kirsty could only politely feign enthusiasm. This was not her Ireland, she felt nostalgia for the fuchsia hedges, the sea and her room scented with delicate summer riches dispersed from a pink climbing rose

The car halted beside a simple wooden sign positioned on the grass verge. It had, he said, been erected in memory of World War Two Canadian forces. A plaque etched with, 'On this site a cross was erected to the glory of God on 14th April 1944, by men of the 3rd Canadian Division RCASC'.

'Do you miss Ireland?' she enquired.

'I take it that the fact you ask means you do.'

'Yes,' she admitted.

'Very much?'

'Yes sorely.'

'Do you see yourself going to live there?'

'Don't know but I believe it would be good.'

He abandoned the measured response formulating on his lips in favour of divulging information on these Canadian men and their contribution to the war effort. Kirsty could not help but wonder at the significance of the reason for stopping to view this sign. Did he have news?

The best part of their day together was still to come. Sam's surprise was about to be revealed. The car moved on and the tour resumed.

'The Knightwood Oak would be the oldest but the Eagle Oak is my favourite,' Sam said stopping the car again. Kirsty had to marvel at the magnificence of the oak tree towering overhead. But it soon became obvious they were not going to get out and walk. Sam displayed impatience to move on to the Eagle, his favourite. 'I visit it at some point every week. They say that in 1810 an eagle perching on one of its branches was shot by a keeper. It's recorded as one of the last eagles seen in these parts.'

This time when they stopped he was out of the car almost before the handbrake had been securely engaged. Kirsty released her seatbelt to follow his enthusiasm.

The oak trees reminded her of Ireland, but when she started to walk, the forest floor did not emit the same fragrances found in her Killarney wood. This day was starting to feel frustratingly incomplete, fragmented. They were not united or at least not in a way she had hoped they might be. It was coming to the point of deliberating if things she previously envisaged they shared were simply an illusion.

'Hey, hang on a minute,' shouted Sam after her when she strode off along the path towards the huge oak tree. 'You can carry something for me.'

The raised boot of his car revealed a picnic hamper, a plaid rug and a couple of pillow-like cushions. 'I wanted to surprise you and have a picnic. And before you say it's hardly the season, I thought it would be fun.'

He handed Kirsty a tartan rug and four cushions to carry.

'Come on, follow me,' he smiled setting off at such a rapid pace she had to break into a jog to keep up.

When they reached his elected picnic spot she had to agree it was a bit special. Through all weathers, this magnificent tree had endured. Her hand rested on its noble trunk while Sam spread the rug and scattered cushions. The open hamper revealed plates, knives, forks, napkins, and champagne glasses, which he laid out, then lifted several foil-covered dishes and finally a bottle of sparkling apple juice.

'Pretend it's champagne,' he said unscrewing the top and pouring the amber liquid into a glass and handing it to her.

Kirsty smiled, 'This is absolutely fantastic. Thank you.'

She sat on a cushion while Sam removed the foil to reveal sandwiches, a Melton Mowbray pie, salad and a loaf of golden crusted bread.

'Mmm, delicious,' she said, enjoying a sandwich and slice of pie. 'Don't you find things always seem to taste better outside?'

'We need a toast,' said Sam, raising his glass.

'Definitely. It's your call.'

'To a happy future.'

'May it hold all we hope,' she said and they both smiled.

'Cheers.'

Replete, Sam lay back on the rug and rested his head on a cushion.

'Tell me this,' he started. 'How are you feeling now about everything, you know, the whole lot, Biddy, Toby, life? What are your plans?'

A long pause followed before Kirsty answered.

'As you know I am making my return to Edinburgh. Diane is a dear friend and has a room for me in her flat. Then a job search, perhaps teaching or maybe a change, I'm not sure yet. I will take things a stage at a time.'

She didn't add that the prospect of Edinburgh contained concerns that old wounds could become raw. That was for her to deal with by tapping her strength to safeguard from what could become an overwhelming issue.

'Right, moving swiftly on to Toby. All positives in that area, the divorce is forging ahead. My solicitor in Edinburgh has been great and it should be final within the year.'

'Does that upset you?'

'Only in the sense when we married I believed it was forever. Not as in suffering grief over our separation. Suffice to say leaving him brought relief. I'll spare you the gory details.'

'Can't say I took to him, at your mother's funeral.'

'Oh. Why?'

'Too full of himself, boasting a lot about how good he was at his job.'

'Yes, sounds like him.'

'So no regrets?'

'Absolutely none regarding the end of our union. If there is anything to repent it's marrying him in the first place.'

Kirsty looked at the figure stretched out on the rug in front of her. Sam, friend not foe. Sam with his thick mop of golden hair and charming smile. As he shut his eyes she observed the length of his eyelashes. Wasted on a man, she thought.

'And Biddy?' he said without opening his eyes.

She sighed. 'Why are your eyes closed?'

'I like hearing your voice.'

'Oh!'

'Yes, I do. Besides, when something could be difficult to say I don't want to put you off by staring.'

'Oh!' Kirsty said again. 'I don't mind you looking at me. In fact, I believe it would make things easier.'

'Sorry,' he said, opening his eyes and smiling in a way which made her heart leap.

'Well, in terms of Biddy, I have a far greater understanding of everything now. And in spite of it all still hold on to hope that, maybe one day, we shall meet.'

He nodded. 'I believe your time will come.'

'Philippa wanted a child desperately. For them to pretend they produced the child made sense, knowing the dynamics within the family and how cruel Maud can be. Mother used to say her elder sister had a whiplash tongue. Biddy had little choice in any of it, which makes me particularly sad. Barely no more than a child when her world turned upside down through a fault of her own.'

Sam was looking at her in a strange way. Kirsty hesitated, wondering whether to share the moment she saw her father cowering in front of Mattie. She quickly dismissed the thought feeling he might not understand the Mattie dynamics.

Sam wanted to know, 'Could her parents not have dealt with it all in a kinder way? Did she ever tell them she was raped, and if she did, why was the horrible Joseph not brought to justice and made to face his deeds?'

'I wish she had and all you say was true. But, sadly none of it is.'

'I'm optimistic sometime in the future Biddy will feel strong enough to meet you.'

'I truly hope so. It helps to believe. I don't think the words exist to explain this properly. It's like a constant ache, missing pieces, but has to be, relegated to a place where normal function can resume. To harness a favourite old cliché, life goes on.'

Kirsty tried to smile, she was anxious to show she appreciated his concern saying, 'At least now I can try and understand lots of things at work in the whole sorry mess. Like the impact of infertility, why it led to lies and deceit, the impact of rape, and I can condemn the weaknesses within Irish society and the Catholic beliefs that contributed to changing Biddy's life.'

Sam reached out and squeezed her hand. 'Wouldn't it be nice if we could make things better for that poor unfortunate woman?'

The warmth of his hand resting on hers travelled up her arm. Sam is not just Sam, she thought. He's the nicest man I have ever met.

'When is it you go to Canada? Exactly when?' She tried to sound upbeat and cool as a breeze.

It came as a shock when he divulged he would be starting his new job at the beginning of the following month – in ten days' time. Attempting to disguise her distress she pretended to be pleased for him.

They stayed beneath the ancient oak and she managed to resist the urge to lie beside him and rest her head on his shoulder. Ultimately it was a crisp chill in the air and the damp rising from the ground which forced them to pack up and return to the car.

Their day together had, after all, turned out to be special. There was never anything resembling plotting or a scheming between the two of them, only a refreshing honesty in their communications which felt so natural. With sorrow she parted from Sam that evening as he kissed her on the cheek saying, 'Remember, Canada is not so far. You could come and visit sometime.'

Immediately she became distressed he'd selected the word sometime which was vague, non-committal, something you might say to anyone.

That night her dream of the lady outside a church on a hill replayed. The woman turned and smiled, for the first time appearing serene. With no fairground visible, all the previous pandemonium ceased. The woman turned and walked away, as if to signify 'her job was finally done'.

If fate dictated she would never see Sam again at least she had memories from this special day. To remember Toby occasionally was alright. It reminded her how good life was without him. To remember Sam and their unique day together would waken wistful notions of what might have become possible had circumstances been different.

Kirsty checked-out of her accommodation after breakfast the following morning, thanking the owner whose face resembled a work of art. To apply war paint to this level of perfection Kirsty guessed would require a hideously early start to the day. The desired effect diminished by bright right red lipstick bleeding onto her obvious false teeth. Periodically these were shifted from side to side with a misguided notion this would go unnoticed.

About four minutes into her journey, a text arrived on her phone from Sam:

CAN U DO ME A FAV PLS REVISIT THE EAGLE AND COLLECT SOME ACORNS. WANT TO PLANT THEM IN CANADA SEE IF THEY GROW

Kirsty - OK NO PROB EMAIL UR POSTAL ADDY

Sam - WILL DO. THE WORLD JUST GETS SMALLER EVERY DAY

Finding the tree again was easy. Walking towards it the phrase 'we are programmed well how to forget' weighed on her thoughts. Nearing the parking area they'd used the previous day she quietly spoke aloud, 'But now I can differentiate and know it is not possible or wise to forget completely.'

Beneath the boughs of the noble tree she noticed their rug, or one uncannily similar, lying on the ground. An enigma, for she felt sure they had not forgotten to lift it when they packed up the picnic items. Closer examination confirmed beyond doubt it was indeed an identical rug. A second text arrived.

Sam - IT'S A GREAT DAY TO COLLECT ACORNS

She put the rug down again and started to reply.

beep beep… and a third.

Sam - BEST PLACE TO LOOK IS BEHIND THE TREE

Kirsty - OK

Sam - HURRY UP HAVN'T GOT ALL DAY

'Sam!' she exclaimed as he stepped out from behind the tree, he laughed at her obvious bewilderment. 'What are you doing here?'

'I got to thinking,' his lovely smile and brilliant blue eyes seemed even more hypnotic as Kirsty was barely able to accept the reality of his presence.

'Come here,' he said.

She stepped easily into his waiting arms. It felt so natural.

'Come to Canada with me,' he whispered. 'Let's see what happens. No pressure. After all, there is nothing to keep you here.'

'Me to Canada?'

'Yes, you and me, or if you want to live in Ireland eventually, that's all good too. Let's give coupledom a go; I'd like us to share the adventure.'

'Oh yes, yes, please, together we can go anywhere and do anything.'

She responded experiencing a wealth of pleasure she'd never imagined achievable.

The wise old oak tree watched over them.

19733426R00152

Printed in Great Britain
by Amazon